Manchester Christmas

A Novel

John Gray

PARACLETE PRESS
Brewster, Massachusetts

2021 First Printing This Edition

Manchester Christmas

Copyright © 2020 by John Gray

ISBN: 978-1-64060-744-6

The Paraclete Press name and logo (dove on cross) are trademarks of
Paraclete Press, Inc.

The Library of Congress has catalogued the hardcover edition of this book as follows:
Names: Gray, John Joseph, 1962- author.
Title: Manchester Christmas / John Gray.
Description: Brewster, Massachusetts : Paraclete Press, 2020. | Summary: "A
 searching young writer is drawn to a small town where she is pulled into
 a mystery centered on an abandoned church and the death of a special
 girl. This novel illustrates how God often uses the most unlikely among
 us to spread healing in a wounded world"-- Provided by publisher.
Identifiers: LCCN 2020034543 (print) | LCCN 2020034544 (ebook) | ISBN
 9781640606401 (hardcover) | ISBN 9781640606418 (epub) | ISBN
 9781640606425 (pdf)
Subjects: GSAFD: Christian fiction.
Classification: LCC PS3607.R3948 M36 2020 (print) | LCC PS3607.R3948
 (ebook) | DDC 813/.6--dc23
LC record available at https://lccn.loc.gov/2020034543
LC ebook record available at https://lccn.loc.gov/2020034544

10 9 8 7 6 5 4 3 2 1

Published by Paraclete Press
Brewster, Massachusetts
www.paracletepress.com

Printed in the United States of America

For Courtney
Who makes every day Christmas

1

lost and found

"There's no question, Scooter, that's the same barn." Chase was tired of driving in circles and was about to take the GPS device she'd won in a Christmas party raffle two years earlier and throw it out the car window. She didn't, because her vintage cherry-red 1967 Mustang convertible was stopped on a dirt road somewhere in the vicinity of Manchester, Vermont, and this perfect country setting, with tall pines and hidden streams, was far too pretty for her to be a litterbug. She'd been driving in circles for a half hour, but Scooter, her passenger, didn't offer an opinion on which way to turn because the four-year-old Australian Shepherd wasn't very talkative at the moment. He was busy nosing through her Louis Vuitton bag that rested comfortably on the passenger seat, searching for the snacks she had packed earlier. Sour cream potato chips, if he remembered correctly.

Up ahead, Chase saw a tractor slowly making its way across a faded brown hayfield, so she reluctantly pulled the car forward to ask for help. She put the Mustang in park and stood on top of the front seat to make her five-foot-six frame taller and get the farmer's attention. He was right out of some old Hollywood Western, with a weather-beaten face and bib overall jeans that were only half snapped at the top, exposing his wrinkled red flannel shirt underneath. He looked like half-folded laundry to her.

The old-timer shut off the tractor and put his hand up to his ear, letting her know she'd better shout whatever she had to say. "I'm lost. Trying to get to Manchester," she yelled.

The farmer scratched the top of his faded blue baseball cap, looked around, a bit confused, then said, "Let me get my son." With that he put two fingers in his mouth like a fork and gave a loud whistle. It was so loud, blackbirds taking a nap in the nearby maple tree sprang to life and flew off into the bright blue November sky.

The huge wooden door to the nearby barn she'd already driven by three times suddenly swung open as if Hercules was on the other side commanding it. "My Lord," Chase said to herself, and for good reason. Out stepped a man who looked like he belonged on the cover of one of those cheesy romance novels they sell by the rackful at the dollar stores back home. He was six foot two if he were even an inch, with the athletic build of a man who did hard labor every day of his life. His thick, dirty-blond hair was untamed as it pushed out in all directions from under a tan cowboy hat. Even from this distance there was something from the squint of his eyes that made her nervous and excited at the same time.

Chase looked down at her ninety-dollar jeans and the leather boots she'd bought on sale at Nordstrom, thinking she'd dressed the part of a country girl, but these two, this father and son, they were the real deal. As the young cowboy walked from the barn toward the tractor and this beautiful young woman in the cool car, his father spoke. "This is my son, Gavin Bennett." With that he turned back to his son, directing his next words to him. "She's trying to get to Manchester."

Gavin took a hard drink out of the half-gallon plastic jug that Chase had just noticed was in his hand the whole time. She was so fixated on his face and strong shoulders he could have been holding a purple ostrich and she wouldn't have noticed. The jug looked a bit dingy, but the water was clear and refreshing as he took a long swig. She could see his eyes were blue—not light blue, but a darker shade, making them more mysterious. She thought a girl who wasn't careful could get lost in those eyes.

He just stood and stared at her with those ocean-blue eyes until Chase finally spoke. "Trying to get to Manchester and I seem to be going in circles."

"What's your name?" Gavin asked her, wiping the excess water from his chin. "Why does that matter?" she shot back playfully.

He liked that she did that, showing some spunk, and smiled back at her saying, "'Cause I don't give directions to strangers unless I know who they are."

She stepped down from the car seat she was still standing on, opened the car door and walked around to the front bumper, giving him a good look at who he was talking to. "I'm Chase. Chase Harrington. I'm from Seattle; I'm lost and trying to get to Manchester sometime this century. How's that?" she added sarcastically at the end.

The handsome young cowboy and his father shot each other a look and the old man chuckled. "Best not mess with this one, Gavin. Now stop giving her a hard time and tell her."

The young man pushed his cowboy hat back, revealing the rest of his handsome face, and he smiled wide, changing the entire mood in an instant. "I'm just messin' with you, Miss Harrington. Turn your car around and go down this road until you see a Christmas tree farm on your left. Take the first right after that and stay on that road until you hit Route 7A. Hang another right and it will take you straight into Manchester."

Chase smiled back and put those imaginary pistols she seemed to be carrying back in her holster as she told him, "Much obliged, paht-nuh." Gavin gave her a confused look and then burst out laughing.

"What did you call me?"

Chase was suddenly embarrassed, her cheeks turning red. "Um, isn't that how you country folk talk?" Chase wondered aloud.

Gavin sized her up as he bit down playfully on his bottom lip. He then unzipped the jacket he was wearing to reveal a sweatshirt that read "Boston University." He moved a step toward her so she could read it better, which made Chase's stomach twirl in a good way, and said, "I went to B.U.—master's degree in agricultural science. So, not so country after all, darlin'."

Chase smiled warmly and said, "Okay, touché, Mr. Bennett. Thanks for the directions. Maybe I'll be seeing you around town."

Gavin climbed up on the tractor, now resting his hand on his father's shoulder, and said to his dad, "You think I'll be seeing her again, Pops?"

His eyes never left Chase's soft auburn hair that framed her smooth white skin and full lips, as his father responded, "Oh, having a front row seat for this introduction between you two, I'd pretty much count on it."

Chase climbed back in the car and fired up the engine, giving Scooter a pat on the head. "He's trouble with a capital 'T,' buddy," she whispered so only the dog could hear. Scooter just looked at the two farmers and wagged his tail with approval, still thinking about those potato chips.

Before she could put the car in gear Gavin shouted, "Hey! Chase? Isn't that a boy's name?"

Chase shrugged her shoulders and said, "What can I say? Daddy wanted a boy."

Gavin wasn't quite done. "By the way," he asked, "what brings you to beautiful Vermont right before the holidays?" Chase put her sunglasses on and checked her face in the rearview mirror to make certain her makeup held up to all this driving, and this cowboy was getting the best version of her.

She then put the car in drive and yelled back, "License plate, cowboy. License plate."

As the Mustang made its way toward the Christmas tree farm and the turn that would take her to a new adventure, Gavin spied the back plate on the car and saw one word—W R I T E R.

Gavin glanced back at his father, giving him a look that said he really liked her. Reading his son's mind, the farmer said playfully, "With a name like 'Chase' you better get moving if you wanna catch her." The two of them let out a laugh so loud it echoed a half mile across the meadow.

2

Owen

Owen Johnson put on one of his favorite sweaters. It was solid black with three buttons at the top and complemented the Lucky Brand jeans he was wearing. It was one of the perks to selling real estate: nobody much cared if you wore jeans or a business suit; they were only interested in the house you were selling and the price. He checked himself in the mirror and felt good about what he saw. A couple of years shy of forty, he still had all his hair and had managed to keep the weight off, something most of his old high school buddies couldn't boast. His brown, soulful eyes that made the high school prom queen fall for him all those years ago were still engaging, just looking a bit sad today. Why today? There was nothing special about it, just another day. *Sadness has a way of dropping in unexpectedly like that for some reason*, he thought.

He went into the garage to grab up a handful of Realtor signs with a photo of a gorgeous woman who looked strikingly like Jennifer Lopez smiling on the front of them. Above her picture it said, "Buy from Amazing Grace," and below was the Realtor's phone number, which rang directly to Owen's cell. "We can't be missing calls and leaving money to the wind," Grace used to say. Owen would remind himself of her words every time that phone rang late at night.

His plan today was to place the For Sale or Rent signs in front of the old abandoned and empty St. Pius church that sat on Main Street in the heart of Manchester. But first things first; he needed to go back into the living room for a quick word with his wife.

"Well, Grace, I'm about to head out," he started. "It's another perfect late fall day, just the way you like them. Most of the leaves have fallen, so the leaf peepers have had their fill of Vermont, and Manchester is getting quiet again the way we like it." Owen paused now and collected himself for what needed saying next. "I miss you. I hope you know that. Every single day." He looked toward the stairs that led up to their family bedroom and continued, "Tommy is doing well. The teacher thinks he's getting a little bit better, more connected to things." Owen looked away from his wife's face now, down at the boots she bought him at L.L. Bean for his birthday a few years earlier. He glanced up at the clock on the wall and realized he really needed to get moving. He wasn't sure what to say anymore besides telling her he missed her.

The sound of a teenager's feet stomping down the stairs in the quaint Cape Cod-style home broke the silence, and Owen's son, Tommy, came bounding around the corner, breaking up this private chat. "You talking to Mommy again?" Tommy asked, giving his dad a big hug. You'd never know he was on the autism spectrum unless you sat and talked to Tommy for a bit. "He's sharp as a tack, he just lacks some social skills," is what Grace told people, especially those administrators at school.

Tommy walked over to the table by the big bay window where the late-day sun was drenching the mahogany wood and shining brightly on the neatly framed photo that Owen had been talking to. A beautiful woman with a light in her eyes was smiling. Tommy picked up his late mom's picture and gave it a kiss before returning it to its home. "We'll see her again someday, Dad?" he asked his father. It's a question he asked almost every day since she died. Owen scooped up the real estate signs, tucking them under one arm, and gently grabbed Tommy's hand. "You bet, sport. Someday."

Owen popped the trunk to his jet-black Jeep Grand Cherokee and laid the signs with his wife's image down carefully, as if she'd feel it if he tossed them in with abandon. "Amazing Grace. What a great name for a Realtor," he said to himself. She'd been gone three years, but there was no way he was changing that name or taking her face off those signs. Owen checked his watch and realized he was going to be late. He had to place those signs in the lawn outside a church that was now for sale, then get to the Empty Plate Diner in the heart of town by 5:00 p.m. Some out-of-towner who had emailed him from Seattle was searching for a house to rent for the holidays, maybe even longer, depending on how things went.

As he drove down Potter Hill Road, past the old mill with the pretty waterfall and the pond where he used to ice-skate as a kid, Owen's phone came alive with a beep. He would never text and drive, so he pulled off to the side of the road and touched the screen, revealing a one-line message that said, "Got lost but I'm close to Manchester now. Sorry if I'm a bit late. Thanks for understanding, Chase."

Until this text message, Owen had only communicated with Chase through email. It occurred to him at this moment that he had no idea if this "Chase" was a man or a woman. It certainly sounded like a boy's name. To his pleasant surprise, he'd soon find out he was wrong.

3

Harlan

Harlan loved this part of the job: parking the big SUV with the word "Sheriff" stamped on the side and walking his rounds down Main Street in Manchester. It was about a mile long with beautiful shops and discoveries on both sides of the street. Harlan's keys, the ones that hung from his belt and opened the police station's single cell that rarely had any occupants, jingled as he made his way down the block saying his "hellos" and "how are ya's" to the town folk who passed him by. They rolled up the sidewalk early this time of the year, so, many businesses closed by five p.m., save for the diner, which seemed always to be open.

If a building was dark with the "closed" sign hanging in the window Harlan would grab the doorknob and give it a quick check to make sure the owner had remembered to lock it. If they didn't, he had everyone on speed dial in this quaint New England town, and they always picked up when Harlan's name appeared on their cell.

He was breathing a bit heavily tonight. He'd like to blame it on the thin mountain air, but as he adjusted his belt, he saw his belly was not thinning at all. "Too many of Margaret's muffins," he said to no one in particular. He glanced down at his gun, the standard pistol they'd issued him when he'd taken the job twenty years earlier, but he'd never had need to take it out of the holster. Heck, he hadn't even unsnapped the cover that kept it in place.

In his right hand was a small plastic Ziploc bag with saltine crackers inside. His left hand was needed for waving to everyone who called out his name with a smile. "Hey, Harlan," they'd say. Never Sheriff Harlan, just plain Harlan. That was Manchester for you; formality had little use around here.

As he worked his way up the block, he saw a pretty young woman standing next to a fancy old sports car, craning her neck this way and that. "You lost, ma'am?"

Chase was waving her cell phone around as if it was going to tell her which way to walk now that she finally found the town she'd driven 3,000 miles to get to.

"No. Yes. Kinda," she said, confused.

"Can I ask your name and where you're trying to get to?" Harlan inquired.

"My name? Oh right, this is the town where nobody will help you until they know your name. Chase, Chase Harrington. Can I ask your name?" she said.

"I'm Harlan, the sheriff around these parts. And it's Chase, you said? That's a strange name for a girl. Is there a story behind that?"

Chase was tired and late already, but there was something disarming about this older gentleman, so she played along. "Yes, there is. My daddy loved what he called chase movies. You know where the good guy, who's kind of a bad guy, gets chased around by the cops."

Harlan thought for a moment as he noticed her dog in the front seat of the car and said, "Like those *The Fast and the Furious* movies. What's your dog's name?"

"No," Chased replied. "Older ones with Burt Reynolds. Smokey and the Biscuit or something thereabouts."

"Bandit," Harlan corrected her.

"No, not Bandit, his name is Scooter," Chase answered, clearly confused.

Harlan laughed now. "No, no. The movies you're talking about were called *Smokey and the Bandit*, not Biscuit. Hi, Scooter." He walked over and began petting her dog.

Chase liked this man; he had a kindness about him. "So, now I'm curious; don't you have a first name?"

Harlan kept playing with Scooter as he said, "Erastus."

"Erastus? Are you kidding? And you thought Chase was a funny name. Okay, tell me how you landed with that?"

Harlan leaned on the car now, giving his sore back a rest. "Well, since you asked, my grandfather once lived in Albany, New York. It's about an hour and a half from here. For a time, he found himself unemployed and feeling sorry for himself. One day he was in the park and a well-dressed man sat down next to him on the bench and they started chatting."

Chase was enjoying this story. "Go on," she said.

"So, my granddad tells this guy how he can't find work anywhere. When he's done complaining, the man gets up and writes a phone number on the back of a business card. He says, 'Call this number and mention my name and they'll give you a job.'"

"Just like that?" Chase asked with astonishment.

"Yep, just like that," Harlan said.

Chased thought for a quick second and asked, "So, who was the guy?"

"Glad you asked, young lady. My granddad turns over the card and it says 'Erastus Corning, Albany Mayor.' He got him a job in the water department, and he worked there nearly thirty years. I guess the family figured we owed old Erastus a favor."

Chase laughed now. "And you're the favor. That's a great story."

"Well, thank you, darlin'," Harlan said, and then, "Oh wait, not to interrupt you, but my friend is here."

With that an orange tabby cat emerged from the dark shadows next to a bakery and walked straight over to Harlan. He rubbed up against Harlan's leg, making it clear they were old friends, and Harlan took a cracker out of the plastic bag he'd been carrying and gave it to the cat. "He looks for me every night," Harlan said to Chase.

Harlan then remembered his manners, saying, "I'm sorry, rambling on like that. Where was it you were trying to go, dear?" Chase didn't want the conversation to end, but she knew the Realtor must be sitting in a booth, checking his watch. "The Empty Plate Diner," she said.

"Easy as pie, Chase. Walk three blocks down and you'll smell the bacon. The diner is on the left."

"And what if they aren't cooking bacon?" Chased asked playfully.

"It's a diner, sweetie," the sheriff said. "They're always cooking bacon."

Harlan patted Scooter's head one more time as Chase took him by the leash and started walking those last few blocks. Bacon and eggs sounded fantastic right about now.

4

the empty plate

If Chase had any hope of entering the diner quietly with her dog in tow, that illusion was quickly dispelled by the loud cowbell fashioned directly above the front door. As she pulled the door open, *CLANG* it went, causing every head in the place to turn and take a look at who was coming in. Chase's eyes were as big as saucers, taking in the fifties-style diner complete with an old-fashioned counter and shiny silver stools with red leather seats. It was real leather too, not that fake stuff used today. She could tell because of the cracks in it. Booths lined the walls to her left and right, with about a half dozen four-top tables filling in the rest of the open space. The chairs around the tables didn't match, giving it even more charm.

As Chase slowly moved inside, a familiar country song hung in the air. *Kenny Chesney*, she thought, but she couldn't be sure. Strong and delicious aromas hit her nose: pot roast and mashed potatoes, apple pie and syrup. It smelled like everything she'd expect in a small-town diner like this. It had the familiar scent of your grandmother's house on a Sunday afternoon before she set the table for a family dinner.

Behind the counter was an older woman in a pretty blue dress chatting up the guests, passing out the plates and cashing people out all at once. "If I ever own a restaurant, remind me to hire her," Chase said to Scooter.

Farther beyond the counter was a wide window that gave patrons a view directly into the kitchen, where a heavy-set man with salt-and-pepper hair was wiping his hands on his already greasy apron. He put two hot plates up on the window ledge that separated the kitchen from the space behind the front counter. Waitresses walked back and forth, grabbing up the food for table delivery as it came out. If they weren't paying attention, the cook would hit a small bell, letting everyone know the food was ready. The cheap bell was held down to the counter with duct tape to keep it from hopping around when he smacked it too hard. *Better Homes and Gardens* this was not, but everything that looked wrong with this place felt just right to Chase.

She surveyed the room, looking for a man who might have his head up looking for her, but there were no takers—not yet. She guessed the Realtor must have been running late too. Before she took another step, the woman behind the counter walked around with a keen eye on the dog leash in her hand and the four-legged guest who was probably violating a half-dozen health codes just by being inside.

"Hi, I'm the owner, Shayla. Is that a service dog?" she began. Chase brought her hand down gently on Scooter's head, looked sheepishly at the floor and shaking her head. "Don't you speak, dear?" Shayla asked.

"Yes. I'm sorry. No, he's not a service dog, but . . ."

Chase began to explain before she was cut off by a loud, "BECAUSE the only pets we allow in here are service dogs. I'm not crazy about animals being in places where you serve food, but state law says we have to let in service animals. So, I ask you again, is that a service animal?"

"He's not," Chase answered a second time. "I'm new in town and haven't had a chance to get myself sorted out. I would have left him at the inn I'm planning to stay at tonight, but I haven't even had a chance to check in yet. I'm supposed to meet a Realtor, who must be even later than me, and we're both starving."

"You and the Realtor are starving?" Shayla asked, only half kidding.

That made Chase chuckle. "No. Me and my friend here are starving—Scooter. We've been driving all day and got lost, which wasn't a total loss because I met a cowboy who looks like . . . Well, let me put it this way, if Brad Pitt and a Victoria's Secret model had a kid and he grew up to be a cowboy, that pretty much nails it on what this guy looked like. I mean, WOW."

Shayla smiled, enjoying this stranger rambling on this way. "Continue," Shayla said.

Chase thought for a moment, then said, "Tell ya what. I saw a bench outside. I can tie his leash to it when the Realtor shows up and let him quickly show me some places he thinks I might want to rent. It's a bit chilly outside, but Scooter can tough it out."

Chase turned to walk toward the door when Shayla yelled after her, "You didn't let me finish, dear."

Chase looked back. "I'm sorry. Go ahead."

Shayla bent down and scratched the dog's belly, and Scooter gave her a fast kiss on her nose. "I was saying I only allow service dogs in here, but I'm not much for paperwork. When someone comes in with a dog I ask them if it's a service dog and if they tell me 'Why, yes it is, Shayla,' well, I just take their word for it and tell them to pick any booth they want, keep the dog under control and by their feet, and we'll have no troubles at all. Do you understand, dear?"

Chase finally picked up on what the nice lady who ran the diner was trying to say. "So," Shayla asked for the third time, "is that a service dog?"

Chase looked down at her pup and back into Shayla's kind eyes and said, "Why, yes he is, ma'am."

Shayla scooped up a menu and handed it to Chase, adding, "Here's your menu. Pick any booth you want, just keep your dog under control and by your feet."

Chase nodded in agreement and chose the booth in the corner with a good view of the room so she could see her Realtor when he arrived.

The table was tiny, but Chase could tell it was vintage too. Probably pulled out of some diner that closed fifty years ago when people came in three sizes: medium, small, and extra-small. Chase's frame was tiny, though, so the small table suited her fine. She was about to look through the menu when she noticed a mini jukebox mounted on the wall next to her. It was no bigger than a loaf of bread and had a clear glass front with those little tabs you turn showing all the song choices. She'd seen something like this on a TV show once and thought it was so neat. She noticed it took quarters, and the small print told her just twenty-five cents bought you two songs. "Elvis, Aerosmith, Lady Antebellum. Oh, there's the Kenny Chesney song I heard," she said under her breath. She'd have to dig a quarter out of the bottom of her purse before this visit was through.

Chase opened the menu, and it offered the usual fare with one exception. There in bold print across the front cover it said, "Home of the World-Famous Blueberry Corn Muffin." "That's odd," she said. "Never heard of that."

The waitress, wearing a tag that said *Brad*, overheard her reading the menu and said, "Oh, the muffins, yeah. How about that?"

Chase couldn't help noticing the nametag and asked, "Brad?"

The waitress giggled at the question every time she got it. "Yep. It's actually Brenda, but you see that guy in the kitchen talking to himself and slamming plates and abusing that poor little bell?" Brenda said. Chase had noticed him earlier and was looking at him now. "He's the owner, along with his wife, Shayla, the nice lady who seated you. His name is Colgan. Anyhoo, about my nametag: I'm terrible about losing stuff, and in the eighteen months I've been here I've lost three *Brenda* nametags. To punish me, Colgan made me a *Brad* nametag, and if I don't lose this one, he says he'll think about giving me one with my real name on it again."

Chased smiled. "So, Brad it is. I was curious about these muffins."

The waitress looked around to see if anyone was listening, giving dramatic effect to what she was about to say. "Legend has it, one day Colgan was out drinking all night with his buddies and forgot it was his turn to cook breakfast in the morning. So, he comes in on no sleep, still half in the bag, and he can hardly see straight. Idiot that he is, he accidentally mixes a big can of blueberries into the corn muffin mix. He's cheap as they come, so there was no way he was gonna dump it in the trash. Instead, he baked them as is, and a new muffin was born. I have to admit, they're pretty incredible. Total fluke."

Chase immediately went for her bag and pulled out a notepad and pen. "What'cha doin'?" Brenda wondered.

"Oh, I'm a writer. Whenever I hear nutty stuff or something I love, I immediately write it down. This place is great. I mean, that duct tape on the bell: priceless."

As Chase jotted down some notes, Brenda shrugged her shoulders and said, "Well, let me know when you want to order."

Chase kept her head down, continuing to write. "Yeah, I'll just yell for Brad." Brenda snapped her gum and giggled as she made her way back toward her grumpy boss in the greasy apron.

Chase had turned her attention back to the menu when the cowbell on the door made another announcement. She turned, looking for the Realtor, but her hopes were dashed when a teenaged boy came through and yelled, "Hi, Shayla." Chase could see the boy was older, yet he talked like a small child.

The lady in the pretty apron lit up immediately and said, "Thomas James Johnson, how's the handsomest young man in town?"

Tommy smiled and made a beeline for the tip jar on the counter, stopping himself before reaching in. "Can I?" he asked Shayla.

"Sure, hon. You know I can never say no to you."

He reached in deep and fished out a shiny quarter, then ran over to the nearest empty booth, pushing it in the slot on the tiny jukebox, making it light up. He quickly flipped through the pages that he knew by heart, resting on the second-to-last one, punching in R-17.

A moment later the sound of beautiful piano music filled the diner, and Chase looked up as a memory stirred. "My mother used to play this song when I was a little girl," she said out loud to anyone who would listen. "What's this song?" she asked louder to the customers in the diner, hoping someone would answer.

Tommy did. "'The Gift.' Music by Jim Brickman. The singer is Collin Raye."

Before Chase could try to remember the lyrics, Tommy started singing them loud enough for all to hear: pretty words about snow falling and a perfect town that resembled something from a fairy tale.

Just then came another clang of the cowbell, and a good-looking man in his thirties bounded in, wearing a black navy pea coat with a red scarf tied neatly around his neck. Chase saw he had wavy brown hair and sad brown eyes, gentle eyes that looked as if they'd been broken and put back together again. Owen Johnson heard the music that was already playing as he shouted, "Tommy, really? Again?"

He looked at Shayla as if he were sorry, but she didn't care, she loved Tommy. "He can play that song every day of the year if he wants, Owen."

Shayla then went over to Tommy and took hold of his hands as if to dance with him, singing along to this song she'd heard far too many times. As the last note sounded, Shayla pulled Tommy close and gave him a loving hug. There were only about a dozen people in the diner at that moment, but all of them spontaneously burst into applause, and that brought a roar of laughter out of Tommy. Even Chase was clapping, and they hadn't even met yet.

When the applause died down the metal bell taped down on the kitchen counter gave a ding, and Colgan called out in a playful tone, "If Cinderella is finished with her dance we have some pancakes that need delivery to the kingdom. By that I mean table five." Shayla gave her husband a wink and went back to work. Chase could see these two really loved each other.

Owen scanned the room and saw a beautiful young woman who looked about thirty studying a menu, and he just stared at her. He felt guilty for what he was feeling at this moment; it was something he hadn't experienced since Grace died. He wasn't ready to feel anything for another woman, not yet. He thought, *My, she's pretty. But I doubt that she is . . .* "Chase?" he said, loud enough to get her attention. *Don't look up, don't look up,* he was saying to himself. Then she did.

Chase smiled, and the two locked eyes for what felt like a minute but was merely a second. "Yes. I'm Chase. Are you Owen?" The handsome Realtor moved with ease across the diner and extended his hand to shake hers. Instead of using just one hand like he normally did, Owen brought his second hand down over the top of hers with its perfectly manicured pearl-white nails. It was more holding hands than shaking. *What the heck are you doing?* he thought in that instant. She didn't seem to mind, though.

"Is that your doggie?" a child's voice asked, breaking up the moment. Chase looked up and saw the teenaged boy who had been singing and dancing a moment earlier, standing next to her booth now. "Can I pet him?" he asked politely.

Owen jumped in, "I'm sorry, this is my son, Tommy. He loves animals. Do you mind?"

"Of course not. His name is Scooter, and you can pet him all you like, Tommy," Chase offered with a smile.

As Tommy sat on the black and white checkered linoleum floor, Owen took out a binder and started leafing through some of the properties available for rent. They were all fine, and most looked identical, except for the last one. "This one may seem strange to you, but I want you to give it a serious look," Owen said. It was a beautiful, small gray stone building with a lot of character.

"Wow, this is pretty cool," Chase reacted. "What's the deal with this place?"

Owen leaned in so she could see the photos better, close enough that she could smell his cologne. If he wasn't attractive enough with the jacket and scarf and hair a girl could run her fingers through, he smelled like the kind of guy who surprises you with dinner in front of the fireplace and a dozen roses.

Focus, girl, focus, she thought to herself. Chase looked at the photos and saw this stone building had everything she was looking for: a cozy bedroom, full kitchen and a den with a leather couch parked right in front of a gorgeous old fireplace. It also seemed to have a big empty space that looked like a dance floor. That could be a fun spot for Scooter to play.

"Technically, Chase, this isn't even on the market yet," Owen said to her. She liked how he said her name. "The reason I'm late is because I had to put signs out in front of the place. The owners told me I could sell or rent it; they're okay with either."

Chase told him she loved it.

"So, why don't you get some dinner and check into your hotel, and we can agree to meet here at nine a.m. tomorrow morning," he said.

Chase smiled and liked the idea of seeing him again that soon. "Sounds like a plan," she responded.

As Owen got ready to collect Tommy from the floor and pry him away from Chase's puppy, Shayla walked over with her ordering pad in her hand and pen behind her ear with a big grin on her face. She'd been watching the two of them chat in her booth and could see by the body language there was more than just real estate being appraised.

Shayla nodded and kept smiling at Chase as if she knew something Chase didn't. Finally, Chase said, "What? Have I got ketchup on my face or something?"

Shayla looked at her and Owen and said, "Remember earlier you told me you met some cowboy when you got lost?" Chase swallowed hard, a bit embarrassed; she did not need Owen knowing about that earlier conversation. So, she faked confusion asking, "Cowboy? Giving me directions? Hmm, yeah, I vaguely remember that. What about him?"

Shayla shot a look toward the front window that faced Main Street. "He just pulled up in his pickup truck. I'm guessing he's hungry." Shayla paused now and laughed, adding, "For something."

Right on cue the cowbell clanged and in walked Gavin Bennett. He'd changed out of the dusty barn coat and Boston University sweatshirt. Now he had on a crisp white dress shirt and painted-on jeans that stretched down to a pair of work boots. He'd seen Chase's Mustang down the block so he knew she was likely here, but he played it cool, walking over to the front counter and grabbing up a menu. "What's good tonight, Colgan?" he asked, loud enough for all to hear. He glanced at the specials and said, "Well heck, I'm gonna go with the pot roast."

Gavin reached into the tip jar to borrow a quarter, shooting Shayla a look like the cat that ate the canary, asking innocently, "May I?" He then strutted over to the booth where Chase and Owen were sitting and reached right between them, depositing the quarter in the little jukebox.

He didn't need to flip through the song list to see what he wanted to play. Without hesitation he punched in B-4, as if he'd done this before.

"Oh, I'm sorry, Miss Harrington. You'll have to excuse my crude country ways." As he pulled back his strong arm and got ready to walk away, he exchanged a glance with the Realtor, who was looking right back at him. Chase thought they looked like two red-tailed hawks about to claw each other over the same piece of territory.

"Owen," Gavin said in a manly low tone, tipping his cowboy hat the way knights do before a joust.

"Gavin," Owen said back, matching his intensity.

Gavin returned to the counter and put his muscular frame down on the cracked red leather stool, taking his hat off and resting it next to him. Just then the song he played on the jukebox came on. Chase recognized it from the first few guitar chords. It was an old country song by Toby Keith, "Should've been a cowboy." The statement Gavin was making about Chase's boothmate wasn't lost on anyone in the diner.

"Seriously?" Chase said out loud, causing everyone to look at her. The only person not looking was the cowboy at the counter. Gavin's blue eyes were fixed on the kitchen and Colgan, who was looking back, smiling. They gave each other a wink that said the game was on.

5

the sleepy panther

Chase wrapped up her business with Owen, and then took hold of Scooter's leash, saying, "It was great to meet you, Tommy. Thanks for playing with my dog." The special boy smiled broadly, giving the pup one more hug before Chase made her way toward the door, saying to Owen, "So, we reconvene in the morning and we go look at that property, Mr. Johnson?"

Owen ran ahead to get the door for her and said nervously, "Owen, please. Call me Owen."

Chase made certain not to give Gavin the satisfaction of looking back at him and said, "Owen it is. See you tomorrow."

The Mustang's seats were chilly as she hopped back in and turned the key. It had grown dark since she went into the diner, and the streetlights were on. "How pretty. See that, Scooter?" She was looking at the lampposts that lined Main Street; the white globes on top looked like something Bob Cratchit from *A Christmas Carol* might recognize. A light snow had fallen while she was in the diner talking to the Realtor and trying to ignore the handsome cowboy, making the sidewalks and trees all the more enchanting.

She reached for the radio, but there was no point turning it on, because a purple and black sign jutted out from a building just ahead with the words *Sleepy Panther Inn*. Just below the name on the sign was a painting of a black panther, sound asleep on a tree branch.

The car trunk was full of bags, but Chase was too tired to bother dragging them all in tonight. A set of white wooden doors with purple trim and etched glass greeted her at the top of the wraparound porch. The gray paint was peeling on the porch, but it seemed to suit the Victorian structure that had to be at least a hundred years old. Chase stopped before going in and looked up at all the windows that were looking back, each one jutting out with a different story to tell—some open, some closed, some with pretty curtains, others with shutters. "Nice," she said to herself as she turned the knob on the front door and went inside.

As she stepped onto a thick rug that covered a beige hardwood floor, the inviting smell of a fresh wood fire filled her nose. And another nice scent. "What is that?" she wondered. It was so familiar. Then she saw the source, resting on a plate that sat on the front desk right next to a vintage cash register. It was fresh oatmeal and chocolate chip cookies. She wasn't even hungry, having just left the diner, but she wanted one anyway. Scooter looked up with ravenous eyes that said, "Grab two of them, please."

As she considered the cookies, a man with a straw hat and a long beard came around the corner, stomping his feet to get the fresh snow off of them. "Right with ya, miss. I'd shake your hand but . . ." He was holding a healthy stack of firewood that had already been cut into the perfect size logs to toss on the fire. The gentleman dropped the wood into a wrought iron basket that sat next to the fireplace, wiped his hands on his dusty pants, and walked straight over to where Chase waited patiently by the front desk. "Ned Farnsworth. Proprietor, manager, and official head cheese at the Sleepy Panther."

Chase let her one bag fall to her side on the floor, freeing up her hand to shake his. "And I'm . . ." she began to say, before he cut her off.

"You're Chase Harrington. Driving in from the West Coast and said you'd be here sometime today," he finished her sentence.

"That's right, Mr. Farnsworth. Sorry I'm a bit late," Chase offered, while still glancing at the cookies but trying not to be obvious.

"First off, it's Ned, and you're not late, Miss Harrington. You said "today," and it's still today until it ain't. You want a cookie? My wife Abigail makes 'em fresh every afternoon." Chase stared at the cookies, which looked lumpy and delicious, and was about to decline when Ned added, "I'm not supposed to eat them, so you'd be doing me a favor because every cookie I get a guest to eat helps keep me out of Dutch with the missus."

He was smiling at her now as he picked up the plate and moved it closer. Chase obliged. "Well, I will take two, one for me and one for Scooter here."

"Yes, yes, you did mention you had a dog. He's sweet. There's no extra deposit, just promise me you'll clean up after him if nature calls and he can't make it outside in time," Ned said in a friendly tone.

Chase nodded with approval. "Of course, Mister—I mean, Ned."

There was no computer set up behind the desk, just a big leather ledger that Ned flipped open and began thumbing through until he found a page marked *November*. He had what looked like an antique pen hiding by the register and gave it a dip in the ink well before handing it to Chase. "Just need your John Hancock right here, my dear," he said. "You're paying for twenty-four hours, so since you're checking in late you can stay this late tomorrow if you like," he added. Chase had never heard such generosity from any hotel she'd ever stayed at.

She responded, "Well, that's very kind of you. You don't see Marriott doing that for guests."

Ned looked over his shoulder, making sure his wife wasn't watching before grabbing up a cookie and giving it a big bite. Then with his mouth full he said, "Well, this ain't the Marriott."

Chase nodded in agreement and said, "Oh, I love the name, 'The Sleepy Panther.' Who came up with that?"

Ned finished his cookie and said, "Me. We took a tour of a zoo once in California and it was a hot day, so none of the animals were doing much of anything. Most just sat there or hid in the shade, but up on a branch was a beautiful black panther, fast asleep. I thought to myself, what a sleepy panther. I guess the phrase just stuck in my head."

"Well," Chase came back, "it's a great name."

She reached for her wallet and Ned put his hand over hers to stop her. "Don't worry about that now, dear. We can settle up tomorrow." Chase couldn't believe how kind the people in Manchester were. Was it the Christmas season making them this way, or had she stumbled onto the nicest place on earth? She retrieved the bag from the floor and led Scooter up the narrow staircase to the second floor. All along the wall she noticed pretty oil paintings that were framed and hung with great care. They were beautiful paintings of nature, and each seemed to be signed by the same person in the bottom right corner of the frame.

Attached to the room key was a tag that didn't have a number on it but a name instead. The tag said "Taylor." She stopped near the top of the stairs, about to call down and ask which room that was, but Ned was already reading her mind.

"The rooms upstairs are named after my kids because they used to live in them. We had three: Scott, Brian, and Taylor. You'll see names on the doors, can't miss it."

As tired as Chase was, the writer in her was curious and always probing, so before taking another step she asked, "They're all grown up now? What do they do?"

Ned's face took a somber turn. He looked toward the fire and stared for a moment, not answering right away, and finally saying, "It's late. Let's make that a conversation for another day."

Chase knew not to push, so she said, "Sounds good, and thank you— for the cookie, the room, everything." Ned bowed his head forward and tipped his straw hat as if he were conversing with the Queen of England.

"Sweet dreams."

Chase took the last few steps up the stairs, hearing a creak with each shift of her weight. At the top of the stairs she glanced right and saw the word "Taylor" on a pink door. She walked over and slipped in the key. She realized when she went to turn it the room was already unlocked. She guessed the key was for her in case she wanted the door locked behind her. Something told her that in this house you were safe with it unlocked.

Inside she found a four-poster bed with a down comforter and an ivory-handled brush and a sterling silver mirror already laid out for her on a gorgeous antique vanity. Fresh mints were on the pillow, and the bedspread was pulled back just a smidge, making the soft sheets look even more inviting.

She dropped the bag and leash at the same time, and Scooter immediately jumped onto the bed and curled himself up like a warm croissant. "You stinker," she said lovingly, as she kicked off her Nordstrom boots and flung them whichever way they wanted to go. "My gosh, I'm tired," she announced to the quaint room, falling face-first into the heavenly cotton sheets.

As she closed her eyes, she could already hear Scooter was snoring. Her mind raced with everything she'd seen that day: the sheriff, the Realtor, that ridiculously good-looking cowboy. Feeling exhausted, she was quickly overtaken by sleep, with her last thought being, *I wonder why the innkeeper didn't want to talk about his children? Tomorrow, Chase, worry about that tomorrow.*

6

fresh waffles & fresh men

Chase's bedroom at The Sleepy Panther faced east, so when the sun rose over nearby Equinox Mountain it beamed straight through the lace curtains and soaked the warm bed. After rubbing the sleep from her eyes Chase reached for her cell phone, which was charging on the nightstand, and saw she had no new messages. "Good," she thought to herself. She liked quiet.

She rose and found her way to the bathroom, which had a large cast-iron tub. The prospect of soaking in that thing for about an hour was so inviting, but she had a handsome Realtor to meet at the diner, and Scooter would need to be walked soon. She splashed water on her face, put on a minimal amount of makeup, grabbed that exquisite brush she had seen the night before on the vanity, and chased the tangles out of her hair.

After slipping into a black T-shirt with a Big Brothers/Big Sisters logo across the front, Chase searched through her bag for something that would be kinder to her feet. "I could have sworn I packed them. . . . There you are." She grabbed up a pair of pink and white Converse sneakers, the kind with the old-fashioned star on the side. Chase loved wearing things that were long out of style and about to come back into fashion. She looked over at Scooter, who was being beyond patient. "We're going old school today, buddy." He wagged his tail in agreement.

Before going downstairs, Chase took her first good look at the room in the light of day. It was small but pretty, definitely a girl's room, with violet-colored paint on the walls and a pretty vanity and bed. She could imagine herself in a room like this growing up. Curiosity got the better of her, so she opened the dresser drawers; all were empty. Then she moved to the closet, where a white terry cloth robe hung inside next to about a half-dozen empty wood hangers. She was about to close the door when some bright colors in the corner of the closet floor caught her eye. "What are those?" she asked herself aloud.

Chase reached down and picked up three canvas paintings. One of them showed a pond with lilies on it and a yellow house in the background; that painting was nearly done. The other two had splashes of paint on them, but she couldn't tell what they were supposed to be or were going to be, since they weren't near finished. In the opposite corner was a folded-up wooden easel trying to hide from sight and a small cloth tarp covering up more artwork.

Chase took the one finished painting out of the closet into the light to see it better. "Beautiful," she said to Scooter. It was then she realized the style of painting looked a lot like the paintings she'd noticed last night on the walls when she was coming up the stairs, exhausted. Chase glanced at a clock on the nightstand and realized she should probably get moving, so she returned the painting to the closet, carefully closed the door, and clicked on Scooter's leash to lead him downstairs.

She wasn't three steps down the long staircase when she smelled something sweet and amazing. The creaking of the steps and Scooter's nails on the hardwood floor gave her entrance away, and Ned Farnsworth emerged from the kitchen with a pitcher of fresh-squeezed orange juice. There was a room to the side she hadn't noticed the night before, with a long table that could easily seat a dozen people.

"After you bring him outside to go potty there's a rope tied to the back porch you can hook him on. If you didn't bring dog food, I have some leftover chicken and rice we can feed him. He'd probably like that better," Ned began, talking to Chase like they were old friends. "Sit anywhere you like. I have OJ, coffee, and water all on the table. For grub you'll have to grab up a plate and come to the kitchen. I make the food but I don't serve it," he said, adding quaintly, "In Manchester we pick up the slack in our own rope." Chase wasn't sure what that meant exactly, but it sounded a lot like, "Get off your butt if you want to eat."

Chase was barely awake, but coffee sounded great about now, so she did as she was told with Scooter and the chicken and rice, spooning it out in a dented metal dish on the back porch. Scooter took one whiff and was in heaven. As she made her way back into the house by way of the kitchen, she saw the old man's waffle machine and couldn't help giggling. "Is that electrical tape holding it together?" she asked, looking at a waffle maker that appeared to be from the Civil War era. The electrical cord had several places where the original coating had worn off, exposing the wires, and was now patched together with black tape.

Ned chuckled and said, "Now, don't you make fun of my waffle cooker until you've tried my waffles, young lady."

Chase thought for a moment: *Was I supposed to meet that Realtor Owen at the diner and eat with him? Or just meet him and go look at the property I might rent?* Just then a sizzling sound came from the old waffle iron as Ned poured in some fresh batter. He clamped the top shut and used a clothes pin over the ends of the two handles to keep it closed tight. "This will only take about four minutes, Taylor. Why don't you go grab a seat at the table?"

Chase was about to leave the kitchen when she caught herself and asked, "Taylor?"

The old man looked confused for a second, and then his face turned to a mixture of embarrassment and sadness. "I'm sorry, Chase, meant to say Chase. Sorry, sorry," he continued as he fiddled with some kitchen utensils, looking for something to draw his attention away from this conversation.

Chase could see pain in his eyes, so she instinctively crossed the kitchen and touched his arm. "It's all right. You mentioned those were your children's rooms upstairs, and I stayed in a room called "Taylor." That was her bedroom?"

Ned didn't answer right away. He kept busy cleaning up the now-empty batter bowl and put the milk back in the fridge. Finally, as Chase was about to leave for the other room to sit, Ned said, "Yes, it was. Taylor was my daughter. We lost her a few years ago."

"I'm so sorry, Mr. Farnsworth," Chase said, almost in a whisper. A moment later she asked, "Are those her paintings I see around the house? They are beautiful."

Just mentioning her artwork seemed to cheer him up in an instant. "They are, Chase. She was a wonderful artist. She never went to school for it or anything. It was just something that came natural to her. She'd paint in that room you were in or sometimes she'd find something she wanted to paint in nature and spend all day in a field somewhere with her canvas and brushes." He was lost in a nice memory, now looking out the kitchen window at the pretty trees that had only recently dropped their last fall leaves.

"Oh shoot," he said, quickly taking the clothes pin off the waffle maker and opening it up. "Good, I thought I burned them." The waffles looked as perfect as any you'd order in a restaurant, thick and brown with deep trenches to hold the pure Vermont maple syrup. "The key is, the minute they come out you put lots of butter on them so it melts," he said, with a smile in his eye.

Chased helped herself to a waffle big enough to cover the plate and went into the other room to find a place to sit. She thought she might see others at the table, but it was just her.

"I'd eat with you, but I already had some. If you're okay alone I'm gonna make up a fire and drive the chill out of this place," said Ned, sounding every bit the caretaker that he was.

Chase dug in, and from the very first forkful her mouth was filled with the best breakfast she'd ever eaten. She took out her notepad to jot down all the things she needed to get done today, when from the other room she heard the front door opening and the sound of voices. Ned was talking to someone. A moment later the old man appeared and said, "There's someone here to see you—a gentleman caller."

Chase thought she must be late or maybe just she'd gotten her wires crossed with the Realtor and he had come by to fetch her. She quickly wiped her chin clear of any syrup. "MY GOD, that was good," she said to herself, downed the last gulp of coffee, and walked into the room with the fireplace. There in the shadows was a man with his back to her, poking the fire with a stick. "I'm sorry, Owen," she said, "I thought we were meeting at the diner."

Suddenly a familiar, rugged face and frame turned toward her with a smile and said, "Not Owen, Miss Harrington." It was Gavin Bennet in a brown leather jacket and black wool scarf. His thick hair was under control with some kind of gel, and the day's stubble covering his face gave him the feel of an outlaw. He looked like he'd fallen off the cover of *G.Q.* magazine.

"What are you doing here, cowboy?" she began, trying to mask the fact that his popping up this way, unannounced, excited her.

"Well, I'm off today at the farm and figured, you're new in town, and maybe you could use a guided tour. I know all the pretty places a lady might want to see."

Chase instantly put that chip back on her shoulder, the one she'd had the first time she met Gavin, shooting back, "Who says I want to see pretty things?"

Gavin loved the spunk in her and without hesitation responded, "Well, then, maybe I'll just show you all the places a girl can get in trouble."

Chase was so tempted to blow off the entire day and see what this cowboy was really up to, but at the moment she had nowhere to live, a dog tied out back, and a Realtor no doubt standing outside the diner looking at his watch. So, she said with a smile, "Tempting, but I can't. I have an appointment. So, if you'll excuse me."

Gavin stepped toward her in a friendly way, giving her a full view of his sturdy frame. "Maybe I can tag along. My schedule is wide open today."

Chase considered his offer for about two seconds when she decided to drop the pretense, walking straight over to him as he stood next to the warm fire, putting her face only six inches from his. "Gavin. I've been in Manchester less than twelve hours. What's the burning rush? Why are you giving me the full court press?"

Gavin turned his attention back to the fire now, instinctively kicking a burning log with his heavy boot in a reckless way. "Well, I guess you could say I'm a guy who goes after something he likes when he sees it. I don't know why you ended up on that dirt road near my family farm, but I'm glad you did. I like you. And I think you maybe kinda like me a little. I wasn't talking marriage; just a drive in the country is all. But listen, if you have stuff to do, you best get to it."

Gavin started backing away, looking like a little boy who just got yelled at for eating the last piece of pie, and Chase felt her heart pull toward him a bit. "I didn't mean any offense, Gavin."

He zipped up his leather jacket now, bracing for the chilly November air, saying, "And none taken. Like you said, you just got here and it's a small town. I'm sure we'll bump into each other again, if you want."

As the handsome cowboy walked toward the door Chase could feel an opportunity about to slip away. "How about later today? I have things to do, but a girl has to eat. How about dinner later, say five?"

Gavin stopped just as he put his hand on the doorknob and turned around, giving her his biggest country-boy smile. "Five it is."

Chase looked at her watch and saw she was now fifteen minutes late. "What in the world am I doing?" she said out loud, thinking no one was listening.

Ned emerged from the hallway and said, "Sounds like you're having dinner. Nothing wrong with that."

She guessed he was right. As long as she kept that cowboy with the devil in his eye an arm's-length away she'd be fine, right? Right? She glanced at herself in a mirror on the wall and said, "Oh, who are you kidding?" Ned laughed and started whistling as he retreated to the yard to grab more firewood. Something told him the fire wasn't the only thing about to heat up around here.

7

St. Pius

Despite being late, Chase decided to walk to the diner instead of driving. It was only three blocks, and the crisp morning air woke up her lungs. Before she reached the Empty Plate she saw the Realtor, Owen Johnson, standing outside with his son, Tommy, and talking to a familiar face. It was that sheriff she'd met, the man with the funny first name, shooting the breeze with them. "I'm so sorry I'm late. You can blame it on a cattle rustler," Chase said, jokingly.

Harlan stood up straight as if he were snapping to attention, pretending to put his hand on his gun. "Well, that sounds like a crime I should investigate, Miss Harrington."

Chase knew he was kidding. *God, everyone is so friendly in Manchester*, she thought. She said, "Please, Harlan, call me Chase, remember?"

The lovable officer patted his belly and said, "I do, that I do. And do you remember my first name and how I got it? I should have told you there would be a quiz later," he said with a grin.

Chase put her hand on her chin and looked up at the sky as if she were struggling to remember, then said confidently, "Erastus, and it comes courtesy of the Albany mayor, who likes handing out business cards and jobs."

"Bingo," Harlan said.

Owen chimed in, "I had no idea you two knew each other."

Harlan reached into his pocket and pulled out a lollipop and handed it to Tommy as he said, "Oh sure, old friends."

Chase then got down to business, asking Owen, "Did you need to eat? Because I accidentally ate a big breakfast at the place I'm staying. I'm sorry."

Harlan jumped into their conversation again. "You're at the Sleepy Panther, so let me guess: Ned broke out the waffle machine."

Chase nodded. "That he did. Nice man."

Owen then said, "Actually, Tommy and I ate earlier, so we are good to go." Chase was surprised the teenage boy would be tagging along on his father's business, but she could tell there was something special about the child, so maybe it did make sense after all. He seemed like a sweet boy who needed a little extra looking after.

Just as they were about to depart, Harlan intervened. "Tommy, do you really want to go look at boring houses with these two, or would you rather help me walk the beat and check on the jail?"

Tommy lit up. "Can we inspect the cell?"

Harlan put his arm around the young man with great affection and responded, "Absolutely. In fact, just to make sure it still works we can take turns locking each other in. How's that sound?"

Tommy jumped to hug his father and said, "Bye, Dad."

As Harlan turned to go with the boy at his side Chase's voice took on a serious tone. "Sheriff? I mean, Harlan."

The old officer, sensing the change in her, got serious himself. "Yes, Chase."

"The room I'm staying in at the inn belonged to a girl named Taylor. Her father told me she died a few years back and I didn't want to pry. I was just wondering . . ." Chase trailed off.

"You were just wondering how she died?" Harlan responded. Moving closer now to make this conversation more private, he said, "It was a car crash, Chase. Six years ago, right before Christmas. Everyone was coming back from the big tree lighting and bonfire up on Mount Equinox when it started to snow. Taylor took her little car instead of Ned's four-wheel-drive truck and, well, it didn't handle well in the snow, especially on those steep hills. He begged her not to drive that car in the snow but, ah, you can't tell kids anything. She lost control on a patch of ice, jumped the guardrail, and went into a tree."

Chase could picture the pain on poor Ned's face in that instant, and she winced, just thinking about that talented young woman being taken that way. "That's terrible," Chase finally responded.

Harlan nodded in full agreement. "Yes, it was. It was also the last time we had the Christmas ceremony up there. Too dangerous, is what people said. Although, if we're being honest . . ."

Chase waited for him to finish that thought but he went quiet. She finally asked, "If we're being honest, what?"

Harlan's aging hazel eyes locked with hers. "I think everyone felt it would be downright disrespectable to celebrate up there again after what happened. What Ned lost. What this whole town lost."

Tommy was growing impatient with all this adult conversation. "Are we going to inspect the cell, Sheriff?"

Harlan could sense the hurt in Chase at that moment, thinking about poor Taylor's fate, so he squeezed her hand and said, "Yes, we are, Tommy, right now. You take care, young lady, and good luck finding a place." With that, Harlan led Tommy south down Main Street toward the Manchester police station, such as it was, situated in between the barber and florist shops. It only had the one cell, but luckily, in these parts, crime was about as common as bad waffles; it just didn't happen.

Owen broke the awkward silence. "So, no breakfast needed and ready to look at places, shall we?"

Chase refocused her attention and said, "Yes, let's do that. How many places do we plan to see?" .

Owen opened a leather satchel and pulled out a tan folder stuffed full of flyers for real estate that was currently available for purchase or rent. He started thumbing through them and then stopped on the stone building Chase seemed to like the night before, when he showed her the photos in the diner. "Well, Chase, you seemed to really like this one, but there's something I didn't mention. Are you much of a religious person?"

Chase was confused. "Um, no, not really. My parents took us to church on Christmas or if someone got married, but no, not really. Why?"

Owen flipped over the folder and pulled out a new listing he had just put a sign in front of the night before. "You said you liked this one, and I remember you telling me over email that you weren't afraid of something different, if you could get it at the right price. How am I doing so far?"

Chase nodded. "Right, right, but what does that have to do with going to church?"

"This," Owen said pointing. "The stone building you like used to be St. Pius Church. They built it like 150 years ago when the village was first founded and there were only fifty Catholics living around here. But over the years the congregation grew, and this old relic was just too small. So, they gutted it and moved all the church stuff over to the big new church they built on the edge of town. It's the one with the tall white steeple." Owen realized Chase was brand new to Manchester, so she had no clue what he was referencing. "Anyway," he pressed on. "The old stone church just sat there empty for years until some couple from Boston, teachers I think they are, bought it dirt cheap and converted it into a really cool one-bedroom castle of sorts. I say 'castle' because of all the gray stonework. Very *Game of Thrones*."

Chase smiled, half liking this idea. "Oh, and you think I'm Khaleesi the dragon lady?"

Owen smiled back. "I don't know, but it just came on the market, and they told me they are happy renting or selling it, doesn't matter. The living quarters are gorgeous, and I'm telling you, you'd never know it was a church. Well, except for the windows."

Chase tilted her head to the side curious. "The windows?"

"Tiffany glass. Very expensive, apparently. The church folks were going to take the glass with them when they moved, but something about the way they were installed made it impossible to remove them without damaging them. They didn't want to wreck them, so they just left them be."

Chase looked at the photos again, and it looked even prettier the second time around, with its hardwood floors, a marble countertop in the kitchen, and that huge empty space where the pews had once sat. "So, no crosses on the roof, and I'm not going to trip and fall into a tub of holy water?" Chase jokingly asked.

"Nope. Like I said, except for the four Tiffany windows, you'll think you're in a private castle," Owen said.

Chased considered another moment, and said, "Let's go take a look."

The two of them climbed into Owen's Jeep, and for a moment it felt like a date when he closed the door behind her like a gentleman. As he made his way around the vehicle to get in the driver's side, Chase glanced behind her and could see Realtor information scattered on the back seat. All of it, the signs and pamphlets, had the photo of a beautiful woman on the cover with the words "Amazing Grace."

After slipping the Jeep into drive, Owen began pointing out some of the local landmarks. "That's the post office there. Our movie theater with all two screens is here on your left." Chase was only half listening as she watched this handsome father in his thirties with soft brown eyes and mild manner treat her with such tender care. He was saying something about the Revolutionary War and the Green Mountain Boys' secret headquarters in Manchester when Chase threw him a complete curve. "Who is the pretty lady on all the signs? Who is Grace?"

That brought Owen's guided tour to a halt fast as he swallowed hard and said, "Grace was my wife." That word, *was*, hung in the air for a moment and Chase knew by the way Owen said it that she wasn't his former wife because of some fallout or divorce. She took a chance and asked, "When did you lose her, Owen?"

He responded, "About three years ago. I know it may seem weird keeping her on the signs and stuff but I uh, I just . . ."

Chase understood completely. "You loved her."

Owen pulled the Jeep over to the side of the road and put it in park, given the sudden turn of this conversation. "Yeah I do. I did. I do. You know what I mean."

Chase squeezed his hand without realizing she was even doing it. "How did you lose her?"

Owen liked how her tiny hand felt in his. He hadn't held a woman's hand since he lost Grace, and in those final days and hours it seemed that all he did with his lovely wife was hold her hand and let her know she wasn't alone. Never, ever alone.

"It was cancer. Breast cancer. She was so young, thirty-one." Owen let out a deep breath as if just saying those words again, *breast cancer*, took some small piece of him away.

Chase locked eyes with him now. "I'm so sorry, Owen. And Tommy, he was so young to lose her."

A single tear tried to make an appearance on Owen's cheek, but he pushed it away and cleared his throat at the same time, hoping to mask his emotions. "Yeah. Tommy took it hard. You can probably tell, he's, um, special. He loved his mom, so trying to make him understand why she'd leave . . ." Another deep sigh came from him now. "Anyway, we're doing a lot better now."

Chase could tell he was mostly telling the truth about "doing better," but the wound to his heart was still fresh, and she wasn't sure what to say next. She realized they were still holding hands, and nobody wanted to be first to pull away.

"SO," Owen said dramatically. "We're here. This is St. Pius or what you fondly called 'Khaleesi's castle.'" This seemed to break the spell they were both under in that moment.

Chase and Owen stepped out, and the home was prettier than in the pictures. Short boxwood hedges lined the property and stone walkways. Not the kind of stones you buy today at Home Depot, these were cobblestones, no doubt chipped together two hundred years before Chase or Owen existed. The building's front door was large, of solid oak wood with wrought iron fixtures, a handle, and a large knocker that looked like a growling lion's head.

"My God, I love that," Chase said when she gently placed her fingers on the knocker.

A turn of the key opened to a woodworker's paradise inside. Thick wide beams made up the floor and the pillars that held the old building sturdily in place. The walls were stone, as advertised, with splashes of modern touches that made you feel like a contemporary home was placed in a time machine, transported back, and stuffed inside an old English castle.

The tour continued, and Chase found a comfortable bedroom and living area with an elegant kitchen and bathroom. Rather than your typical shower, there was a cast-iron bathtub with lion's claws where the tub's footing would be. *They certainly love their tubs here in Vermont,* she thought.

The back door opened to a private garden filled with perennials that were timed to bloom in intervals, so you were never without fresh flowers—except in the dead of winter, of course. Her last stop on the tour was the large common area that used to house the altar and pews. It looked like an open dance floor waiting for a party to begin. "Holy cow, you weren't kidding. You'd have no idea this was ever a church," Chase said to Owen.

A large rolltop desk was tucked neatly into one of the corners with an old-fashioned typewriter sitting on top. The name of the device was stamped in big white letters across the front of it. "The Chicago? Oh my, I've read about these but never actually seen one," Chase said with amazement.

Owen had never noticed the antique typewriter before this moment, and said awkwardly, "Oh is that a good one or something?"

Chase laughed. "Yeah, more 'or something.' These were only made for about fifteen years back around 1890. So neat." She was gently touching the typewriter keys now, but not pushing hard enough to make them come to life.

"Well, you said you were a writer in one of your emails. Maybe this is a sign?"

Chase looked around and spun herself in a full circle with her arms stretched out. "Ha, ha, maybe it is, Owen." Owen thought she looked like a Disney princess when she twirled that way, about to conjure up magic or perhaps change into a ball gown with a flash of lightning and a puff of smoke. Owen realized he was staring a bit too much now, but he couldn't help himself because Chase sure was pretty.

Before she could say, "I'll take it," Chase spotted the four Tiffany windows Owen had mentioned on the way over. They were breathtaking in color and details, each one capturing a different moment from the Bible involving Jesus. Chase wasn't lying when she said she wasn't much for going to church, but seeing these windows made the place even more welcoming.

"How soon can I move in?" she asked Owen.

Owen smiled with surprise. "Well, I'd say, grab your stuff at the inn and your pup, sign some paperwork, and you can sleep here tonight if you want."

Chase had been in the old church for only twenty minutes, but something felt right. It felt like home.

8

the broken sunset

Chase didn't bother looking at the other properties Owen had available for rent. She wanted the vacant church, which felt like a castle waiting for a queen. It was a beautiful November day with the sun playing peek-a-boo with big white puffy clouds. She buttoned up her faded jean jacket and made the ten-minute walk from St. Pius to the Sleepy Panther Inn. She took the front steps on the wraparound porch two at a time as she bounded in to let Ned know she'd be moving on faster than she thought. For some reason that made her feel a little sad, because she felt comfortable in that upstairs bedroom with the name *Taylor* etched on the door.

Before she could even speak Ned took the burden of delivering the bad news off her shoulders. "Lemme guess: you found a place and you're moving on, young lady."

Chase smiled and said, "Well, not before I have another one of those cookies you keep behind the desk and I get a chance to thank you for the waffles."

Ned went to the kitchen to fetch a small plastic bag. "Seeing you're leaving us, I'm packing a bunch of these cookies to go, for you and the puppy." Chase gave him a wink and went up to her room to toss yesterday's clothes, which lay strewn on the floor, into her overnight bag. It didn't take more than a minute to collect everything, but she couldn't leave just yet. She was thinking about the young woman who used to sleep here and her sad and tragic death. Chase's eyes traveled back to the closet, and her feet moved her over to its door without even thinking about it. She turned the knob and opened the wooden door, which gave a loud squeak, and looked down at the half-finished artwork still keeping residence on the dusty floor. She realized there were more than the three paintings she'd seen earlier. There must have been more than a half dozen hiding from view under that cloth tarp.

Chase scooped them all up and placed them carefully on the bed. She slowly started looking through them, noticing all the details and nuance in the bright colors. "Gosh, she was talented," she said out loud to the room, hoping in her heart the artist who painted them might somehow hear her praise.

Ned was giving Chase her privacy as she packed her things, but he was lingering in the hall and did hear her say it. He smiled with pride as he knocked gently on the half-open door and came in the room. "Yes, she was, very talented. Imagine if she'd gone to college for it, studied it," Ned said. Then he paused and let out a sigh when he added, "Imagine if she'd lived."

There was silence in the room for a good long minute before Chase offered, "I spoke to Sheriff Harlan earlier. He told me how it happened. I'm just so sorry, Ned."

The old caretaker of the inn could tell Chase meant this, and he could sense her sadness. "Thank you, darlin'," he said, and then instinctively he gave Chase a hug, the kind a grandparent gives you to say hello or goodbye. "Ya know," Ned continued. "It would mean the world to me if you picked one of those and took it with you, as a gift, something to remember us by."

He was pointing at the paintings now spread out on the bed. "I couldn't," Chase said, startled by the generous offer.

"Sure you could. Which one do you like?" Ned said, seeming to cheer up with the prospect of sharing his daughter's talent.

Chase looked through them all, and her eyes were drawn to a painting of an open field with a single weeping willow tree in the center and a small stream running nearby. Behind the tree was the outline of a mountain, and a bright orange sun was saying good night into the horizon. You could see nearly the entire sun slipping away except for one cloud that jutted up from behind the mountains, spoiling the image.

"I really like this one," Chase said to Ned.

He looked closer at it now and said, "Oh, I remember this one. She did it about eight years ago over near Dorset. Flip it over."

Chase turned the painting over, and on the back of the canvas were the words "*Broken Sunset* by Taylor Farnsworth." "Hmm, Broken Sunset?" Chase looked at Ned, confused by the name.

"She liked to title all her paintings by what she saw the day she did them. If you flip it back over you'll see that one cloud spoiled a perfect sunset by getting in the way. That's probably why she called it that," Ned said.

Chase turned the painting back over and studied it more closely, focusing on that one cloud. "If it bugged her, why didn't she just leave it out?"

Ned sat on the bed, now giving his seventy-two-year-old frame a break. "No, no. I don't think it bugged her. Taylor saw beauty in the world's imperfections, and she'd never take something out of nature to, um, fix it. That wasn't her way. She may have called it 'Broken Sunset,' but trust me, she thought it was beautiful or she wouldn't have painted it."

Chase picked it up now. "Well, I think it's beautiful too. Are you sure?"

Ned stood up and grabbed Chase's bag so he could carry it downstairs like a gentleman. "It's yours. You honor me by taking it."

The old man went ahead, taking the leather bag with the long strap slung over his shoulder, outside to her Mustang. Chase came down not long after, placing the unframed artwork in the back seat, and gathered up her dog.

"Do you mind if I come back and visit you sometime?" she said in a hushed voice.

Ned smiled. "Having a beautiful young woman back in that room, well, you made an old-timer happy. So, yes, Chase, you are always welcome here."

She gave him a big hug before placing Scooter in the front seat and turning the key. Chase had come to Manchester to write something special, and up until this moment she'd had no clue what that would be. But she decided in the driveway outside the Sleepy Panther Inn, that whatever she wrote, that old man and his late daughter would be part of it.

9
Gavin's surprise

Chase turned the key to open the front door at St. Pius, and instantly it felt like home. There was something warm and inviting about being surrounded by all that wood and stonework. She brought in her four Briggs and Riley travel bags chock-full of her life and plopped them on the large, soft bed. Scooter cuddled up next to a bowl of fresh water she poured, as she decided to take a private tour of the building. It was just as she remembered from earlier: a large, empty space that used to be the church, a beautiful kitchen with oak cabinets, marble countertops, a large island with stools, and a Viking stove for those times she might not feel like Chinese takeout. She knew nothing about cooking, but Chase had watched enough of those cooking shows on cable TV to know a Viking stove was the best you could buy.

There was a ladder above her head in the hallway that dropped down, giving her access to the attic, but she couldn't see why she'd need to go up there. A small breezeway on the side of the building led to a one-car garage that would be a welcome sight in the heart of those harsh Vermont winters. She lifted up the garage door to reveal a spotless parking space with some fresh-cut firewood stacked neatly to one side. "Nice," she said to herself.

After going back in, she wandered into the big open space where they used to hold Mass when this place was a church. The altar and pews were all gone; it was just one large dance floor with gray stone walls, a vaulted ceiling, and those four stained glass windows that harbored the secret of what this place once was. Chase hadn't really looked at them earlier, but now she was curious.

The first window, the one closest to the door, was an image of Jesus standing on a hillside preaching to a crowd. Tall brown grass lapped at his feet, and his long white robe gave him the appearance of almost floating.

Chase walked down a few steps to take a closer look at the second window on the same side of the building and said out loud, "Oh I know this one." Even though she wasn't much for church, her parents would drag her under protest a couple times a year on the big holidays, and some of what the preacher was saying must have sunk in. The image in the stained glass was Jesus again, only this time he was walking on water, and some men were sitting in a boat, clinging to its side, afraid. The sky was dark and the waves looked angry, having their way with this tiny boat, tossing the men about. "I think he asks one of them to get out of the boat and try walking on the water with him, but the guy sinks like a stone," Chase said to herself. "Heck, I wouldn't get out of that boat, buddy," she said, directing her words to the image of one of the men in the boat. She thought hard for a moment, staring at the stained glass image as Scooter walked in, his nails on the hardwood floor giving away his stealthy entrance. Then she remembered: "Apostles, that's what they called them, Scooter, apostles."

She turned around and walked over to the other side of the empty hall to check out the last two windows. The first was of a woman standing against a wall with people gathered around her, holding stones. It looked like some of them were dropping the stones to the ground and hanging their heads in shame. Chase thought this image felt familiar too, but she shrugged her shoulders and moved on to the last of the stained glass windows.

The final window was very bright with light, and it showed the backs of the apostles, who were all looking up toward the sky. Above them was an image of Jesus rising toward the sun. Chase thought it was pretty, but again the image held no real meaning for her. *They're just windows*, she thought, as she bent down to Scooter and gave him a kiss on the top of his head. "I love you, buddy. You like it here?" The dog wagged his tail in approval.

From the shadows behind her she heard a voice. "I do. Very nice." It was then that Gavin knocked on the wall with his knuckles, the sound echoing through the empty space. "Sorry, I should have called first."

Chase stood up from smooching her dog and said, "No worries. I thought we were meeting up later."

Gavin looked at his watch, a black Timex with silver trim that he wore on his left wrist, and said, "Um, it is later."

Somehow talking to Ned Farnsworth about his daughter's painting and getting a feel for this place had eaten up more time than she imagined. "Wow, you're right. Sorry, Gavin. Give me a minute to change and we can head out. I'm getting the nickel tour, right?"

Gavin put his hands in his pockets the way a little boy does when he talks to a girl he likes and said, "Yeah, something like that. Hey, maybe a quarter's worth."

Chase ran into the bedroom and shut the door behind her. She took off the blue Gap sweatshirt she'd been wearing all day over a T-shirt and upgraded to a pretty purple sweater. Her hair was up in a ponytail, so she pulled the tie and let it flow gracefully down onto her soft shoulders. Her makeup only needed a bit of a touchup, and, true to her word, she was ready in no time flat.

It wasn't until she came out that she realized how handsome Gavin looked. He wore dark brown khaki pants and a light beige Ralph Lauren button-down dress shirt tucked in neatly. She knew it was Lauren from the little emblem of the polo player on the left side of his strong chest. It wasn't tight, but just snug enough to tell anyone looking that this was a man who works out and takes care of his diet. Looking down, she saw he had on a pair of brown shoes that complemented the pants perfectly.

"You look great," she said without thinking.

Gavin smiled broadly and responded, "You too. Ready to have some fun?"

She recognized his truck from that night he came into the diner, and she liked the way he walked around the back to open her door first before letting himself in. She knew nothing about engines, but when he fired it up it roared like a rocket ship. Gavin put the truck in gear and slowly drove down all of the important streets in Manchester, pointing out things along the way.

"That's the barber shop. A nice guy named Fred has been cutting hair there for, well, since I was a kid. He's getting a bit old now, so if you don't mind your hair a little crooked, you can get a cut there for ten bucks."

Chase smiled. "Ten bucks? The girl who cuts me back in Seattle charges ten bucks just to give you a shampoo. A cut there is more like sixty."

Gavin nodded. "But I'll bet it's straight."

Chased laughed back. "Ah, yeah, at least it's straight."

They drove some more, and then Gavin pointed. "I know you've eaten at the Empty Plate, but if you want something different for breakfast, Aunt Nolly's bakery is up on the second floor of this building. Freshest and best rolls you've ever tasted. Just know she lives below the bakery, so she gets up early and bakes the fresh rolls at five a.m. If you don't get there fast, they're all gone by eight o'clock, sometimes sooner."

Chase pretended she was taking notes with her finger, using it like an imaginary pen. "Aunt Nolly's by eight or no hot rolls for you." She was enjoying this drive and chat.

Gavin was more relaxed and not as cocky as he appeared when she first met him, or later that night in the diner when he was playing the role of the strong, silent cowboy. She had to remind herself to stop staring at his face; those deep eyes and strong jawline were downright distracting. He caught her looking a little too long, and she quickly darted her attention out the window, turning a light shade of red.

Gavin kept driving and slowed down on the play by play of everything they saw out the truck windows. He didn't want to talk her ear off. After a gentle pause he said, "You hungry? I kind of packed us a picnic."

Chase hadn't eaten in hours, and pulling over for a bite to eat did sound inviting. "Sure, I'm famished," she said.

After another five minutes of driving away from the town Gavin pulled up a dirt road that lead to a small stream. He opened her door and took her by the hand, carefully leading her over the uncertain footing, bringing her to within just a few feet of the rushing water, which made a loud roar. The water looked cold as it tumbled over the jagged rocks, big and small, in this wild country creek.

"We swim here in the summer," Gavin said to her. "Well, the water is shallow, so it's more like lying in the rocks as the cool water runs over your body. Trust me; it's better than any air conditioner or pool." Chase believed him and could almost picture the rugged farmer and his friends lounging in the creek bed with a six-pack of beer chilling in a cooler nearby. Almost as if he was reading her mind Gavin added, "And the cool part of coming here in the summer is, if you bring something cold to drink, you don't need a cooler. You just find a big rock in the middle of the stream, one that isn't going to move, and you put the bottle or can of what you're drinking down in the sand behind it."

Chase was fascinated by this. "Right in the water, you put it?"

Gavin nodded. "Yep, they call it 'sinking the beer.' And when you're thirsty you pluck it out and that beer is ice cold."

Chase looked up at the stream and then at the hills surrounding them, and for the first time in her life she understood why people like living in the middle of nowhere. She said to herself without thinking, "Who needs a mall when you can sink your beer." Gavin couldn't hear her over the rushing water, but he could tell she liked it here by the joy on her face.

The handsome cowboy then spread a large checkered blanket out on the shore and retrieved a wicker basket he'd carefully hidden in the back of the truck. Inside was a $20 bottle of Merlot, fresh bread, a brick of sharp cheddar cheese, and an uncut stick of pepperoni. He produced a sharp hunting knife from the cab of the truck and proceeded to cut up the delicious food.

"Oh my God, I don't know if it's just because I'm starving, but that looks amazing right now," Chase said.

Gavin smiled as he lay out the unexpected treat onto a plate and popped the cork on the wine. It had a picture of a windmill on the label, with the words "Wind Spring Vineyard" written out in block letters. "A college buddy of mine owns the vineyard where they produce this, out on Cape Cod. The windmill is actually a photo of the one on his property in Yarmouth. It's pretty good wine, considering it's not from Napa."

Chase looked at the wine and said, "Your friend has his own windmill? Cool."

He poured Chase a healthy amount, and she swirled it around in the pristine glass before bringing it to her ruby-red lips and taking a small sip. "Mmm, you're right, it *is* good. Go Cape Cod!" she added playfully.

There was silence for a while as they sipped their wine and stared at the rhythm of the stream. It was perfect and almost hypnotizing watching the water break over the rocks. Gavin broke the silence, saying, "Isn't it kind of crazy? This little stream leads to a bigger stream and that to a river and eventually to the ocean. So, the water we're watching, right now, will someday be part of something so much bigger."

Chase smiled at the thought and said back to him, "I wonder if it will remember us. The water. I mean, someday when we're swimming in the ocean, does the water we see today remember us like an old friend? Does it embrace us?"

Gavin liked the way she thought, and as he tossed a small stick into the stream he said, "I keep forgetting you're a writer. That was beautiful, what you just said." He wanted to tell her she was beautiful too, but it felt too soon. *Don't rush and blow this*, he kept saying to himself.

When the picnic was done and their tummies were full, they returned to Gavin's truck and started back toward town. It was just beginning to get dark, and Chase was glad Gavin was driving because she knew she'd be lost on these unmarked country roads. Gavin looked more than once at his watch, and Chase noticed and asked, "Are you late for something?"

Gavin smiled and said, "No, actually right on time. Can I show you one last thing before I bring you home?"

Chase trusted him. "Sure."

Gavin took a few more turns and then pulled off the side of the road, next to a big field to the right. It didn't look like anyone's property because it wasn't well kept, and the weeds and trees seemed to just grow wild there. Gavin got out and told Chase to stand in the back of the truck on the big flat metal bed. "You'll be able to see better up there," Gavin added.

"See what?" she wondered.

Just then he walked down the hill into the tall weeds. She could only make out his silhouette now because it was really getting dark. He looked back over his shoulder at Chase and said with a grin, "Watch this." Gavin then started running through the weeds, clapping his hands loudly. All at once Chase noticed something rising from the clumps of tangled grass, something small and dark at first that suddenly started to light up like tiny candles. They were lightning bugs, thousands of them.

Suddenly the dark field was filled with little dots of bright light flying in every direction. It was like a private fireworks show provided by nature. Well, nature and a kind farmer with a college degree and good taste in wine. Gavin stood in the field with his arms stretched out to his sides and yelled a very proud, "Ta da."

Chase laughed so loud and uncontrollably, she put her hand over her mouth to contain it. It was the silliest and sweetest gesture someone had ever done for her.

After Gavin returned to the truck, he helped her down off the back and into the cab. To do this he had to momentarily put his hands around her small waist, and she liked the way he felt as he held her. He opened her truck door again like a gentleman and helped her with the seat belt. As she was about to click it, and he was about to shut the passenger door, Chase said, "Wait. Come here." With both hands she grabbed him by his strong shoulders and pulled Gavin close to her, making certain to lock eyes with him before what happened next. Staring in each other's eyes, three seconds felt like three hours. Then she pulled him in all the way to kiss him. It wasn't a hard, awkward kiss. It was soft and perfect. She held him there for a second and wanted more, but she stopped herself and said, "Thank you for a perfect day."

Gavin did something that he rarely did with women he dated: he pulled her closer and gave her a big strong hug. He liked this girl, this stranger in town. He liked the way she talked and thought and felt in his arms at that moment. He then released his unexpected hug, looked Chase directly in the eyes and said, "You're welcome."

No one spoke for the rest of the drive home. Both knew that moment was perfect, and neither was going to ruin it with idle chatter. The comfortable silence put a bow on an evening that couldn't have gone better.

10

has anyone seen Rudy?

It was late November when Chase slept her first night in the comfortable bedroom at the old St. Pius church. Even though she'd only been in Manchester a couple of days, she could already tell you two things for certain. The sun came up that time of year a few minutes before seven a.m. She knew this because it was streaming through the window and hitting her directly in the eyes as she sat up, wondering who had turned the light on in her pitch-dark room. That led to the second thing she could tell you, which was that whoever built this place a couple hundred years ago placed the bedroom facing directly east; not a smart move if you were a writer who liked to stay up late working on your laptop.

Scooter was on the bed next to her and stretching his front paws forward as he stuck his furry backside up toward the ceiling. "My dog is doing downward dog," Chase said to herself with amusement, thinking of the yoga class she tried once back home and didn't much care for. Too much sitting around, she thought. She was more of a "spin girl."

She put her bare feet on the hardwood floor with its thick boards, much wider than the wooden floors they make today, fumbled through her top dresser drawer, and retrieved a pair of wool socks that would cut down on the chill her toes were feeling. She slowly made her way to the kitchen and opened the side door, allowing Scooter to go back into a fenced-in area to do his morning business. Lucky for her, the kitchen came equipped with a small Keurig coffee maker, and there were some pods in the cabinet above. Her eyes were not quite awake yet, so the task of making a simple cup of coffee seemed to take twice as long as it should.

Soon enough though, the aroma of fresh coffee filled the kitchen. She took her warm cup into her small, soft hands and curled up on a couch that faced a fireplace in the living room area. "I will definitely have to make use of that firewood," she said out loud, as if someone were listening. As she started to finally wake, her mind went back to that perfect date with Gavin the evening before. "It was a date, right?" she asked herself, with some measure of doubt. "Of course it was. We kissed and had a meal and he did that firefly thing in the field. Definitely a date," she told herself with more confidence now.

She took her time sipping the coffee, and the silence of the quiet Vermont November morning was broken by the sound of scratching at the door. "Coming, Scooter," she yelled. Chase bounced up off the warm couch and flung open the kitchen door, and her puppy ran in with the morning chill chasing after him. She fixed him a quick bowl of dog food and water and took a seat in the kitchen, watching him eat. As he finished up his kibble, Chase realized her own stomach was growling. In her haste to rent this place from Owen and take the tour with Gavin she had never had time to stop at the grocery store. She didn't know much about Manchester, but there were two sure solutions to an empty stomach this morning: that bakery Gavin had mentioned on the other side of town with the fresh rolls, or the Empty Plate Diner, which was just a few blocks away. Quicker and closer sounded better in her mind.

Chase changed into a hooded sweatshirt and jeans, pulled on a pair of brown leather boots, and grabbed her purse and laptop before heading out the door. She took some of Scooter's toys and placed them in the big open area of the church with the stained glass windows and told him, "Be a good boy for Mommy. I'll be back in a bit."

As she strolled down the block, she noticed how awake the town of Manchester was, even at this hour, reminding herself of the cliché that country folks tend to rise and fall with the sun. Perhaps building a home with the bedroom facing directly east did made sense after all, because you could use the sun as an alarm clock long before cell phones were invented.

A few people passed her as she walked, and every single one of them said hello, even though they had no clue who she was. Whether you were a tourist or a local, the attitude was, "You're in Manchester today, so you're one of us." Chase liked that, and she gave a very welcoming smile and waved back at everyone she saw.

Walking with the laptop would be a daily occurrence no matter where Chase lived, because, as a writer, she never knew when an idea would strike, and she'd need to get busy writing it down. If ideas floated invisibly in the sky, that laptop was Chase's butterfly net to scoop them up and cage them before they got away.

It took her less than four minutes to go from the church to the Empty Plate Diner. She hadn't even cleared the front door when a familiar voice bellowed, "Good morning, Miss Harrington," from a booth to her right. It was Sheriff Harlan, polishing off some scrambled eggs and bacon, extra crisp, waving hello to the new girl in town.

"Hey, Sheriff," Chase returned with a smile. It felt as if she'd known him for years.

Chase then heard, "Grab a seat anywhere you like." It was a female voice that also sounded familiar.

"Hey, Brad," Chase said with a teasing grin. It was Brenda, the waitress she had met the night she arrived in town. Before Chase could even ask, Brenda was on the way over to her table with a pot of coffee in one hand and a clean white ceramic cup in the other.

"What's shakin' bacon?" Brenda said playfully, as she poured a cup of coffee, acting like they were two old pals.

Chase thought for a second, making a list in her mind and said, "Well, I rented the old church with the pretty windows even though I'm not religious, I got a tour of town and a lightning-bug show from a cowboy, and a very nice old man gave me a painting."

Brenda had grown up in Manchester and knew every last stitch of this place, so she pondered for about five seconds before saying, "So you're living at St. Pius, handsome Gavin got you into his truck, and Ned Farnsworth told you about his daughter."

Chase was impressed. "Wow, pretty good, Brenda. Or should I say Brad?"

Brenda put a menu down on the table in front of Chase adding, "You can call me Brad until Friday. That's the day, I'm told, I get a real name tag again."

Chase laughed at the silliness of it all and said, "You'll always be Brad to me."

Brenda put both hands over her heart in an exaggerated gesture and let out an "Aww," as if she were swooning.

Shayla, the owner, walked by and recognized Chase from the other evening, adding, "Looks like we can't keep you away."

Chase glanced around at the old-fashioned diner with those precious little jukebox machines at every booth and the greasy counter and said, "No, you can't."

As Shayla went to walk away, the writer in Chase had to know something. "Hey, Shayla, is it? Can I ask you a question? What's with the name of this place?"

Shayla got this question a lot from *out of towners*, so she moved close to Chase's booth and said, "Well, think about it. We have the best food in southern Vermont. If you order anything off the menu here, what do you end up with fifteen minutes later?"

Chase got it now. "Ah ha, an empty plate."

Shayla pointed her finger at her like a little pistol, pretended to pull a trigger and made the sound of a tiny gun going off. "Pshooo." With that she was back behind the counter to berate her husband for falling behind on the orders.

"Mind if I join you?" It was Sheriff Harlan, looking a little lonely in the big booth he was sitting in by himself.

Chase gave Harlan her million-dollar smile and said without hesitation, "Of course you can. Come on over."

Harlan had finished his eggs and toast but was taking his time on his third cup of coffee. He took the chair directly across from Chase and asked, "So, how do you like us so far? I hope you write something nice about us."

Chase considered the sheriff's request and said, "Hey, wait, how did you know I was a writer?"

Harlan gave her an aww shucks grin and said, "Miss Harrington, word gets around real fast in a small town like Manchester. Plus, the license plate kind of gives you away."

Chase nodded. "I guess it does. And to answer your question, I do plan to write something, but I haven't started yet. I'm kind of intrigued by that old man at the inn and the daughter he lost, Taylor."

The sheriff's face turned more serious now, and his voice took on an almost protective tone. "Oh, and why is that?"

Chase struggled to explain her exact reasons. "I don't know. Young girl, an artist, so pretty and she dies that way. Now the town doesn't even celebrate Christmas like they used to."

Harlan put his coffee cup down and leaned closer. "We still celebrate the good Lord's birthday. We just don't have the big bonfire and tree lighting like before. Out of respect."

Chase listened carefully but was confused. "Because a young girl died? That's really why you stopped having it?"

Harlan could see from her face she wasn't picking up on what he was trying to say, and suddenly he was growing weary of this conversation, adding, "Yes. Driving up and down that road on the mountain to celebrate just doesn't sit right with a lot of folks, not after what happened. You'd have to live here for a while to get it, young lady."

Chase didn't want to press the lawman any further, so she bowed her head and said in an apologetic tone, "Fair enough, sir."

The two of them sat in silence for a moment, not sure how to restart this conversation on a happier tone, when the bell on the diner's front door let out a loud *clang*. It was an older woman named Maria Millington, holding a stack of papers. When she got closer, walking by the table that Chase and Harlan were sitting at, they both noticed an image of a little Scottish terrier on every piece of paper. They were identical copies of the same dog with some words beneath his photo.

"What's wrong, Maria?" Shayla asked from near the register.

The old woman looked disheveled, with messy hair and no makeup on. A closer look at her eyes revealed she'd been crying. "It's Rudy. He's missing." With that she handed a flier to Shayla, and below the pup's picture were the words, "MISSING. Answers to the name Rudy. If you see him, please call." Maria's phone number was printed out as well.

Shayla held the flier in her hand, and as her heart sank, Maria asked, "Would you mind if I posted one on the bulletin board, Shayla? I know this is a diner, not a lost pet center, but . . ." With that, she started to cry.

"Shhh. Of course you can, sweetie," Shayla said, while rubbing Maria's arm for comfort. "Of course. We'll find him."

As the small flier was attached to the brown cork bulletin board with a tiny red thumbtack, Maria handed out copies to a few people sitting at the counter. Chase and Harlan were watching all of this from their booth a few feet away.

"Her dog is lost," Chase said to Sheriff Harlan. "That stinks. Do you think you can help her?"

Harlan was a small-town cop, but even this was a bit under his pay grade. "Missing people, missing cars, missing laptops," Harlan said, pointing to Chase's computer sitting on the table between them. "Those cases I work and investigate. But missing dogs? If I did that, I'd spend half my time looking under every back porch in Manchester. Her pup will turn up—they almost always do."

Chase sipped her coffee and felt uneasy for the woman with tears in her eyes at the counter. "I hope so," she said to Harlan.

Just then, her cell phone dinged from her jacket pocket. She always kept the volume on loud so she'd hear it no matter where she had tucked it away. "Excuse me, Harlan, not to be rude, but," Chase said taking out her cell and looking at who was messaging her. It was a Manchester area code and a number that vaguely looked familiar. Once she started reading the message things crystalized quickly. "Good morning, Miss Harrington. This is Owen Johnson. My son Tommy hasn't stopped talking about your dog. I was wondering if you were up for a little lunch today and maybe Tommy could play with your pup? I can bring sandwiches and we could eat right at your new place if that's okay. Let me know."

Chase took care to look at it twice, giving the sheriff enough time to read Owen's name upside down from the other side of the table. "Interesting. Gavin gives you a tour last night and now the mysterious widowed Realtor fancies a little lunch." Harlan took a drink of his coffee with a very satisfied look on his face, like a man who thinks he's being amusing.

Chase suddenly felt embarrassed, but she wasn't sure why. She then blurted out to Harlan, "Wait. What? I don't think . . . Listen, he's my Realtor, and his son wants to see my dog. That's all this is, and you should not jump to . . ." Chase stopped herself as if another shoe was about to drop in her brain, looking a third time at the message for some secret meaning.

"Conclusions? Is that the word you're looking for dear?" Harlan finished her thought.

Chase threw her shoulders back as if ready to tell someone off. "What I mean is . . . Hey, I am not your dear, and what I'm saying is . . . Hey; hold up, how did you know I was out with Gavin? And don't give me that small-town nonsense. There wasn't another car for miles when we . . ." She stopped herself again midsentence, feeling a bit silly.

"When you what, Chase?" Harlan said with a chuckle.

Chase glared at him, but she wasn't really upset at all. "None of your beeswax. Hey, Sheriff, shouldn't you be getting home to the missus and explaining why you're eating bacon and toast smothered in butter when you're supposed to be watching your waistline?"

Harlan took another sip of his coffee and said, "Oh, I think the life and times of Manchester's newest resident are far more interesting than anything going on at my house." There was a pause now between them when Harlan let her off the hook. "Listen, kid, I'm just teasing you. I know about Gavin because the two of you drove by the barber shop and I recognized his truck out the window."

Chase relaxed her tone. "Yeah, I thought your hair looked crooked."

Both of them laughed now, and Harlan added, "He's a nice guy and so is Owen, although . . ." Harlan stopped himself there.

"What?" Chase asked seriously.

"Nothing," Harlan responded. Chase gave him a look that said, hey, buddy, you can't start a sentence like that and not finish it. Harlan continued, "They're just in very different places of their lives. Owen is still trying to find his feet after life knocked him down. You know what I mean?"

Chase did, adding, "His wife, you mean? Yeah, that's rough."

Harlan nodded. "It is, but he's a good father and guy, so, oh, I don't know. I guess what I'm saying is, be careful with his heart."

It sounded like an overstatement to Chase. I mean, after all, the guy was just bringing his son over to play with the dog and maybe they eat a sandwich in the kitchen. Still, she could tell he was fragile from her brief time with him, so she gave Harlan a reassuring look and said, "I hear you and I will. I mean, how do you even know he's interested in me that way?"

Harlan sat up from his chair and put on his hat, which had been hanging on a hook to his left. "Um, have you looked in the mirror lately, Chase?" It embarrassed her when people gave her compliments like that, but it also made her feel good.

"You're sweet, Sheriff." Harlan made his way toward the door and gave it a yank, waking up that bell again that hung above it.

Chase noticed the napkin holder was made of shiny metal, which also meant it could work as a mirror in a pinch. She picked it up and glanced at her own reflection. Everyone saw a beauty that somehow eluded her. "Why was that?" she thought, as she looked into her own green eyes.

Her breakfast arrived: egg whites and turkey sausage with whole wheat toast. As she picked up her fork to dig in, she said out loud to herself, "It's just lunch. That's it. His boy likes Scooter, nothing more." Something inside knew different, and Harlan's words still hung in the air like the scent of burnt bacon long after he left. "He's damaged goods, so hands off." That's what he was telling her. Plus, there was Gavin and those fireflies. Chase had been in Manchester a grand total of seventy-two hours and her life was turning into a romance novel. Maybe that's why she hadn't opened the laptop yet to write a story; at this moment her real life was so much better than fiction.

11

the unexpected posse

The temperature was in the low fifties, which was downright warm by Vermont standards for late November. More sun than clouds occupied the light blue sky, and fallen leaves covered the sidewalks that lined Manchester's Main Street. Chase had grown up on the West Coast, so she'd never heard what dried-up leaves sounded like when they crunched under your feet. It was a bit addictive, like those people who pop BubbleWrap after opening a package.

So, "crunch, crunch" went her feet as she strolled down to the town square, taking in the beauty and simplicity of a small New England town. "I can see why people live here," she said to herself, as she returned to St. Pius to grab Scooter for an early morning walk. Scooter liked it here too, if you counted how many times he wagged his tale as a measure of happiness.

The two of them made their way around the town, taking time to explore some small side roads she had driven by but never ventured down. Manchester's architecture was beautiful and untouched by time. It was almost as if they had passed a local law that said you can't build a home that looks like anything older than the 1920s. Many of the homes were small, almost cottage-like, with lots of property around them. And every single one had a view of something nice. Equinox Mountain stretched up to the northwest, and open valleys, fields, and streams greeted your eyes if you looked south or east. She could see why people would have settled and built their homes here hundreds of years ago. The mountains stood like big brothers protecting you from the harshest of winters. The Battenkill River ran the stretch of the entire town on the west side, supplying ample fishing and fun for anyone with a paddle and canoe.

Scooter's nails needed trimming, because Chase could hear them clicking along the stone walkways as they made their way through town. She had brought a bottle of water and a small dish in case he or she got thirsty. Most young women would be lonely, being off on their own like this, three thousand miles from friends and family, but Chase viewed everything as an adventure and source material for her writing. She could sit in a coffee shop for hours just watching people and come up with ideas for a half-dozen stories. She'd sold a number of them as a freelance writer to major publications, enough to fund these trips. This time something told her she might find a larger story to tell, one that could fill a whole book.

As the two of them circled the entire town and were ready to make their way back home, Chase noticed a small group gathered in a place they called "Monument Square." It was a large green space with benches, and in the center stood a soldier's statue with a stone wall listing the names of local heroes who had fought and died in America's wars. Each name was someone local who had put down their farm tools and taken up a weapon to protect their country.

There were about a dozen people gathered there, of all ages, having a loud, animated discussion with pieces of paper in their hands. As Chase got closer, she saw they were holding fliers for the missing dog she had learned about in the diner earlier that morning.

Chase and Scooter approached gently, knowing they weren't invited to whatever this gathering was. She smiled sheepishly and looked toward the ground, uncertain how to proceed. "Can we help you?" asked an older woman in a winter jacket that looked much too warm for this weather.

Another man she didn't recognize interrupted, "Oh, I know you. You're the new girl who rented the old church. What's your name?"

Before she had a chance to answer she heard, "Chase. Chase Harrington. She's all right." It was Ned Farnsworth, with a walking stick in one hand and a small silver flask filled with something he called *grandma's medicine* in the other.

Chase was happy to see a friendly face. "Oh, hey, Mr. Farnsworth. Watcha doin'?"

The first woman spoke up again, addressing the entire group. "This is Maria Millington's dog Rudy. He jumped the fence going after a squirrel and she hasn't seen him since. Usually he comes right back, but he didn't this time, so she's worried." The woman pushed a flier with Rudy's picture on it into Chase's hand. "So, we're forming up a posse and we're going to fan out and see if we can't find him and get him back where he belongs."

Chase was astonished by the kindness of what they were doing. "Wow, okay, well, that's so nice of you."

Ned moved a bit closer to Chase now and spoke in a hushed tone to keep what he said a bit more private. "Since her husband, Al, died ten years ago, she's been very lonely, and that dog is her only company," Ned whispered.

Chase nodded. "Got it. Well, Scooter and I don't have plans for a couple of hours, so how can we help?"

The first woman jumped in again. "Glad you asked. We are all taking a section of town and looking for Rudy. Since you don't know your foot from your elbow, 'cause you just got here, why don't you and—what's your dog's name again?"

Chase patted his head. "Scooter. This is Scooter."

"Why don't you and Scooter walk south down Main Street and check every back yard you see on the right side of the road. When you hit the garage with the big sign that says *Tire Service*, turn around and hit all the back yards on the other side as you walk back."

The small group parted with their assignments, and Chase did as she was instructed, making her way down the block with her dog leading the way. Scooter sniffed the ground as if he understood they were on some kind of a detective case looking for missing jewels or something. A few people came out on their porches when they saw her poking around their back yards, but Chase just held up the flier and said, "Trying to help a woman find her dog."

More than a few of them said, "Rudy? Maria's dog is missing again? Darn it."

As she passed a big Victorian house with a large front porch, she noticed the sign outside said "Valenti's Funeral Home." Back in Seattle the funeral parlors were very modern, but this one looked like someone's home. "Nice," she said to herself, as she looked at the spires jutting up toward the morning sky. She saw a flock of twenty or so geese cutting through the blue above like a big black arrow and heading south for the winter. They were loud, she thought, for being so high in the sky.

"They're smart, getting out of Dodge when the getting's good," a voice said to her from the bushes to her left. It was a man in his sixties, balding but wearing a Boston Red Sox baseball cap to hide the worst of it. "I'm Roddie Valenti—this is my place," he said, gesturing to the funeral home.

Chase was caught off guard and forgot her manners for a moment. "I'm sorry—Chase Harrington. What were you saying about getting out of where?"

"Dodge. Getting out of Dodge. It's an expression. I was talking about the geese. We get about ninety inches of snow every winter, which works out to about ten small storms and four doozies."

Chase laughed at her slow-wittedness. "Getting out of Dodge, right. I'm sorry; I guess I'm not quite awake yet."

Roddie smiled. "No worries, I shouldn't be sneaking up on you like that. I saw you going in and out of yards. You lose something, dear?"

Chase held up the flier. "Not me, a woman named Maria Millington lost her dog, Rudy."

Without hesitation he said, "I'll get my coat."

Chase wasn't sure what that meant, exactly. Was he going to walk with her, or was he going out to look on his own? Before she thought too hard about it the door swung open and Roddie emerged with a thick brown Carhartt work jacket on. "I'll help you look. You must be new around here 'cause I don't recognize you. Unless you're Marsha Willburn's granddaughter, the one who went to Chicago to study finance?"

Chase giggled. "No, no, I'm Chase, remember? Chase Harrington."

Roddie scratched his head. "Duh, you did say that. Sorry. Let's see if we can find her dog."

Chase looked back at the funeral home and said, "You can just leave like that?"

Roddie let out a big laugh. "Oh yeah, no croakers today. I'm free as a bird flying south."

Chase smiled at him and said, "This is Scooter."

Roddie rubbed Scooter's chest and got a kiss on the face in exchange for the kindness. He then showed her a cell phone in his left hand, adding, "Besides, if someone decides to meet the Grim Reaper while we're out, they'll just give me a call." He paused for a moment, adding, "The family of the dead person will call, not the Grim Reaper. I don't think he has cell service from the afterlife." With that he laughed again so loud it made him cough.

Chase started walking again with Scooter, thinking to herself, *For a guy who spends all day with dead people he sure is happy.*

She looked at Scooter and said, "It must be Manchester. Right, buddy?"

Roddie heard her and said, "What is?"

Chase looked over her shoulder and said, "Oh, nothing."

Over the next hour the two of them walked together and snaked their way through the fifteen blocks of downtown Manchester, searching every nook and cranny they could find. Scooter's presence seemed to spook a number of dogs who were in their own yards, but for all the barking and carrying on there was no sign of little Rudy.

Chase got more comfortable with the man from the empty funeral home, so she said, "I have to ask: Roddie? That's an interesting name. Is it short for something?"

The funeral director nodded and said, "It is: Rodney. But that's not why I got it."

Chase was intrigued, "Okay, so?"

He continued, "When you drove into Manchester a couple days back did you happen to notice a huge store called Orvis?"

Chase searched her memory. "Is that the one with the big pond next to it and fishing stuff all over the place out front?"

Roddie smiled. "That's the one. If you go in that store they have a section where they sell fly-fishing stuff, and they have thousands of fake flies. You tie them on the line and use them to catch trout and bass."

Chase replied, "Okay, okay, continue."

"In the corner you'll see a little section with flies that I tied. I sell them there."

Chase was lost now. "I'm not following. What does that have to do with your name?"

Roddie brought the story home for her. "I've been fly-fishing and tying my own flies since I was seven. I'd go down to the Battenkill and fish ten hours straight. When I was a boy, every time anyone saw me walking through town I was always carrying a basket to hold the fish I'd caught, and resting on my shoulder was my . . ."

He paused now, waiting for Chase to catch up. "Your fly rod!" she finally said.

"That's right," he continued. "Since my name was already Rod-ney, everyone just started calling me Rod-eee."

Chase nodded, understanding now. "It makes sense. Erastus, Shayla, Roddie, you people have names that belong in a James Joyce novel."

Roddie responded, "James who?"

Chase smiled. "Never mind."

The two of them stopped chatting and realized they had covered the entire area Chase was told to search and found everything but a dog named Rudy.

"I guess we're done. I'm sorry we didn't find him, but it was sure great to meet you, Roddie." Chase extended her hand to shake his.

The older gentleman took her small hand with both of his and said, "The pleasure was mine, young lady. Bye, Scooter." With that, Roddie

Valenti crossed the street and headed back to his home and business, waiting for the phone to ring.

Chase looked at her watch and said to Scooter, "We should probably start heading back. You need lunch and I have a . . ." She stopped herself midsentence, realizing that she'd almost said *date*. Then, as if Scooter were waiting for her to finish, she added, "Friend. I have a friend coming over and a little boy who wants to play with you."

With that the wind picked up, and as Chase and Scooter crossed Main Street and made their way back to the old church, a sidewalk full of orange and red leaves, all curled up and extra-crunchy, blew with the wind and seemed to chase them home.

12

taco tuesday

There was an antique clock that was left in the empty church when the congregation moved on to greener pastures. It was nothing fancy, rosewood with a white face that was now stained yellow from the rigors of time. It looked as if someone had taken a new clock and dipped it in tea. Still, for an old thing, it worked with precision and counted out the gongs when it was the top of each hour. First it played a brief melody and then counted out the hours, letting you know where things stood in the day. As Chase finished feeding her pup, making the bed, and tidying up, the clock counted out, one, two, three, four . . . not stopping until it clanged twelve times, telling Chase it was indeed noon and her non-date should be arriving any minute.

Right on cue there was a loud knock at the door, and Scooter barked and ran to greet their lunch guests. Before she even had a chance to open the door, she smelled something good and no doubt bad for your waistline. The large wooden door pulled open to reveal Owen and Tommy side by side, dressed nicely as if they really were going to church for a service instead of lunch. Before she could even get a proper "hello" out, Tommy screamed, "SCOOTER," and pushed passed her to almost tackle the dog.

"TOMMY," Owen yelled in embarrassment at his son's lack of manners.

"It's okay, it's okay. Scooter will love the attention," Chase responded.

Owen wiped his feet on a mat outside the door that Chase hadn't even noticed was there until this moment. She saw Owen was holding a rather large fast-food bag in his hands. "And what have we here?" she asked in a playful tone.

Owen looked embarrassed again. "Listen, I'm sorry about this. I told Tommy he could pick what we ate for lunch and . . ."

Before Owen could finish his thought, Tommy barked out, "Taco Tuesday at Taco Bell." Then, without prompting, in a fake deep voice he started reciting a TV commercial he'd seen so many times, "Don't forget, taco fans. On Taco Tuesday you can get five tacos with all the fixin's for just two bucks. No, don't adjust your TV dial; you heard that right, five tacos for two bucks. Only on taco Tuesdays and only at Taco Bell." Chase laughed out loud at Tommy's spot-on impression of a TV announcer.

Owen looked up with those kind, brown deer eyes and said, "Epic fail on my part letting him pick, especially since it's Tuesday. I was thinking more Caesar salad or something healthy, but . . ." Chase cut him off right there. "Well, I'll have you both know I'm starving, and I absolutely LOVE tacos."

With that they made their way to the large oak island that sat at the center of the kitchen and spread out the feast on top. "Just do me a favor, Tommy. None for Scooter, okay? It may bother his stomach."

Tommy smiled as he patted the dog on the head, and said, "Sorry pal, no Taco Tuesday for you."

As they crunched away Chase couldn't help noticing how adorable Owen really was. He was nothing like Gavin, but certainly right in all the ways that matter to a woman looking for a steady man to lean on. Handsome in the "boy down the hall at college" kind of way, the one you never really noticed back then but wish now you had flirted with or asked out on a date. He was wearing jeans and a white dress shirt with a black sweater vest over the top. The sleeves carefully rolled up on each side gave him the look of a man who could hop under the hood of your car and fix something at a moment's notice. He smelled good too.

"What is that you're wearing?" Chase asked curiously.

Owen had a mouthful of beans and rice, and the question caught him off guard. "Oh, this?" He swallowed before continuing. "Sorry. This is Polo. The green bottle, not the blue."

Chase smiled, not sure what that even meant, and Owen could see it in her expression.

"I'm sorry. I'm terrible with names of things. Polo sells a few different fragrances, but the two most popular come in a green or blue bottle. The green is the original and it smells nice without knocking people over. The blue is a sporty style and it's too strong for me. See . . ." He extended his wrist toward Chase's face, and she hesitated before leaning in and taking a good whiff.

"Oh my, that is good," she said in a sultry tone one uses when describing a hot fudge sundae, not one you'd use talking to a man you have no interest in. She didn't, right, have any interest? As she looked him up and down confusion was quickly replacing certainty. *Good grief, woman, what are you doing?* she immediately yelled in her head. *STOP.*

Owen saw her react to the cologne, and that pleased him in an unexpected way. He told himself this was just lunch with a new friend and Tommy playing with a dog, nothing more, and now he had her smelling him. *Slow down, tiger,* is all he kept thinking.

Then he did what he always did when he was around an attractive woman in the years since his wife died. "Grace loved that scent too," he added. *Why in God's name am I bringing up my dead wife,* he thought to himself. It was no wonder he hadn't dated anyone since her passing.

Chase just smiled and said, "Well, she had good taste."

Tommy finished his tacos and asked if he could take Scooter out in the yard to play fetch. Now it was just the very tender Owen and the new girl in town, who had no clue what she was doing with her dating life, sitting together in the kitchen.

A silence filled the room, both searching for something to say to get them back on track here. "Tacos were good," Chase began.

Owen cut her off immediately. "You don't have to say that. It was a bit of a disaster, but it made Tommy happy, so . . ."

Chase smiled and looked into Owen's eyes now. "You adore him, don't you?"

Owen got up and tapped a plastic spoon in his hand nervously as he paced the kitchen before saying, "I do. He's my everything now. Since my wife died."

Chase just smiled gently, not saying a word.

Owen then said, "Jesus, I never say it that way. You know? It's always, Grace is no longer with us, or Grace passed. I never say she died. It's almost too, oh, I don't know."

"Final?" Chase offered.

Owen put the spoon down and hopped onto a stool closer to her. "Yeah, I guess that's it."

There was more silence now with Chase, uncertain where to tread and if so, how lightly. Then Owen surprised her. "You know, I know this isn't really a date, but this is the first time I've asked a woman to meet me for a meal, even if it was just tacos, since Grace died. I know it's not a date, but I guess I wanted you to know that."

Chase smiled and appreciated his honesty. "Well, I feel honored then. As for this being a date? I don't know why we have to label things, Owen; sometimes life should just be lived and experienced."

Owen suddenly had a burst of courage or recklessness, he wasn't sure which, when he interrupted Chase, blurting out in a loud voice, "Are you seeing Gavin Bennett, the Chippendale farmer with the fancy degree? Wow, why did I just ask that? Why did I just get so snarky there? I'm so sorry." Owen couldn't believe the words that just came rapid fire out of his mouth.

Chase didn't mean to, but his avalanche of very personal questions made her laugh out loud. "Um, well, we had one sort of a date, but I wouldn't say we're dating. Not yet. I think you need more than one picnic by the water to call it dating."

Owen leaned back and ran his tongue across the front of his teeth. He did this whenever he was concentrating or trying to solve a puzzle and was totally unaware he was doing it. "He took you to the Battenkill for a picnic? Oh, he's good. He's always been good. That guy can have any girl in the county and you're new and beautiful so why am I surprised he brought his A game and . . . Ya know, I'm gonna just stop talking."

Chase was smiling again, not certain how to respond to that. So much for Owen the sad Realtor being a shrinking violet. *Once you fill him with tacos he's a regular chatterbox*, she thought to herself.

Chase couldn't resist teasing him now, asking as she looked down at her nails, pretending to inspect them, "So, you think I'm beautiful?"

Owen suddenly responded, "No. I mean. Yes. Come on, you know you are. Don't torture me because I ran on at the mouth that way."

Chase stepped down from her seat and imitated Frankenstein's monster extending her arms like a zombie in a trance and started marching around the kitchen saying, "Well you haven't seen me in the morning without my makeup. Raaaahhhhhhhhhhhhhhh!!!"

With that the door swung open and Tommy and Scooter bounded back in. "Oh, are we playing monster?" Tommy asked.

Owen was usually unhappy when Tommy barged in on his conversations, but in this case the boy had just saved him. He then lowered his voice to a whisper and said to Chase, "Something tells me you are beautiful, even in the morning."

He hated retreating this way from a brutally honest conversation, but Tommy's return gave Owen a chance to make a break for the door before he blurted out something else he wasn't ready to admit. "We should probably hit the road, champ."

Chase was surprised he was leaving this soon and wasn't sure what to say next, given the conversation they'd been having not ten seconds before.

Tommy intervened, "I'm 'champ,' in case you're wondering. He's talking to me," he said to Chase. His childlike innocence that went hand in hand with his autism made him such a delightful, honest, and loving boy. Before she could respond Tommy stepped forward and gave her a big hug. "Thank you for letting me play with Scooter."

He then started toward the door, making certain to give the dog one more back rub.

Owen's soft, sad eyes returned, replacing his momentary courage, as he said to Chase, "I really did have a good time. Maybe we can have another non-date someday."

Chase took his hand and gave it a squeeze. "Do me a favor. Don't overanalyze everything so much, Owen. You can be 'just friends' with a woman and have fun and not worry where it's going. Time has a way of sorting things out, ya know?"

Owen truly appreciated the soft landing she was offering him, because he did want to see her again, but he wasn't sure if he was ready for "dating" and all that came with it.

As if she were reading his mind she added, "And you don't have to stop loving her. I think your real estate signs tell the truth. She sounds amazing. Amazing Grace. Don't run away from those feelings. When you're ready you'll know."

Owen pushed his shoulders up high and broadened his chest now, the confidence returning. "I think you're right. But I do want to see you again, if that's okay," he said.

Chase nodded. "Of course it is."

Owen turned to go. "Oh, and sorry about that Chippendale crack."

Chase made a funny face and replied, "Ya know, he does kind of look like one."

They both laughed now and caught each other looking into the other's eyes again. Owen felt in that instant he might be ready for a real date sooner than Chase thought.

"Are we going, Dad?" Tommy shouted from the door, destroying the romance completely.

"Yes, champ. Say thank you again to Miss Harrington."

Tommy suddenly shifted back into his best TV announcer voice saying, "Thank you, Miss Harrington, for sharing TACO TUESDAY with us. Until next week, watch out for that hot sauce."

Chase and Owen laughed as the sweet child with a heart as big as the mountains made his way outside into the cold November day.

Owen stopped before stepping outside, glanced up at the trees, and without looking back said, "Smells like snow." With that the door closed slowly behind them, the scent of fresh tacos and cologne from a green bottle still dancing in the air.

13

Duke's call

It was now December third, and by Chase's count she'd been living in Manchester for exactly one week. Aside from the occasional call or text home to her parents or younger sister her only contact with the world was happening right here in this quaint New England town.

When she was a little girl Chase used to like going to the mall right before Christmas and wandering in and out of the various stores. While most people loved the decorations and music, Chase was always looking for something specific: those little snow globes they'd put out this time of year. Some of them would wind up and play music, but most were just simple little toys that a child could shake in their tiny hands and then watch the snow fall on some holiday scene inside the glass bubble.

At this moment, Chase felt as if she were living inside one of those snow globes, with the adorable little downtown, decorations abounding, and friendly shopkeepers everywhere she turned, eager to give her a friendly wave hello. She wondered if things were always this nice here. Or if perhaps she'd caught Manchester, Vermont, at exactly the right moment when things seemed brightest. Well, almost everything was bright. That story she heard about beautiful Taylor Farnsworth losing her young life on an icy mountain road had certainly left a scar that was still visible in this place. Every time she pressed anyone for more details, it was clear they wanted that scar left alone to heal.

Still, it was wonderful being here, with Christmas just three weeks away. She'd almost forgotten why she'd traveled the three thousand miles from Seattle in the first place. She was here to write something special. But what? Who knew at this point? She didn't want to press it; when she wrote anything, she preferred to let the story reveal itself.

Chase sipped her morning coffee next to the small fire she'd made with the wood she'd seen stacked in the garage. She was proud of herself for doing that, as she'd never built a fire before in her life. It wasn't even that cold this morning, but she wanted to see if she could do it, and besides, she'd learned in the short seven days that she'd lived in Vermont that she loved the smell of firewood burning. They didn't make fires like this back in Seattle. Not cold enough, I suppose, to warrant having a stack of firewood sitting outside your back door.

Scooter was curled up in front of the fire with his eyes closed, his little paws slowly moving in a circular motion. "You dreaming, buddy?" she said to him softly, so as not to wake him. "Probably chasing a rabbit, I bet," she said, adding, "I hope you catch him."

The moment, the stillness of the old church, was just perfect. The only sound in the world was the occasional snap of the fire, as if to remind her it was burning. She stared at it, thinking about everything but writing; her mind was on Gavin and his sweet picnic and kiss, and Owen and that dear child who had already stolen a piece of her heart. She was thinking about the sheriff who watched over these people like they were his own children, and all those wonderful, colorful people at the diner.

Yes, she was thinking of everything but writing when her cell phone, which was set on silent, started humming and dancing around the edge of the coffee table. She walked over and let out a sigh when she saw the name lit up on the screen: "DUKE." It was her agent wanting to know when she'd have something for him.

Chase didn't want to answer, but they hadn't spoken in nearly a month. At some point it would get rude to keep ducking him, so she picked up the phone with a hearty, "Duke Ellsworth. How are you, sir?"

She called him "sir" out of habit and respect, because Duke was older, in his sixties was her best guess, and he seemed to have earned it by being a literary agent for so many writers over the past forty years.

"Chase, is this really you? I was about to send out a search party," Duke joked, with a smile in his voice.

"Ha, ha, yes, it's me, Duke, and no, I don't have anything for you yet," Chase answered confidently.

Duke continued, "Well, last we spoke you were thinking of taking a big road trip to some place with snow. Where did we land, Alaska?"

Chased laughed. "No. Manchester, Vermont."

Duke was genuinely surprised. "Really. I went skiing there once a million years ago. Or some place near there—Mount Snow. I only remember the name because I thought it was too obvious. Like calling a volcano Mount Lava or something. Anyway, there was a girl there who ran the ski lift, blonde hair that went down to her waist. She was like a Norwegian goddess."

Chase jumped in: "Duke, seriously, you called to tell me about some girl from the 1800s?"

Duke came back at her: "Very funny, smarty pants. It was more like 1975. I think the Bee Gees were her favorite band."

"DUKE," Chase shouted at her phone.

He relented. "All right, all right, enough of memory lane. So, you went to Vermont, but you don't have anything for me yet. There's no pressure, but *Vanity Fair* loved the piece we sold them on Mardi Gras back in the spring. They love your style of writing, so if you find another four thousand words on whatever it is they do in Manchester in December, we should be able to sell it."

Chase looked at the fire and didn't answer right away. Scooter was still snoring, free from worry about agents and deadlines and how much to get paid per word.

"Chase, honey, you still there?" Duke asked, concerned the line had gone dead.

"I am, Duke. I'm just thinking. This place, these people. There *is* a story here. I just haven't nailed it down quite yet. But when I sit down to write it, I think it's going to be a lot more than four thousand words."

Duke's spirits lifted right up. "Are you saying you may finally give me that book I've been begging you for, for what, five years now?"

Chase looked back at the phone and at his name still lit up in text. "Maybe, not sure. I'll know more when I know, Duke. But for now, for me to do this, you have to leave me be."

Duke understood how particular writers could be, having represented so many over the years. "Fair enough. Just tell me this. Is this a travel book? Fiction? Dare I say romance?"

Chase smiled while staring down at the phone. "Hold on to what hair you have left, Duke, but you may get all of those and more."

Duke was now content, and this call put the agent at ease. "Well, I love what I'm hearing, and I won't bug you again. Are you flying home for Christmas or staying?"

Without hesitation Chase said, "Staying. There's a story here and I don't want to leave it."

Duke wished her an early merry Christmas, knowing it was unlikely they'd speak again until the New Year. "Stay safe, and if you need anything," he added without finishing the thought.

"I have the number. Give my love to Molly," she said lovingly, before hanging up. Molly was his wife of thirty years, and they'd met on a few occasions when she was in Los Angeles visiting friends and Duke needed a business lunch to write off on his taxes. Sweet woman, she thought, perfect for a man named Duke. *Duke and Molly*; it sounded like a sitcom.

Chase turned, because Scooter was stretching now, waking himself up from his morning nap in front of the warm fire. He looked up at Chase, and she said, "Morning, sleepy head. You must be thirsty; do you want a drink of water?" He sprang right up and ran from the room without looking back.

To the kitchen she went to give Scooter a drink, unaware the story she was searching for was about to start writing itself and that she, Chase, would be one of the central characters.

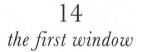

14

the first window

Chase was a beautiful woman who took care of herself. At five foot six she was careful to watch what she ate, except for old Ned's waffles the other day, and she enjoyed exercise. She took spin classes back home, and when the weather was nice she'd often go for a two-mile run. Looking out the window at the bright sunshine and the crisp December air, she decided it was a perfect day to stretch her legs. She fumbled through the small antique dresser that came with the old church she was renting, looking for sweatpants and a heavy pullover with a hood. As she pushed her mess of clothes side to side looking for the right outfit to run in, Chase heard barking coming from another room. It was Scooter, carrying on about something. He didn't need to go out, because she'd just brought him in.

Black pants and a gray top were the best she could do. So Chase changed into them and started searching for her running shoes. They looked a lot like her other sneakers, only the salesclerk at the sporting goods store back in Seattle had told her this style of Nikes was lighter and built for running. It was a good sales pitch, so she spent the $65 to buy the pink and white size six sneaks. As she laced them on, there was more barking, but even louder this time.

"Scooter, here boy," she yelled into the mostly empty old church. More barking. "SCOOTER!!" she let out even louder now, with what bordered on an angry tone. That kind of angry shout always brought him, but Scooter didn't obey and just kept up the barking. "Seriously?" she said to herself, now legitimately getting upset.

Chase stomped out of the bedroom and started craning her head from left to right, trying to figure out where the dog was making such a racket. One by one she eliminated rooms, until the only place left was the large, empty space where the church itself used to be filled with pews and people. She marched in, pounding her feet along the way as if to give the puppy a warning that she was coming and she was not pleased.

"Bark, bark, bark," was all she could hear as she turned the corner and went in.

"Scooter, what the heck, didn't you hear me call you?" Her dog gave her a quick glance out of respect but then immediately returned his fixed gaze to one of the stained glass windows up on the wall. It was the first one on the right if you were walking into the church from the front door, the one with Jesus in a white robe preaching in a field. Chase walked down to touch her dog and see what had made him so upset.

"You okay?" she asked sincerely, as she bent down on one knee to inspect him more closely. He looked and seemed fine except for the barking and staring up at the picture in the glass. He'd done this once before back home when he had cornered a mouse behind a couch. This was different though, as there certainly couldn't be a mouse hiding behind Jesus's feet in the field of grass in a picture.

Chase looked up at the image, and for the first time since she'd moved in she really studied the detail. It was beautiful, and she said to Scooter, "Ya know, whoever made this thing all those years ago really did a nice job. The detail is exceptional." Scooter stopped barking now and seemed to be looking at Chase for help understanding something.

"What is it, boy? Did something spook you? It's just a picture. Can't hurt you." Chase patted his head and was making her way toward the door to start her morning run. As she turned the knob Scooter started up again with the barking and staring. "What?" she said out loud. "You have to stop." But he wouldn't. Scooter kept looking up and barking and then back at Chase as if he were trying to tell her something.

Confused and getting frustrated, Chase took him by the collar. "Let's go, freak boy." With that she dragged him out of the large area and into the hallway that led to the kitchen. "There," she said, shutting the door firmly behind her and keeping Scooter from returning to the room where he was causing so much commotion. Chase then walked back through what was once the church and toward the front doors of the building to finally get to her run.

As she walked by, she couldn't help looking up at the stained glass window that was spooking her dog, and she noticed the morning sun hitting the horizon and making the sky behind Jesus glow and come alive. "Gorgeous," she thought to herself, and then she continued walking toward the front door. Then, out of an uncontrollable impulse, she turned her head back to look a third time at the image, and something made her stop in her tracks.

Behind Jesus in this Tiffany glass window was a field, a rolling hill, and the sun rising on the horizon. But at the top of the hill was something she hadn't seen before. "What is that?" she said out loud to herself. She inched closer and squinted her eyes to help see more clearly. There at the top of that hill in the glass image was an old well. It had very specific details. It was made of round black and gray stones that had been patched together to form a perfect circle. The well was about three feet high and had a wooden structure above it that was used to hold a rope and a bucket. She knew from watching old movies that before we had plumbing and running water in our homes, people would drop a bucket like that one deep into a well to collect fresh water.

Chase was puzzled, because the well was very clear in the image in the stained glass, yet somehow she'd never noticed it until this moment. "That's weird," she said to herself as she turned toward the door, flung it open, and let the fresh morning air wash over her face. She pushed her earbuds into place, turned on some music, and set out. She hadn't run in a couple of weeks, so this might be a sluggish endeavor, she thought to herself. "Who better to get me going than Kelly Clarkson?" she said out loud. With that she pushed play and was off on a twenty-minute jog.

The town was alive with people and smiles and waves, just as always, and Chase did her best to return the "hellos" with a nod or a wave back. She went down Main Street, past the funeral home and the man who liked to fish, turned left near the bakery with the great rolls, and dodged a woman pushing a baby carriage near the barber shop where Sheriff Harlan had spotted her on her date with Gavin. For not having run in a while, Chase was happy with how her legs and lungs were holding up. Eventually the loop around the town brought her back to the old church where she was staying and the front door she'd left not so long ago.

Before she could even open it, she heard Scooter barking faintly from inside. She turned the knob, entered the church, and could hear him scratching at the door behind which she'd closed him for his own good. As she approached the door his bark got louder and more persistent and didn't stop until she set him free. "Sorry to make you a prisoner, buddy, but you were driving Mommy nuts," she said with love. Scooter jumped up and gave her a kiss hello, and Chase made her way to the kitchen for a glass of cold water.

As she filled the glass and before she could even take a sip, Scooter was back at it, barking in the church. Chase downed the water quickly and made her way back into the large common area, not surprised at all to see her dog in exactly the same place, barking at the same window. She wasn't mad this time, she was intrigued.

"What is it, boy? I wasn't paying attention before, but I am now. What's wrong?"

Chase got down on the floor with her dog to put her arm around him. Once she started looking up at the window, Scooter stopped barking. She did a quick inventory and said out loud, "Okay, we got Jesus in the golden grass, white robe, hand in the air, check. We have the beautiful horizon behind him and the hill, and up top we have the well which I didn't see before today." She looked down at Scooter now. "I'm not seeing it, bud. Did Jesus wink at you or something? Because I don't get the nonstop barking."

She hugged her dog and was about to pull him away from the window and the room when her heart stopped. She looked again more closely at the well and saw something sitting on top of the stones to the right of the bucket and rope. "What is that?"

Chase stood up quickly, as her mind was trying to catch up with what her eyes were seeing. She said to herself, "That was not there before. That was not there when I went out for the run." It was something thin and round and brown, but that's all she could make out. It was sitting on top of the well only inches from the black hole where you'd drop the bucket below to fetch water.

Chase ran into the kitchen to grab one of the stools that sat around the wooden island where she'd had breakfast each morning. She dragged it back into the common area and placed it right in front of the stained glass window. She carefully climbed up on the chair to get a closer look at the brown thing on top of the well. "Darn it. It's too small," she said to Scooter. "I can't make it out."

She looked around and saw a chair in the corner next to the antique desk. She dragged it over and placed the stool carefully on top. She knew this was stupid, because if her weight shifted the wrong way she'd most certainly come tumbling down. As she slowly climbed up to raise herself higher and closer to the window, she thought, *Manchester's version of Cirque du Soleil at your service.* Once she was on top of both chair and stool, she could finally make out what the small item was that was resting on the stone. "It's a dog collar," she said to her pup.

After climbing back down to safety, Chase took Scooter out to the study where she made a small fire and sat in a large, comfortable chair with a cup of tea. She stared at the fire and over at Scooter, confused at what was happening. She kept thinking, "It's possible the well was in that glass image all along and I just never noticed it. That, I'll buy. But that dog collar sitting on top, no way. It wasn't there earlier."

Was it possible someone was playing a prank on her? But why? And how could they get in the church, find a thirty-foot ladder, climb up and paint something on a window, all in twenty minutes? It made no sense at all.

She looked at Scooter and just asked, "If you have a clue what's going on, now would be the time to tell me." Her dog looked back with loving eyes but no explanation for what was happening here. She realized in that moment the door leading back to the church was wide open, but Scooter no longer had any interest in running in there and barking at the window. Maybe he'd just needed her to see what he saw. But what did it mean?

"Maybe we're both going nuts, bud," she said to him, only half kidding. Scooter cast his eyes on the fire, now content with what he'd accomplished.

Her phone let out a loud "ding," indicating a text message had arrived. It was from Gavin Bennett. "Hey, miss you. Wanna grab lunch at the diner? Noon?" Next to the message was an emoji of a cowboy hat.

Chase quickly typed her reply, "See you at noon." She decided in that moment she wasn't going to mention what she and Scooter had seen in the window. Handsome men generally don't date crazy people. Still, something told Chase, deep inside, she wasn't as crazy as it seemed.

15

of muffins and men

It had been four days since Chase had seen Gavin and they had shared that perfect kiss. A few text messages back and forth and one short phone call was it so far. Both of them were trying to take it slow, and slow it was certainly going. Still, for someone who only seemed half interested in getting serious with a man, Chase felt anxious pangs in her stomach as she walked the few blocks down to the diner. She was careful not to overdo the outfit, a simple yellow top with jeans that fit her nicely and her other pair of Nike sneakers.

As she pulled the door open the bell above gave her entrance away. The handsome cowboy was already sitting at the counter with his tan Stetson hat covering the stool next to him. He looked like he hadn't shaved in a day or two, giving him a gruff look that Chase liked. She thought to herself walking toward him, *Why do we women love that look on a man when it's hell on your face to kiss them? Too scratchy.* As she moved closer, she wondered how this greeting would go. A hug or kiss? It certainly wouldn't be a handshake. If he did that, she'd be very confused.

Gavin ended the suspense by hopping off the stool and coming in for a quick peck on the lips followed by a nice strong hug. The kind a boy gives a girl he adores when he hasn't seen her in a couple of days. It was very familiar but not over the top, which Chase liked. Everything about this guy was solid, from his body to his manners to his instincts.

Shayla worked the counter as always, leaving the waitresses to tend to the tables. She waltzed over with two glasses of water and a menu. "I assume you two don't mind sharing," she said, referring to the greasy menu. She continued the teasing with, "Was that a kiss I just saw or is my mind playing tricks on me?"

Both looked away a bit embarrassed, and before either could answer, Shayla's husband, Colgan, yelled out, "Darn it, woman, leave those two alone. I'm sorry, kids, ignore her." Colgan was about thirty years older than Chase and Gavin. He called everyone that much younger than him "kid."

Shayla just rolled her eyes back at her husband and said, "I'm just funning with them, grumpy." Turning back to her guests, she added, "He's always so grumpy back there." Shayla motioned with her thumb toward the kitchen. She then shifted to all business. "Coffee? Or are we eating?"

Gavin looked at Chase and said, "I had kind of a late breakfast, but you go ahead." Chase was hungry after taking her run and that bizarre encounter with the stained glass windows at St. Pius, but there was no way she was going to shovel food in her mouth with a man she liked sitting there watching. There are some things a girl just won't do.

So, she played it cool. "Hmm, I'm not that hungry, but I could have something small. Hey, I know. I heard so much about these blueberry corn muffins this place is famous for. Want to split one with me, Gavin?" she asked.

Gavin folded up the menu and handed it to Shayla, saying, "Done!"

Before she could even turn to the kitchen to grab a fresh muffin from under a glass cover, Colgan chimed in, "See that, woman. They were probably going to order steak and eggs until you opened your big yap." Anyone watching could tell he was teasing his wife. Colgan gave off the impression that he was gruff and hard, and I suppose standing over a hot griddle does toughen a man up, but he was a gentle giant. And watching him watch his wife as she chatted up customers and delivered gravy and gossip, you could tell he still adored her as much as their first date all those years ago. She knew it too. Sometimes, and today was one of those days, when they were giving each other a hard time, one of them would give a wink or a signal that it was all just for play. On this morning, after Colgan griped about the steak that wasn't ordered, Shayla strutted by the counter into his view with an exaggerated wiggle, then flipped up her apron like a tease.

He smiled at the gesture as she said, "You love me and you know it." And he did, and everyone at the diner knew it.

The muffin came out slightly warmed, but before they could dig in Gavin said, "Wait."

Chase wasn't sure why they couldn't eat it yet, when Shayla suddenly took a butter knife and cut it right down the middle, releasing steam. She then took a healthy slice of butter and dropped it into the slit. Then, using a fork and knife, as to not touch the muffin with her fingers, Shayla pushed the two halves back together and held it for about five seconds. When she released the pressure the muffin fell away, each side dropping back and revealing the melted butter smothering the insides of the muffin. Without saying a word Shayla turned to go help another customer. Chase looked at Gavin's handsome unshaven face and said, "Oh, I see we have a bit of a ritual with the world-famous muffin, huh?"

Gavin said, "Ladies first," pushing the small plate closer to Chase. She picked up her half of the muffin and saw the blueberries were almost liquefied in the breading.

After she took a healthy bite, "Oh my God" came tumbling out of her mouth.

As Gavin nodded and took a bite of his own, Colgan said from the kitchen, "We were thinking of changing the name to the 'OH MY GOD' muffins, but it didn't fit on the sign." Chase and Gavin both laughed as they devoured what was left.

"So tell me how a B.U. graduate with a master's ends up plowing fields. And please don't take that as some kind of disrespect—it's just unusual," Chase said.

Gavin looked out the diner window at the busy Manchester morning, with people and cars hurrying to places they needed to be. He said, "I'm a farmer. I grew up in it and I really do love it. My dad's ways are the old ways, but they aren't always the best ways. Things change, and technology and science change with it."

Chase was listening intensely and finished the handsome cowboy's thought: "So the prodigal son leaves home, learns the new ways of doing things, and returns to make the farm even better."

Gavin smiled. "It's a bit more complicated than that, but yeah, that's pretty close. But it wasn't a prodigal son thing. He wanted me to go off to school and have those experiences college kids have. In fact, he told me I had no obligation to return and help run the farm."

Chase sipped her water, wishing they had ordered two muffins. "But you did come home, but not out of obligation." Chase was staring into his deep blue eyes, sizing him up at this moment and adding, "It was love. Love for that farm and what you do. That's why you returned?"

Gavin leaned back on the stool as if proud of himself. "Hey, what can I say? We feed America. Or at least a couple counties of Vermont, with what we grow." He smiled, adding, "Plus, I know you've only been here for a week, but you see how pretty it is."

Chase nodded in agreement, but asked, "Don't you miss stuff bigger cities have?"

Gavin was intrigued. "Such as?"

Chase replied, "Oh, I don't know. Like a mall."

Gavin had heard this question before from his college friends and was ready for it. "Point in any direction and you can be at a mall in one hour. That's not so far to drive to live in paradise. Next question?"

Chase wasn't prepared for this debate, but she pressed on. "Lemme think. Okay, arts, theater, that kind of thing."

Gavin was ready again. "If you like plays we have a small theater in Dorset about twelve minutes from here, and the bigger theater in Williamstown, Mass., is only forty-five minutes to the south of us. Oh, and before you talk about stars, they actually get them there in Williamstown at the theater festival every summer. We should go if you're still around in seven months. And if all that doesn't float your boat, we have something called Amtrak, and you can look out the window at the pretty trees and be in Times Square in about four hours."

Chase could see he had an answer for everything. Then Gavin surprised her. "Why are you here? I know you're a writer and this is probably some kind of assignment, but why here? Why Manchester?"

For this tough question Chase did have an answer, but she was a bit embarrassed to share it. "I, um, you'll laugh at me."

Gavin put three fingers in the air and said, "I won't. Scout's honor."

Chase liked and trusted him, so she decided to share a very personal story. "Well, when I was a kid I loved calendars."

Gavin smiled. "Okay?"

Chase continued, "I didn't have a lot of money. We were kind of poor. So, you know those little kiosks they set up in the middle of a mall where they sell all the different calendars?"

"Yes," he said.

"Well," Chase pressed on, "they're kind of expensive, but the day after Christmas all of them go on sale. At first it's half off and then sixty or seventy percent. Eventually, if you wait about two weeks they practically give them away. Well, I'd wait till the very end and then go buy one to decorate my bedroom wall. Sometimes I'd buy one with kittens or horses, sometimes lighthouses. One year when I was about twelve, I bought one with beautiful pictures of New England."

Gavin nodded without saying a word, knowing now where this may be going.

"So, anyway, I buy this one with all these pretty scenes: little towns like Stockbridge; Newport; Portland, Maine. You know, a different place for each month. That year when I got to December it had a picture of this beautiful village all decorated for Christmas. It had cobblestone sidewalks and was lined with lampposts that were covered in garland and bows. The houses all had pretty wreaths on the front doors. It was surrounded by snowcapped mountains, and in the distance was a white church steeple."

Gavin reached over, touching her hand. "Sounds a lot like Manchester."

Chase's eyes started filling with tears now, and this caught her by surprise, but somehow Gavin seemed to expect it. She continued, "It was. And after the year was done, when I'd tear down all those calendar pictures and go to the mall to get new a one. . . . Jeez, this will sound crazy," Chase added, stopping herself.

Gavin squeezed her hand. "Hey, look at me. It's just us. It's okay. What?"

Chase looked down at his strong hand holding hers. "I didn't have the most ideal childhood. My parents divorced when I was barely two and I didn't get to know my dad. My mom did her best, but you know how it is for a single mom with a kid."

Gavin nodding reassuringly. "Go on."

Chase continued, "I guess those pictures on the wall were an escape for me. They represented what could be for me. They were my . . . someday."

Chase looked out the window now at the sunlight bouncing off the trees. "So that year, after I bought the calendar with all the pretty New England pictures, when it came time to take them down, I did. I took them down, all but one. I left up that one perfect picture of Manchester. I can't tell you why, there was just something about it. It calmed me, ya know?" she added, looking back at Gavin now.

"I do. Art can be that way," Gavin said. "Pictures, music, it can carry you away to a better place." Neither one spoke for the next minute, both thinking about what Gavin had just said.

Then Chase wiped a single tear away from her left cheek and finished the thought. "So yeah, I kept the picture up for the next few years until I went to college at UCLA to get my writing degree, and I even brought it with me and put it up on the wall of my college dorm room. Stupid, I know."

Gavin stood up now. "No, it's not. Not at all. Chase, we need dreams to keep us going sometimes. For you maybe, back then in that time and place, it was that single image of this perfect place."

Chase couldn't believe a guy who looked this big and tough could be so sensitive and get it, get her. "I think you're right. So, to answer your question, three years after you asked it," she said with a laugh, "What am I doing here? I never forgot that picture, and when I finished up my last writing assignment, I realized I couldn't write another word until I saw this place, for real."

Gavin smiled broadly. "And here you are!"

Chase squeezed both his strong hands right back. "And here I am. Living in a haunted church."

Chase couldn't believe those last five words slipped from her mouth.

Gavin almost choked on the water he'd started to drink, asking, "A what?"

Chase caught herself, thinking, *Remember, great guys don't like crazy girls.* So she quickly said, "Oh, nothing. I'm kidding."

Gavin wouldn't let it go. "What did you mean? Did something happen over there?"

Chase quickly explained away her slip of the tongue. "No. No. I was teasing. I think I heard the furnace knocking and making noise, that's all. I'm kidding. Not haunted."

Gavin wasn't so sure she was telling the truth, but said, "Okay, probably just the furnace. Those old places are like that."

"Yes, they are," Chase added in agreement.

With that they heard the bell above the door clang and a sad older woman walked in, slowly taking a seat at the nearest table. It was Maria Millington, the woman Chase had seen days earlier handing out fliers for her missing dog.

Shayla rushed over with her fresh pot of coffee. "How are we, Maria?"

The woman with the sad, tired eyes didn't even look up as she said, "The same. Going on a week now. The vet said they can live a couple of weeks without food but not water. If he doesn't have water . . ." Her voice trailed off. Chase and Gavin thought she'd cry, but she looked like a woman who was all cried out. Shayla poured her a cup of jet-black coffee and left her alone with her thoughts and worries.

Chase looked up at Shayla as she returned to the counter, asking, "She still never found that dog?"

Shayla lowered her voice to avoid upsetting the old woman. "No. It doesn't look good. Probably got lost in the woods and got hurt or some wild animal, you know . . ." Shayla didn't want to finish that sentence.

Gavin looked at his watch and said, "I hate to leave you, but I promised Pop I'd pick up supplies at the feed and tractor store and get back. I really loved talking with you, Chase."

Chase didn't know what this relationship was, or was going to be, but at this very moment she didn't care to worry. She took Gavin's face between her hands, pulled him in close and gave him a real kiss on the lips, adding, "Me too."

Gavin's heart skipped a beat, and he wasn't sure what to say as Chase scooped up his cowboy hat from the stool where it was resting and put it on his head. She then tapped him on the arm and playfully added, "Say hi to your father for me."

With that the pretty stranger from Seattle scooted toward the door like a summer breeze. Gavin was still trying to sort out that unexpected kiss when the bell on the door clanged loudly and Chase disappeared into the chilly December afternoon.

Shayla, watching the tender moment unfold, leaned in with the coffeepot still in her hand and said to Gavin, "She's sweet, Gav. I know you like to hit and run but that one might be worth keeping."

Gavin looked at her wryly and said, "I gotta go." When he left the diner he looked both left and right down the sidewalk, but there was no sign of the mystery girl with the special calendars and sweet kiss. He didn't realize it at that moment, but he'd be seeing her again, soon enough. An adventure awaited, the kind that required blind faith and a working flashlight.

16
midnight hunt

Chase took her time walking home, stopping at a small convenience store that sold a little bit of everything. Beyond the chips, beer, and scratch-off lottery tickets, they also had a small deli where they could slice cold cuts or make you a sandwich. Chase planned to stay in once she got home, so she grabbed some rolls, a half-pound of ham and cheese, and some spicy mustard, the kind with a splash of horseradish. They even sold rawhide bones in the pet section, so Chase grabbed one of those for Scooter. Back home in Seattle he'd chew on one of those things for hours as Chase sat with her laptop, writing away. It was kind of a ritual for them.

Once she got back to the church, she used the side door that led to the kitchen, let the dog out, and fixed him a big bowl of water. After putting the groceries down on the kitchen counter, she realized she was a bit tired from all the running around and decided to make a small fire in the den. She curled up on the couch with a thick wool blanket she found in the closet, and quickly dozed off with Scooter at her feet. The crackling of the wood burning was like a symphony easing her off to sleep.

About ninety minutes later the fire let out a very loud "SNAP," which jarred Chase awake. Her unfocused eyes struggled to take in the cozy room, but seeing Scooter snoring on the comfy cushions brought her back to reality. "I thought we were back in Seattle there for a minute, buddy," she said to the dog, who did not open his eyes. He was sound asleep, and Chase didn't want to wake him.

She retired to the bedroom where a small desk was set up in the corner and took out her laptop. Opening up a blank page in Word, Chase wasn't sure where to begin this story. Should she write a first-person account of what it's like for a young woman to pack up her life and move across the country to a strange place full of handsome men, kindness, and muffins? Or should this be a serious piece looking at how a single event can change a town? She was talking in her head about the Taylor Farnsworth tragedy and how these people still seemed "stuck" in their grief over it, especially at Christmastime.

Just then Scooter slowly came into her room, measuring his steps slowly as if his legs were still asleep. He was a smart dog and had a way of telling Chase what he wanted, so he went over to the door and barked. "Gotta go out?" Chase asked, walking him out of the bedroom and down the hallway toward the door that led to the yard. Scooter turned left into the kitchen and moved over to the counter. He jumped up on the granite and barked at the brown paper bag that housed the ham and cheese Chase had purchased hours earlier at the store. "Oh, man, I forgot to put that away, didn't I? What? You want a sandwich?" Scooter barked again and did this little dance where he wiggled his backside left to right in a kind of happy dance.

Chase was a softy when it came to her puppy. She spread the cold cuts on the counter and was careful to make up two sandwiches. Only one would have the spicy mustard. "We don't need you getting sick," she said to the dog, as if he understood every word. She cut the sandwich in four and laid it on the kitchen floor, parking herself on one of the stools.

"I haven't written a thing yet, Scooter, why is that? That's not like me." Chase was talking to herself because the dog was taken up with his unexpected ham and cheese dinner. When he was done, he looked up at her and did that happy dance again as Chase added, "Maybe I'm not supposed to yet. The words will come when they come, right?" She hopped off the stool, took up Scooter's leash, and decided to take him for a long walk.

She was starting to figure out the town by now, these daily walks with the dog and her occasional jogs for exercise helping her map things out in her head. People seemed to be recognizing her more too as she made her way down the cobblestone streets. It occurred to Chase at that moment how little driving she'd done since she moved here; everything a person would need all felt within walking distance.

After walking for nearly an hour she brought Scooter back home, fixed him an extra-large bowl of water, and decided she'd put off the writing for now. Whenever she was like this back home, trying too hard to come up with an idea, she liked to read someone else's work to shake up her brain. Chase went to her satchel, which hung off the back of a wooden chair in the bedroom, and fished out a novel by author Tim Green. His books were real page turners, and reading a thriller always took her mind away from her troubles for a while.

The sun set right on schedule and Chase finished a few chapters of the book before retiring to the bedroom and sitting up against the headboard of the big plush bed. Scooter took his cue that the day was done and jumped up on the bed to resume his usual position at her feet. He wasn't much of a danger should someone break in, but Scooter could sure bark loudly, and that made Chase feel at ease, having him right there as she slept.

After poking around social media on her phone for a few minutes and listening to music on an app, Chase reached to turn out the lamp that sat on the nightstand. As she placed her phone down she saw it read 10:04 p.m. That hour was still early back home, but kind of late by Manchester standards. She made the room dark, eased back onto the pillow, and stared up at the nothingness above her. She had stayed this way a good twenty minutes when she sat up quickly and reached for the light.

Sleep wasn't going to come this night, and she just figured out why. "That darn stained glass window," she said to herself out loud. "I know that well wasn't in that picture before." Chase hopped up, causing Scooter to rise with her, put on her slippers and made her way toward the large empty area of the church where the windows were. Scooter seemed to anticipate where they were going, running ahead of her into the large empty space of the church. There was no barking this time, though; he just wandered around, wagging his tail, wondering to himself why they were up this late.

Chase flipped on the overhead lights and walked down to look at the first window that was costing her sleep. Light from the lampposts outside illuminated the window in an eerie, beautiful way. She looked up and said, "You've got to be kidding me." She then started walking in a circle and looked back a second and third time at the stained glass window with Jesus on the hill preaching. "Are you serious right now?" she said, even louder to the empty building.

For a moment time froze, and Chase almost pinched herself to make certain she was awake. She then let out a sigh, feeling a bit uneasy and wondering at that moment if she might well be losing her mind. The stained glass window was exactly as it was the day she moved in. Jesus in the white robe, the golden grass at his feet, the hill behind him and the beautiful sky. Just one problem: there was no well. No well and no dog collar sitting on top of it. They were both gone.

Chase paced the floor a few more times, checking the window again and again, even looking at the remaining three stained glass windows to see if something in them was different. It wasn't. All four were exactly as they were the day she set foot in this place, the way they had been for 150 years.

Chase went back to the bedroom and sat up with the light on, thinking hard about what was happening. Obviously she was seeing things, but why? She felt fine; she hadn't been dreaming earlier when she'd looked at the window, twice, before and after her run. It made no sense.

She then went to her bag and took out a large yellow legal pad she'd sometimes use to take notes when she was working on a writing project. She grabbed a plain number two pencil and started to sketch the well as best as she could remember it. Old-fashioned with stones patched together and a large wooden contraption above that raised and lowered the water bucket. For not being an artist she thought she did a nice job recreating it on the blank piece of paper.

Chase tapped the pencil back and forth on the page, thinking and thinking and thinking some more. Then something occurred to her.

She was new in Manchester, so this image of a well that appeared in the glass, and was now stuck in her head, meant nothing to her, but perhaps someone else might recognize it. "But who?" she asked Scooter, who was now back on the bed at her side. Then it hit her. "Owen. A Realtor knows this town better than anyone. Owen."

She picked up her phone and saw it was now 10:37 p.m. and worried poor Owen might be fast asleep. No matter, Chase wasn't going to sleep this night, so she might as well have company. She carefully snapped a photo of the drawing she'd just made and then texted Owen's phone. "Are you awake? It's important."

Chase looked at the phone for about twelve seconds, which felt like an eternity, until she saw Owen had read her message and was typing a reply. "I wasn't awake until my phone dinged. What's up?" he wrote.

Chase then took the photo she'd drawn and texted that to Owen with the words "Does this look familiar? Is there an old well like this anywhere in Manchester?"

Owen was starting to wake up at this point and was confused, texting back, "What's this about, Chase?"

She was growing impatient. "I'll explain later. Would you just please look at the picture? Do you recognize this well?"

Owen thought for a moment and then realized he did. "Yes, I believe there's a well like this at Foster's Dairy Farm. At least there used to be. I haven't been up there in a few years. When Grace was alive she liked to get the milk fresh, sometimes right from the farm."

Chase fired back a text at him in all capital letters. "OWEN. PLEASE. Where is that farm?"

With that message Owen had had his fill of the texting back and forth so he called Chase directly. "Hi, Foster's Farm is just outside of town on the road to Piedmont Pass. It's not that far. Chase, what's going on?"

Chase responded, "I'll explain later, but answer me one more question."

Owen rubbed the sleep from his eyes as he said while yawning, "Okay."

Chase continued, "How far is that farm and well from Maria Millington's house; the lady who lost her dog?"

Owen had to think for a second then said, "Well if you drove it's a few miles away."

Chase came back at him with, "But what if you didn't drive? What if you were a dog who got out chasing a rabbit or something and ran through the woods, how far then?"

Owen cleared his mind. "Actually, if you cut through the woods behind Maria's place, that farm is only about a mile. Chase, are you going to tell me what's going on? You're kind of freaking me out."

Chase wasn't worried about Owen's feeling at this moment. She asked, "Can you take me there?"

Owen responded, "When? Now?"

Chase said, "Yes, now. Tonight, right now."

Owen sat up and slipped into dad mode saying, "Listen, I have a son sleeping in the next room. I can't leave him alone, and I'm not going to wake him when he has school early tomorrow to go to a dairy farm at midnight unless you tell me why."

Chase calmed herself down a bit and realized what she was asking. "I'm so sorry. You're right, Owen. Listen. I'll figure something else out. Thank you for helping me."

Owen sensed she was about to hang up abruptly and yelled, "CHASE!"

It was too late. She was already gone and scanning the contacts in her phone for the only other man in town who'd given her his number.

She pushed his name on the cell and it started ringing.

"You can't sleep because you're thinking about me, huh?" Gavin answered with a smile in his voice.

Chase responded, "No, I mean, yes, sure. I was thinking about you but not for that reason."

Gavin could tell instantly that something was wrong and immediately knocked off the cavalier tone. "What's the matter, Chase?"

Chase came right back, "Do you know a place called Foster's Dairy Farm, up near Peatmoss Drive or something?"

Gavin corrected her politely, saying, "You mean Piedmont Pass. Yes, of course I know it. Why, what's up?"

Chase was pulling her jeans on now with the phone pinched between her shoulder and ear, freeing up her hands. "I know it sounds crazy, but I need you to come pick me up and take me there right now."

Something in her voice told Gavin not to ask any more questions, so he simply said, "I can be to you in twenty minutes."

Before he could hang up Chase said loudly, "GAVIN?"

He responded, "Still here."

Chase said, "Bring a flashlight."

With that, Chase finished getting dressed and waited outside St. Pius, leaning on the black wrought-iron fence that circled the old church and faced the street.

True to his word, Gavin's pickup truck, the same one she had stood in to get a better look at the lightning bugs, pulled up to the curb nineteen minutes later. He was wearing a denim jean jacket with half the collar up and the other side down, which told her he had thrown it on fast and had sprung into action. "Get in," were his only words.

Chase jumped in and took the large flashlight off the seat, placing it instead safely on her lap. Before Gavin could even ask, she said, "I think I know where Maria Millington's dog is. I think he's stuck in the bottom of a well."

Gavin had no clue how this beautiful stranger in town could possibly know that, but he could see in her eyes she was serious and certain. There were only a handful of red lights between St. Pius and that old dairy farm, but Gavin pushed his foot to the floor and ignored every one of them.

17
too steep a climb

Once you left the glowing lights of downtown Manchester, darkness closed in on you fast. "I guess you guys don't believe in streetlights in the country, huh?" Chase asked Gavin, as he maneuvered the dark twists and turns like a race car driver who had seen this track before.

Gavin just smiled and focused on the yellow stripe slicing through the middle of the black road, making certain they didn't end up in a ditch. As they approached the final half mile the dairy farm came into sight. Gavin said, "So, I have to ask."

Chase responded before he could finish his question. "Why do I think the dog is in a well on this farm?" Chase thought carefully before speaking again, because the truth sounded too crazy to say out loud. So, she fibbed. "This will sound nutty, but I had a dream. I dreamt that lady's dog chased after a rabbit, went through the field and ended up falling into a well. I woke up and drew this sketch of the well I saw in the dream. I called Owen and he told me this dairy farm had a well like that. The dog is probably not there, but I at least want to check," she explained, hoping her story sounded plausible.

Gavin pointed out the windshield. "See that light ahead? That's Foster's. Can I ask you something else?"

"Sure," Chase responded.

Gavin said, "Has this happened before, where you dream something and it turns out to be true?"

Chase didn't want to keep lying, so she tried the truth. "Nope. Never. So, like I said, he's probably not there. I just want to be sure."

Gavin nodded. "Makes sense. So, we'll go take a look. If nothing else, I get to share your company again." Chase touched him gently on the arm, her way of saying thank you without the need for words.

The Foster family, like so many who lived in the hills outside of Manchester, had a dog that would raise holy heck if a car drove up on the property, especially at night. In the Fosters' case, it was a jet-black German shepherd named Max who topped out at a hundred pounds. Max let out a very loud bark that wouldn't relent until the lights in the back bedroom came on and Sam and Mary Foster were awake and up.

As he put the truck in park, Gavin turned to Chase. "They don't know you, so let me do the talking, okay? It's kind of weird us showing up this late at night to search someone's property." Chase agreed, and they waited until the porch light came on and Max was on a leash before even thinking about exiting the vehicle.

Mary stayed in the house, pulling her flannel robe tight to stave off the cold evening air creeping in the half-open door. Sam stepped outside with a wooden Louisville Slugger baseball bat in one hand and brought his other hand up over his eyes to help him see better. "Who's there?" he shouted while squinting at the shadows, trying hard to make out these strangers in his driveway.

Gavin opened the truck door with a creaking sound and said, "Mr. Foster, it's me, Gavin Bennett. Frank Bennett's son."

Without hesitation Sam put the bat down, leaning it up against the front of the house. "Gavin? How are ya, son?"

Gavin responded, "I'm well, sir. I'm sorry to come out so late in the evening. This is my friend Chase, and she and I have a kind of bet going on."

Chase glanced over at Gavin and said under her breath, "We do?"

Sam looked back at Mary and then back at Gavin. "A bet?"

Gavin then said, "Yes, sir. You know Mrs. Millington from around the bend? Her dog, Rudy, went missing about a week ago. Chase here had a dream that the dog somehow ran onto your property and found his way to some old well."

With that Chase stepped closer to the porch and held up the yellow scrap of paper with the picture of the well she'd drawn not an hour earlier. "I know it sounds crazy, sir, but do you still have an old well that looks like this on your property? My Realtor friend, Owen, said you used to."

Sam Foster stepped down from the porch and took the piece of paper from Chase's hand. "I do, back on the old lot."

Gavin interjected, "The old lot?"

Sam continued, "Yes. This farm has been here more than a hundred years. As we modernized, we built new on the south side, but up on the ridge is the old lot. We don't use it anymore, mostly weeds now. That's where the well is."

Gavin and Chase were about to ask Sam to take them up there when Mary spoke from the kitchen door. "Wait, did you two say this was about a dog?"

Chase smiled at the older woman. "Yes, and I'm sorry we woke you up."

Mary waved her hand at Chase as if to shoo away her apology. "No worries, dear. Wait right here."

Sam looked confused, not certain where his wife was going in her robe and slippers. Max let out one last bark and Sam scolded him. "ENOUGH, I SAID," and with that the dog fell silent, pushing his ears back and pouting.

Sam Foster looked back at Chase. "A dream, you said?"

Chase hated lying this way, but the truth was a hard sell. So she nodded. "Um, yes, sir."

The three of them fell silent for a moment when Mary returned to the kitchen door and came outside with something in her hand. She said to her husband, "I meant to tell you about this, hon. The other day I saw Max nosing around the fence and found this." Mary was holding a dog collar that looked exactly like the one Chase saw in the stained glass window at the church, the one that was sitting on the well. Mary then explained, "This collar was stuck on part of the fence, almost like the dog who wore it was running through and got hung up. He obviously got loose, leaving his collar behind. I don't know where he got to after that, because I never saw him. Just the collar, that's all I found."

She handed the collar to Chase, and she carefully examined it. Gavin watched her eyes as she rubbed her thumbs along the leather and buckle, almost as if she knew something that she wasn't saying.

Gavin then looked up at Mary and Sam Foster and said, "The old well, do you mind if we give it a quick look?"

Sam said, "Mary, you go back in and get warm. I'll grab my flashlight and we'll walk on up. You have to be careful where you step in this pitch dark. These old farms bite."

After the dairy farmer retrieved his light, Gavin turned his on, and the three of them set off on the winding dirt path that led up a hill behind the house. Even in the dark Chase could see what the farmer meant about his property. The buildings closest to the road were all modern looking, but the farther you walked back the older and more dilapidated they became.

It was black as a witch's cat on Halloween, but after walking about the length of a football field Sam Foster knew exactly where to point his bright light. Chase's heart nearly stopped when the light cut the darkness, and not thirty feet in front of them sat the exact image of the well she had seen in the window back at the church.

Slowly they walked over, and Chase immediately inched up to the edge. "Careful, young lady, those stones aren't sturdy. We don't need you falling in," Sam cautioned.

Gavin immediately got behind her, grabbing a firm hold on the back of her leather belt. "You lean over the edge and shine the light down there, and I'll hold you," he said to her.

Chase slid her tummy up on the top of the well, leaned over the edge and aimed the narrow beam of the light directly into the black hole beneath her. Instantly she saw the reflection of two eyes staring directly up at her and heard a low whimpering. "RUDY!!" she screamed into the darkness. The small dog that had fallen into the well seven days before was exhausted, starving, and weak, but found the courage and strength to let out a loud bark.

"Holy crap," Gavin said. "He's down there?" He pulled Chase back to safety and turned to Sam Foster. "Do you have some sturdy rope?"

Sam was only half awake but sharp enough to say back to Gavin, "Oh you think you're climbing down there? Are you nuts? That well is over a hundred years old, and there's no telling how sturdy the walls still are. If you go lowering yourself down you're more than likely going to kick something loose and bring the whole darn thing down on top of your head. And that poor puppy."

Gavin scratched his chin and didn't like what he was hearing, but said, "He's right. You're right, sir. It's too steep a climb."

Chase immediately offered a possible solution. "Fire department? You guys have those in Manchester, right?"

Sam smiled and said, "We sure do, young lady, and they have a mountain rescue squad that's trained to rappel up and down things. Every summer they pull some lost hiker off Mount Equinox because they got themselves in a tight spot."

Gavin pulled his cell phone out of his pocket. "Do we dial 9-1-1?"

"Give me that," Sam said, taking the phone from Gavin's hand. "I know the chief personally. I'll wake him up and have him get his boys over here with their gear."

The three of them made their way back to the house where Mary already had hot coffee brewing. "Something told me this might be a late night once you three went up there," she said to them as they came inside and shook off the cold.

Because it was an all-volunteer fire department it took a solid half hour before the truck arrived with three men sporting climbing gear. They set up a small generator, fired it up, and turned on spotlights to illuminate the entire area around the well.

The chief took a look in, felt the old clay walls on the inside of the well near the top with his bare hands and said, "Jonas."

With that, one Jonas Miller, the youngest volunteer on the force, all 137 pounds of him, stepped forward and strapped on his helmet. He was the smallest fire fighter and one of their best climbers. So it made sense to send him down.

The chief looked him in the eye. "We lower you down nice and easy, you grab the pooch and we pull you up. Nothing cute, nothing fancy. Oh, and put your gloves on in case he bites you."

The kid in the harness gear pulled thick leather gloves from a nearby bag and said, "Why would he bite me? I'm saving him."

The chief gathered up some rope and was hitching it to the bumper of the big fire truck to secure it when he said, "If you spent the last week in a dark, dirty hole you might be in a bad mood. Just put the gloves on, please."

In a matter of minutes young Jonas was lowered deep into the well and slowly sank down to his destination. He could tell the puppy had fallen about twenty-seven feet from the top of the well to the muddy bottom. When he got close to the bottom he yelled up, "Another half foot and that's it."

Rudy was a mess, covered in dried mud from nose to backside. He was wagging his tail though, excited to see someone, anyone, but kept lifting his right front paw as if it might be hurt.

"How is he?" the chief yelled down.

"Good. I think he's limping. But for what he's been through, he looks okay."

Jonas noticed there was a small pool of water to his left and spoke to the dog. "Hey, buddy, I'm Jonas, and we're going for a ride. You're a tough little man, aren't you?"

His gentle tone put the puppy at ease, so Jonas continued. "That rain we had the other night saved you, I bet. Gave you something to drink down here. Well, don't you worry, when we get you out you can have the biggest cheeseburger you ever saw."

With that Jonas scooped him up tight in his arms, taking off one of the gloves so the dog could feel his warm fingers on his fur. "We're all set—take us up," he said, looking up at the light shining down into the well like a bright harvest moon.

Two firefighters carefully pulled the rope up with the help of a winch. In thirty seconds flat Jonas and Rudy emerged from the top of the well, safely out.

Chase didn't know why, but emotion swept over her the moment she saw the puppy's dirty, tired face, and she started to cry. She put her hand over her mouth, not wanting the others to see.

The old dairy farmer looked at the dog and then over at Chase and said, "Heck of a dream, young lady."

Chase bit her lip, feeling embarrassed for how she had lied about this, and didn't respond.

The chief wrapped the dog in a blanket and said, "I just called Maria Millington, and I think she darn near had a stroke right over the phone. I told her we'd bring the pup over to her now. What was that about a dream?" he asked Sam and Chase.

"Nothing," Chase told him. "Nothing."

Gavin took his coat off and wrapped it around Chase's shoulders to give her some extra warmth and support. He then reached his hand out to shake the fire chief's, and turned to do the same to the old dairy farmer. "Sam, thank you."

Sam shook his hand in return but kept his eyes on the young lady who seemed very emotional, seeing it wasn't even her dog they just saved.

"You okay, sweetie?" he asked Chase.

Chase cleared her throat and said, "Yes, all good. Thanks again."

As they climbed back into Gavin's pickup truck Sam couldn't help teasing her. "Hey, if you happen to dream up any winning lottery numbers, you'll give me a call, right?"

Chase laughed at the notion, and said, "You'll be my very first call, Mr. Foster."

As the truck started to back up, making its way off the Fosters' property, Mary shouted, "WAIT, WAIT . . ."

They stopped the vehicle and could see the old woman trying her best to run over to them with something in her hands. It was milk. "You shouldn't go home empty-handed."

Gavin tipped his cowboy hat as a sign of respect as Chase took the two glass milk bottles from the farmer's wife. "Much obliged, Mary," Gavin said, before putting the truck in drive and making his way off the Fosters' land and back toward town.

Chase reached over, took hold of Gavin's right hand, and locked fingers with him, choosing to look out the window and not speak for the entire ride back. Gavin had so many questions, but he could tell now was not the time. Every mile or so he'd give her hand a squeeze, reminding her that he was there for her, whatever was going on. Gavin knew in his heart this wasn't about a dream.

18
Harlan's visit

Manchester was a small town where everybody knew each other. It came as no surprise that the great dog rescue of Rudy spread far and wide fast. By noon the following day it was all everyone was talking about. The veterinarian told Maria Millington the worst damage the pup had was a sprained leg, and he was badly in need of a few good meals to replace the five pounds he'd lost in the bottom of that well. In fact, had it been summer with temperatures in the eighties, and had they had no rain, the dog wouldn't have made it seven days down there. Luck played a big role in why he was still alive. Well, luck and this stranger in town, who woke from a dream, drew a sketch, and saved the day. That was the story everyone was sharing. "Have you heard about this new girl who sees things in her dreams?" None of it was true, but people didn't know that, and Chase figured that sometimes a small lie is better than a big truth.

She tried to go for a walk with Scooter, but people kept stopping her, wanting to know about the dream she'd had. She was curt with the strangers who interrupted her walk and worried she might be coming off as cold and rude. She just didn't want to talk about it, and that *was* the truth.

As the antique clock near the fireplace counted out eleven gongs, signaling it was now an hour before noon, Chase heard a gentle tap on the church's big wooden doors. Scooter barked and ran. Chase's steps quickly followed after, curious about who was surprising her at home. "Miss Harrington, you mind if I come in?" It was Sheriff Harlan, decked out in his uniform and using a formal tone she hadn't heard from him before. He sounded more serious, more official, Chase thought to herself.

"Sure Harlan, please come in," Chase offered kindly.

As the older gentleman stepped inside and took off his hat, Chase stole a glance up at the stained glass window that started this mess and noticed it looked exactly as it did the day she moved into the empty church. No well, no collar, no surprises. "I must be losing my mind," she thought to herself.

"Chase," Harlan began, "I want you to know I don't like making this call on you today, but I am the sheriff and I wouldn't be doing my job if I didn't stop by and ask a few questions."

Chase's mind was racing, but she was already figuring out what this was about. "The dog rescue, right?" Chase said to him.

"Yes ma'am," he replied. "Can we sit a minute?"

She took him into the study with the fireplace and offered to bring him some fresh tea. "No thank you, I'd rather get to it if you don't mind," he said.

Jesus, he sounds so serious at this moment, she thought. "Okay, what do you want to know?" she asked.

"I spoke with the fire chief and Sam and Mary Foster and they tell me you went up there looking for that dog because of a dream? Explain that part to me, would you please?" the sheriff began.

Chase was not someone who liked to lie. Even as a child if she took a single piece of candy without permission she was not one to lie about it. But, this moment, what was she to do? Should she suddenly have an attack of conscience? How would that go? "Why actually, Sheriff Harlan, it wasn't a dream. It turns out this old church I rented has windows that come alive and change right before your eyes. It was the windows that told me the dumb dog that ran away fell down a well, and if you'll allow me to lead you back to that part of the building, I'll just show you. Oh wait, turns out they look exactly as they always did since the day they installed the things in the eighteen hundreds and it looks like I'm just losing my mind."

The thought of saying that was worse than the lie so she said, "Yes, I know it sounds a bit crazy. I just dreamt that the lost dog was near here, in a well, and when I woke up I drew a quick sketch. I called the Realtor in town, Owen Johnson, and texted him the picture. He said it looked like an old well up at that dairy farm, so off we went."

"You and Gavin? Now how does he figure in this?" the sheriff asked.

Chase got up and grabbed the poker from the fireplace and started pacing a bit with it in her hand. "He doesn't. Gavin is a friend, and I had no clue how to get to the dairy farm, so I bugged him to drive me out."

The sheriff continued, "So you two drive out and then what?"

"Then what?" Chase said impatiently. "Then what happens is we wake up the whole family, walk up with flashlights, and we're all shocked when we look in the well and find the dog. They called the fire department, and that's the whole story."

Harlan didn't say anything for about a minute, almost as if he was turning these implausible events over and over again in his mind.

He then got up, gave Chase a friendly smile and said, "All righty, then. I'm sorry if I upset you coming over like this, I'm just doing my job, you understand."

Chase nodded and relaxed a bit as she led Harlan back to the front door with Scooter following closely next to them. He opened it, put on his hat, and as he turned to go Chase said, "Sheriff Harlan, you don't think I had something to do with the disappearance of that dog, do you?"

Harlan turned and looked her dead in the eye. "Are you asking me if I believe a nice young writer moves here from three thousand miles away, kidnaps a dog she doesn't know from a woman she's never met. Then drives out to a farm on an unmarked dirt road that she couldn't find if I gave her two maps and she had that lady Suzy talking to her on her smartphone. Then tosses the dog in a well and waits a week so she can make up a story about having a dream, just so she can look like the hero. Are you asking me if that's what I think happened here, Chase?"

Chase giggled and said, "Siri. I think you mean Siri."

The sheriff looked confused, so she added, "The lady on the phone who helps you when you ask for it? Her name is Siri."

Harlan said, "Oh right, well, yeah, that lady then. Is that what you think I think?"

Chase looked down, not certain what to say, so Harlan eased her concerns, telling her, "No, Chase, I do not believe that. People around here who've known me all my life will tell you I'm not the sharpest knife in the drawer when it comes to police work, and Lord knows I'm terrible when it comes to controlling my diet." At that moment he patted his belly that was hanging over the thin black belt that was holding up his trousers. "But I am a very good judge of character and I know there's no way you did all that. Like I said, I am their sheriff. These people in Manchester look to me to protect them and do my job. It sounds like a far-fetched story, but that doesn't mean it isn't true and it doesn't mean I don't have to come over here first thing in the morning and at least ask you about it."

Harlan leaned down and petted Scooter, then looked back up at Chase. "By the way, I've seen how much you love this dog, and I heard you let Owen's son come over here and play with him when you barely knew that family. You aren't the type to hurt a flea, Miss Harrington. I don't know about this dream you're talking about, but I do know that about you."

With that he stood up, shook her hand as if they were two businessmen completing a deal and said, "Appreciate your time." And out the door he went.

Chase shut the door behind him and then leaned her cheek against the wood, looking up at the stained glass windows, not knowing what was going on or how she got dragged into the middle of all this. She reassured herself, saying, "The window is back as it was, the dog is home safe, and this nonsense is behind me." What Chase didn't know was this was only the beginning.

19

a call home

Chase decided to lay low the rest of that day, reading the book she'd started, tossing a ball with Scooter on the lawn behind the old church, and wondering when she was going to start writing. That was why she'd come all this way, to write a story, yet somehow a clear idea wasn't presenting itself.

Bored, she went and sat on her bed and opened Facebook. The first thing that popped up was a memory from ten years ago. It was Chase with a wide smile, wearing a cap and gown on her graduation day from UCLA. Her left arm was wrapped around an old and familiar friend who was looking straight at the camera and beaming with pride.

"Mrs. Hood," Chase said to herself. "Of all the days for this photo to pop up in my memories." Maureen Hood was Chase's favorite teacher at college, instructing her in composition, creative writing, and short story. Chase had her for a half-dozen classes over the four years she was in sunny California getting her degree. Somewhere in between the assignments and essays Mrs. Hood also became a good friend. Most students avoided talking with their teachers after class or after stopping by during office hours to go over their work. That was not Chase. She and Mrs. Hood spent so many hours together discussing great writers and works of fiction that by her senior year they were hanging out at the campus coffee shop at least once a month, discussing life, love, and everything that made the world go round.

Chase respected Mrs. Hood because she didn't just study writing in college and then go teach it, she was an actual writer who published books and articles. She had lived in what Chase would call "the real world" for decades before she ever set foot on a campus to teach. That gave her gravitas, in Chase's mind. Just thinking of that word made Chase laugh, because it's the kind of word that if Chase used it in an essay, that would make Mrs. Hood applaud. Chase once used a big word like that and said to Mrs. Hood, "But what if the reader doesn't know what it means?" and Maureen Hood replied with gusto, "Then the idiot can look it up." She was great that way, a big heart with a lot of attitude, for a slender woman in her sixties.

Chase hadn't seen her in years, but they'd talk once in a while, usually because Mrs. Hood had read something Chase had written in *Redbook* or *The New Yorker* and she called to tell Chase how proud she was of her former student.

So here, on this day, when Chase wasn't sure what in the world to write or how to even get started, Mrs. Hood and graduation day popped up on her Facebook page. Chase wasn't religious at all, but that didn't keep her from occasionally looking up to the sky and talking to the heavens. "First the weird windows, and now this. What? Am I supposed to call her or something?" she said to the ceiling above her bed. Scooter sat up, thinking she was talking to him. "Sorry, buddy. Not you." The dog lay back down and let out a big sigh.

Chase glanced to her left and saw the smartphone on the nightstand, reached over, and started thumbing through the contacts. There she was, Maureen Hood, under the M's, just above her friend Nora and right below Luigi's Pizza Parlor back in Seattle. She hesitated, glancing at the time to make sure she wasn't waking anyone up who was on West Coast time. It was noon in Vermont, so nine a.m. for Mrs. Hood. She'd have been up for two hours already by Chase's math. She pressed her finger on Mrs. Hood's name in the contacts and it dialed immediately.

It would take nearly ten rings before Chase finally heard a familiar voice jump from the phone. "Is this world-famous writer Chase Harrington, or have terrorists kidnapped her and are using her phone to call in a ransom?"

Chase smiled broadly, the way she'd done so often back in college when she and Mrs. Hood hung out and shared stories. "It's me, not the terrorists. I sent them out for coffee."

Maureen Hood laughed right back and said, "You know, that's not a bad plot idea for a book. A writer captured by the bad guys, writes a first-person account of the terror."

Chase sat up taller now, since she was talking to her favorite teacher. "Well, yeah, maybe but I'll pass on the kidnapped part, unless the bad guy is Chris Hemsworth."

Mrs. Hood smiled and got serious now. "How are you, dear? Don't take this the wrong way, but you never call, just to call. So what's going on? Something up?"

Chase got up off the bed and paced the bedroom floor now with the cell up to her ear. "Nothing really, you just popped up on my Facebook memories so I thought I'd give you a shout."

Mrs. Hood was surprised but said, "Okay, well hello then. How are you? Actually, where are you? Are you home or off someplace writing something fun?"

Chase looked out the window facing east and could see the top of Mount Equinox was already tipped with snow, like white frosting on top of a cake. She said, "You won't believe it, but I'm in Manchester, Vermont, for Christmas. Maybe longer."

Back in college she'd told Mrs. Hood about her calendar growing up and her fixation on a beautiful village in Vermont that looked so perfect and inviting. Maureen remembered the conversations well and the gleam in the eye of the young lady telling it, and said, "So you finally went, after all these years. Good for you, dear. And what have you found?"

That was a big question, and Chase wasn't sure where to begin, so she let out a deep breath and said, "Everything. Wonderful people, a couple of handsome, special men. It's strange, Mrs. Hood, it's everything I expected and yet nothing like what I thought it would be."

Her former teacher responded, "Maureen. I think it's time you finally drop the Mrs. and call me Maureen. As for what you just said, real places and real people are never what we think, Chase. That's the fun part, peeling back the layers and seeing what's really there."

Chase realized Maureen would always be her teacher, even now in this moment. "Can I ask you a question Mrs. . . .? I mean, Maureen. Have you ever had so many ideas of what to write about you ended up with no clue as to what to *actually* write?"

Maureen sat down in her kitchen chair back in Los Angeles, stirred a cup of hot tea, and said, "Too many ideas means you haven't found the idea yet. You are still circling it but not ready to land. How long have you been there?"

Chase told her, "Less than two weeks."

"Argg," Maureen shot back. "You just got there—give it time. And if you plan to stay for a bit, you can't get to the story, your story, being a fly on the wall watching. Join a club, get a part-time job, become part of the place. Then your story will tap you on the shoulder and say 'Hi, I'm here.'"

Chase was grateful to get the sound advice from someone she respected. "Listen, Maureen, I can't thank you enough. For this and everything over the years."

There was something in her voice that troubled Maureen at that moment. "Sweetie, are you okay?"

Chase bucked herself up. "Yes, absolutely, just finding my footing and dealing with some strangeness, that's all."

Maureen's eyes narrowed now. "Strangeness? What do you mean?"

Chase shrugged off the question, responding, "It's nothing. Someday when I see you, I'll tell you about it and we'll share a good laugh. Listen, I hear my pup scratching at the door, and I promised him a walk. Thanks for the advice, and I promise lunch on me when I get back your way."

Maureen smiled and said, "You've got it, dear. My phone is always with me, day or night. Good luck finding your story."

With that they both hung up. Scooter looked up at Chase from the foot of the bed. Chase had told the white lie about needing to go because Maureen Hood knew her far too well. She could already smell something was up from the other side of the country over the phone. The window thing, whatever it was she thought she saw, was done, Chase told herself. It was best to leave it be.

The sun was shining, with temperatures just north of forty degrees, so Chase put on a thick sweater and hat, and then grabbed up Scooter's leash for an afternoon walk. Her former teacher was right; she wasn't going to find her story sitting on the bed talking to the ceiling. Something told her if she got out and kept her eyes open, an opportunity might bump right into her. She was right.

20
Nolly's ride

Most days when Chase went for a walk or a run she turned right after exiting her home, because much of the town was in that direction. Today she took a left, hoping she and Scooter could happen upon some new sights. She passed the barber shop Gavin had pointed out to her, then a small bank called Vermont First Trust, and eventually she found her way to a place she'd heard good things about but had yet to try.

Her gaze rose up to the second floor and a purple door with a sign hanging above it that read "Aunt Nolly's Bakery." It wasn't a large sign, and if you weren't looking for the place you'd no doubt walk or drive right by. This was Manchester, though, so everyone knew Nolly's and found their way there in the morning for the fresh baked bread, donuts, and rolls. Especially the rolls.

She wasn't hungry, but she wanted to peek in. She tied Scooter's long leather leash to the banister at the bottom of the yellow wooden stairs and went up the twenty-four steps to the top. Just as she got there, she saw an older Black woman shutting and locking the door.

"We closed, hon," the woman said matter-of-factly. "But if you're in a pinch for a birthday cake or something, I can open back up. I closed out the register, so you'll have to pay me tomorrow."

Chase smiled because, once again, the kindness and trust displayed by the people of Manchester simply amazed her. "No, no. I don't need a cake. I just heard wonderful things about this place. I was walking my dog and thought I'd poke my head in."

The woman had her back to Chase now, attaching something to the outside of the bakery window, and said, "Well, you'll have to do your poking tomorrow, child."

Chase was about to turn and go when she saw what the woman was taping to the door. It was a white scrap of paper with the words "HELP WANTED—DRIVER NEEDED—VERY PART-TIME."

The woman saw that Chase lingered to read the posting and said, "You need a job?"

Chase remembered in that instant what her former teacher, Mrs. Hood, had told her about joining in the community. But she didn't want to work too many hours at a job because she needed time to write. So, she asked, "What does VERY part-time mean?"

Nolly Simms took a moment to size up this young lady standing outside her door, then said, "Very means VERY."

Chase laughed. "Okay, so like ten hours a week? Less?"

Nolly took a seat on the bench outside the door that was used by customers when they had a long line and there was a wait. "My legs are talking to me today. Oh, to answer your question. We're a bakery that's open five a.m. until noon. That's it. Most folks come down here to get their bread and pies and such, but a few who are too old or live too far can't, so I run stuff out to them."

Chase was astonished at this. "So you deliver bread and donuts, like someone ordered a pizza?"

Nolly nodded. "That's right, but it's not that many customers. Maybe three or four a day."

Chase interrupted after realizing something, "Oh, wait, so you need a driver? Yeah, never mind. I'm new in town and with all these unmarked country roads, I'd be no use at all."

Nolly responded back, "If you don't mind, I'll finish my sentence now."

Chase was a bit embarrassed at being chastised that way. "I'm sorry, ma'am. Go ahead."

Nolly continued, "We only have three or four deliveries a day, and my husband, Earl, used to do them, but now his legs are giving him trouble. So traipsing up and down stairs and long driveways is hard on him. The job, if I can find someone who wants to do it, is to have somebody ride with Earl and make the runs up to the houses once you get there. He'd be the chauffeur."

Chase understood now. "So instead of Driving Miss Daisy it would be driving Miss Chase?"

Nolly had a confused face now. "Who's Chase?"

Chase laughed out loud saying, "Sorry, sorry. I'm Chase."

Nolly looked dead serious now. "You telling me you want the job? It's only one hour of work from ten to eleven a.m. Monday through Friday."

Chase replied, "So, five hours of work at whatever you pay an hour to ride around the county and bring a basket of bread to a front door or two?"

Nolly nodded. "Yessum, and it pays twelve bucks an hour and all the free baked goods you can eat."

Chase could already see herself gaining twenty pounds on this job, but she loved the idea of seeing more of Manchester. And becoming part of the community in some small way, rather than being who everyone was calling, "That writer from out of town."

So she said, "Ma'am, if Earl is driving, I'm happy walking your goods up to people's homes."

Nolly replied with joy in her voice, "Can you start tomorrow?"

Chase said, "Yes," and with that, Nolly handed Chase her purse and said, "Wait here."

Nolly unlocked the door and went back inside for a good two minutes. When she emerged, she had two large white cardboard boxes that were big enough to hold a car tire. Each was taped tightly shut. She handed them to Chase, saying, "If you're going to work here you need to know what stuff tastes like, so when a customer asks you a question you'll have the answer."

Chase took the surprisingly heavy boxes and asked, "So these are filled with baked goods?"

"Yes, dear," Nolly said. "I don't expect you to eat 'em all, just take the smallest nibble so you'll have an idea what tastes like what."

Chase had no intention of eating them all but simply responded, "Great, can't wait, ma'am."

Nolly took back her purse and the two of them slowly navigated the steep stairs down to where Scooter was waiting patiently. He barked once and wagged his tail as Nolly reached into her right coat pocket and took out a sugar cookie. "I didn't forget you, fella," she said as she opened her hand flat, letting Scooter gobble up the treat.

"I only ask two things of my employees," Nolly said to Chase. "Don't be late and don't talk about other people's business. Driving out to homes you may see all manner of nonsense from people. You just drop the basket and skedaddle. Got it?"

Chase stood up straight and did a playful salute, bringing her right hand up to her forehead and saying, "Got it."

As Chase collected her dog and was ready to continue her early afternoon stroll, she turned and said, "Quick question. Why do they call it Aunt Nolly's?"

The elderly woman with arthritic hands and tired eyes said, "'Cause my name is Nolly and I am an aunt. Any more silly questions?"

Chase bowed her head slightly and said, "Not a one. Thank you for everything." She was going to walk longer, but carrying two large boxes filled with sweets seemed like a silly proposition, so she turned back where she'd just come from and started toward home. There was no way she was going to eat all these treats, so she sent a text to the two men she knew in town to see if they wanted to come over and hang out. Since that first night in the diner when she saw them sizing each other up like wild stags, Chase hadn't seen Owen and Gavin in the same room at the same time. "Maybe we can break the frost between them by breaking bread, literally," she said to Scooter. He wasn't talking again today, his mind on the endless delights he could smell hiding in those big white boxes.

21
when the branch breaks

When Chase was eleven years old, her friends tied a rope to the thin branch of an old oak tree that lived on the shore of Haller Lake, near Seattle. The kids from her county spent days at the lake for summer camp and were told that under no uncertain terms were they to leave the campgrounds and go near the water. Yet there they were, breaking the rules and hoping to use that rope to swing out over the water, let go, and make a big splash.

To the untrained eye of a casual observer, everything about this setup looked wrong; the frayed rope, the flimsy branch, and the need to swing out far enough to avoid crashing onto the rocky shore. One by one as they went around the circle, every child looked at the dangerous drop and decided someone else should go first. It appeared no one was going to test the swing until Chase stepped forward and said, "You guys are all chicken. I'll do it."

She was tiny for her age, so everyone swallowed hard when she took the brown rope in her hands and slowly climbed barefoot up the side of the dirt hill, trying hard not to step on the sharp rocks and sticks as she made her way higher and higher. When she couldn't go any farther she turned around facing the lake, gave everyone a wink and started running down the hill. Within seconds the hill dropped away beneath her and

Chase was clinging tightly to the rope, pulling her knees up toward her chest to make herself into a human cannon ball.

The secret to pulling off this rope trick is knowing when to let go of the line. Do it too soon and you won't clear the hard, unforgiving shore, and hold on too long and you'll swing out and then suddenly rush back toward the hill you just left from, at about a hundred miles per hour. Both guaranteed a trip to the emergency room if you made a mistake.

Chase had never jumped into a lake from a rope swing, but she had a good idea of when to release her grip and fly. After bringing her knees up to her chest, she felt the air rushing by her face as her eyes were focused, not on the lake, but on the sky above. She'd tell her friends later, after the accident, that she actually noticed a hawk slowly circling above the water, perhaps lingering nearby to witness the train wreck that was about to happen.

Chase knew when to let go of the rope, but she never got the chance because the branch had other ideas. They noticed earlier the tree branch was thin but assumed it could carry the weight of a sixth-grader. What they didn't notice was, even though it was mid-July, the tree had almost no leaves on it, which meant it was nearly dead. The branch was about as strong as a piece of uncooked spaghetti, so when the rope went tight and it needed to absorb her weight as she swung out, it snapped.

Every child watching sucked in the air around them with one big gasp as they watched their brave, and slightly crazy, friend drop like a stone toward the shoreline. Chase was lucky that day because she cleared just enough of the shore so that when she crashed down there was *some* water underneath her. Unfortunately, it was only about two feet deep, so she slammed with a loud *thud*. The EMS workers who were called told her parents if she hadn't been in the shape of a ball coming down, had she been standing up straight, she most certainly would have shattered both of her tiny legs.

Instead, Chase slammed her backside on the hard-packed sand in the two feet of water, and it felt like getting kicked by a mule. It looked like it too, leaving her with large purple bruises that made sitting on a chair impossible for three weeks. Still, she walked away from it, a bit of a legend among her friends at camp and school. She was the girl who had defied death.

Chase was thinking about how stupid she had been that day all those years ago as she typed out a text that said "Miss you. I have two boxes of donuts and sweets, come on over and share." What made her feel squeamish and uncertain, much like that day the branch broke, was the fact that she copied that message to both Owen and Gavin. She wasn't sure why she wanted both of them to come over at the same time; perhaps a part of her just wanted them to get along.

She hit "send" and waited. Surely both men would see who else was invited and that this was not a private affair or a date. Silence greeted her text. She looked at Scooter and said, "I guess we'll be eating donuts alone tonight, bud." Then a tiny *ding* jumped from the phone with the words, "Love to." It was Owen. She didn't have to wait another twenty seconds for the second *ding* with the words, "Why not!" That was Gavin. Chase smiled and strutted with confidence out into the kitchen to get some plates and put on a pot of coffee.

The young woman who sometimes courted danger plugged her smartphone into the charger on the kitchen counter, opened up the Pandora app on the phone, looked at her dog and asked, "So, what's appropriate music for this little get together?" She scrolled through a dozen or so artists before landing on Michael Bublé. She tidied up the house, gave Scooter his dinner outside on the patio, and just as Bublé was singing about *wanting to go home* there was the sound of a knock at the door. It was gentle, unassuming, so she knew it had to be Owen. When she opened the door, instead of his smile, she saw flowers hiding a man's face.

"Chris Hemsworth, is that you?" The flowers dropped down, and to her surprise it was Gavin. "Oh, hi," she said. Gavin stepped toward her to give her a peck on the lips as he handed her the flowers and said sarcastically, "'Oh, hi?' That's what I get . . . an 'oh hi'? Don't get too excited to see me. It might go to my head."

Chase punched him playfully in the arm after taking the flowers and said, "By the type of knock I thought it was Owen."

Gavin looked around and said, "Maybe he stood you up and it's just you and me." Chase rolled her eyes as she led Gavin through the house toward the kitchen. He could see she was still getting things ready so he said, "Can I help you with anything?"

Chase thought for a moment then said, "Yeah, grab that metal dish, fill it with cold water and bring it out to Scooter."

Chase stayed in the kitchen laying out the treats from Aunt Nolly's as decoratively as one could on a white ceramic plate with floral designs. The plates, cups, and whatnot came already with the rental, which made her life easier, and besides, she liked the simple country style of it all. She could hear Gavin outside playing with her dog, and that made her smile on the inside. There really was more to this man that she had seen slide open that big barn door a couple of weeks earlier, looking like Thor in denim.

As she checked the coffee she heard a vehicle pull up and then a man's voice. She went to the window to snoop and saw it was Owen, dressed nicely in khaki pants with a blue V-neck sweater exposing just a bit of his chest. "He really is a good-looking man," she thought to herself. "Well, both of them are." She stopped daydreaming to eavesdrop on their conversation.

Owen started by throwing the first verbal punch. "You hoping she'll like you more if you're nice to her dog?"

Gavin kept tugging at a toy with Scooter and snapped back, "You hoping to take her out on a real date because I'm kind of ahead of you on that score, chief?" Owen had always liked Gavin, and once upon a time back in high school they'd been friends. Then he broke the cardinal rule by asking out Grace. You see, back then Owen and Grace were not Owen and Grace yet. Owen had a mad crush on her, and everyone at Manchester Central High School knew it, including Gavin. Back then the strapping, handsome Gavin Bennett jumped from girl to girl. It was only a matter of time before he set his sights on Grace. She shot him down flat because she had a crush on a boy who was still working up the courage to ask her out; that was Owen.

Despite the past, Owen was a gentleman. He walked over to give Gavin a firm handshake. "How are ya, Bennett?"

Gavin stood up, a good three inches taller than Owen, and took his hand saying, "I'm all right."

The two of them lingered a minute when Gavin took in a deep breath and said, "Are you wearing cologne?"

Owen leaned in close to Gavin now and took an exaggerated deep breath of air into his lungs and said, "WOW, it sure beats the cow manure coming off you."

Gavin got his back up, responding sharply, "I guess when you do real work it's hard to wash off sometimes. You know real work? Not like, oh I don't know, planting little real estate signs into lawns and answering the phone all day."

Chase heard every word of it, so she swung the door open quickly and said, "ENOUGH." Embarrassed, both men looked down toward the ground, avoiding her eyes. "You are both my friends and you are both my guests, and as guests at my house you'll both act like it."

Looking like they were five years old and had just gotten scolded for stealing a cookie, both men said in harmony, "Yes, Chase."

She sized them up and wasn't sure if she should kiss them or grab them both by the hair and slam their heads together. Instead, she said, "Now, listen. It's getting cold out and I'm busy getting the food ready, so I need both of you to grab some firewood and come inside and build me a fire. BOTH of you, together." The two of them smiled and went straight to the wood pile to grab up some kindling.

Once they brought the wood into the old church, she pointed toward the other room as if they didn't know where the fireplace was. Both did, of course, having been here before.

There was nothing left to do in the kitchen, but Chase wanted to give the two of them a minute alone before she went in with the coffee and treats. She was glad she did.

"You snap up some smaller pieces there and I'll set up these logs over some newspaper," Gavin said to Owen.

The Realtor did as he was told and said apologetically, "Hey I'm sorry about the manure crack outside. You don't smell like that. I don't know why I get like that with you."

Gavin stopped building the fire for a moment, turned to look at Owen and said, "Probably because we used to be friends and I hit on the girl you liked. I was an idiot back then, Owen, a stupid kid, doing all sorts of stupid things."

Owen wasn't sure how to respond. They'd never talked about this all these years, even avoiding each other at public events in town, and here they were, standing over the unbuilt fire, finally putting the truth out there. After a lengthy pause Owen said, "Yeah, we were friends and you probably shouldn't have hit on her, but we were sixteen, Gavin. I should have smacked you in the head and just gotten past it. I guess it all worked out in the end." With those words Owen looked away, feeling a rush of emotion wash over him thinking about his Grace.

Gavin then spoke in a tone reserved for best friends when he said, "Yes, it did work out, because she chose the guy she was crazy about. That was you, Owen. She adored you. She always did. She still does. Wherever she is right now." Gavin's words meant the world to Owen, and in that instant the ice between them that had taken twenty years to freeze, suddenly melted away. Owen felt tears in his eyes and kept looking away so Gavin wouldn't see. Gavin noticed but didn't dare mention it; he just went back to the fire, saying, "My dad asks about you all the time. And about Tommy."

Owen composed himself now, took in a deep breath and let whatever was left of his anger go, and said, "How is the old guy? He still riding that tractor by himself on the back forty?"

Gavin looked up, smiling. "He is, much as I tell him not to anymore, but he won't listen. Stubborn as a mule."

Owen handed a piece of kindling to Gavin. "Kind of like his son in that regard." The two of them locked eyes and both knew the feud was over.

Chase was about to walk in on them when she heard the conversation take an unexpected turn and needed to hear what happened next. Owen struck a match, lighting the fire, then turned to Gavin and said, "And what about you? I know you like Chase but I mean . . ." His voice trailed off as he measured his next thought.

"What?" Gavin asked curiously.

Owen continued, "I've never seen you with anyone all these years. Wasn't there anyone special in your life after high school? Nobody at college or here in town after when you came home?"

Gavin plopped down in the leather chair, seeing their work with the fire was done, and said, "Honestly, not really. I dated a lot but never got serious. There was one person." Now it was Gavin who stopped talking and suddenly got silent.

"Who was she?" Owen wondered aloud.

Gavin shrugged it off. "Just a girl I knew growing up, then lost touch with. Later, once I came back to the farm, we hung out a bit, but I never got around to really asking her out. It was like a friends thing that probably could have been more."

Owen sprang up now, talking like the friend he used be in high school. "So, idiot, call her. Tell her."

Gavin shook his head. "She's gone, man. She left town for good. That book is closed now."

Owen nodded and said, "Well, forget her then. What about the lady in the other room with the donuts?"

At that very moment Chase almost fell into the room. She was leaning and listening at the door too intensely. Unfortunately, Scooter came up behind her and barked loudly, giving away her secret position. Chase nearly jumped out of her skin and suddenly marched in the room saying, "Hey, you two got the fire going, I see. You guys want to snack in here by the warmth or out in the kitchen on the island?" Chase's tone sounded nervous, like she'd just been caught committing a crime.

Both men smiled and said, "In here is fine."

With that she said, "Well, one of you help me carry stuff in, please."

Owen nodded to Gavin with a wicked grin, saying, "Get in there."

Gavin started toward the kitchen and stopped thoughtfully. He turned back to Owen and said, "Hey I don't want history repeating itself, if you're really into her . . ."

Owen smiled. "You know what? She's a great gal, but I'm not quite ready for that yet. We're just friends."

Gavin went to leave and stopped again, turning back and saying, "You're sure?"

Owen made his eyes big as saucers and in an exaggerated tone said, "YES. GO!" With that, Gavin went into the kitchen and helped Chase carry in the coffee and treats.

She told them about her new, very part-time job, and how nice Aunt Nolly was, but neither man seemed to be listening. Gavin's eyes never left her face and her soft lips; he wished he could kiss the sugar powder left over from the donuts right off them. And Owen was thinking about his Grace and how grateful he was for his time with her. He also looked at Gavin with friendship in his eyes. He was so happy this nonsense between them was over.

After about an hour of idle chatter the two men left together, each going toward their own trucks, but not before shaking hands and pulling each other closer for a quick guy hug, the kind athletes give each other after a tough game. Chase watched all of this from her kitchen window, both hands around a cup of hot coffee she was sipping slowly. She looked at these two friends all patched up and remembered that terrible fall she took at summer camp hanging onto the rope all those years ago. She thought to herself, *Sometimes the branch holds; sometimes something is too strong to break.*

22
hot rolls, cold light

When Chase opened her eyes the following morning, she saw movement outside her bedroom window: not a person, something more subtle. She rubbed the sleep out of her unfocused eyes and then blinked hard, bringing it into clearer view. It was snowing. Not a big storm, just the light morning flurries that winter likes to send Vermont ahead of a cold, harsh season—winter's way of saying, "You'd better go buy a shovel and rock salt because I'm on the way, you silly girl from Seattle." Chase was used to rain, so much rain, but snow would be fun to experience.

She slipped on her favorite sweatpants and baggy sweatshirt, stepped into her fluffy slippers, and made a cup of coffee. Scooter ate his usual bowl of dry dog food, mixed with four spoons of Dinty Moore stew, making it taste better, and the morning was off and running. She promised Nolly she'd go out with her husband, Earl, today and help with the bakery delivery, but what to wear for her first day on the job? It felt like a faded jeans and cable sweater kind of adventure, so she fished out a warm red one her grandmother had given her as a gift on her last birthday. Rubbing the thick pattern of the sweater, she smiled and said, "Nanny."

After taking Scooter out to do his morning business she made sure to leave early. She wanted to be able to walk the nine blocks from St.

Pius to the bakery and be there before 10:00 a.m. The stroll should have taken five minutes, but she made it in four. As she climbed the steps, she heard an older gentleman with a deep voice laughing and carrying on with Nolly. She swung open the door and was immediately greeted with, "There she is, and early no less." It was Earl, an older man with thick gray hair and a bit of a belly that told anyone who noticed that his wife was an excellent cook. "Did you eat?" he asked Chase with a smile. "We can't have you passing out from the heat." It was no more than twenty-five degrees outside.

Chase gave him a confused grin as she said, "Um, no, I'm good. The heat?"

With that, Earl let out a loud laugh that must have carried out the door and halfway down to the street. "I'm just funning with you, child."

Nolly was finishing packing up the deliveries and said to Chase, "Ignore him. I sure do."

Chase smiled and said, "Oh, don't you worry about me, Nolly. I got this." The two of them filled cups of coffee to go and, carrying two large boxes filled with goodies, carefully navigated the steep stairs.

Earl drove a blue 2004 Windstar minivan that must have had 200,000 miles on it. The side door opened with a loud groan as if pulling the latch somehow hurt its arthritic metal structure. "Just place the boxes on the seat there and we'll get on our way," Earl said.

He hopped in the driver's seat, Chase to his right, and the vehicle hesitated twice before coming to life. In a matter of seconds, Earl made three quick turns and they were suddenly outside the town. "We have four deliveries today. First up, Norma Witkowski. She's old and blind as a bat. So when we get there go up to the side door on the porch and rap loud with your knuckles on the black screen door." Chase gave him a look that said, "Should I be writing this down?" Earl saw it and said, "Don't worry, it's easy. You'll see."

Five minutes later the van turned left up a long gravel road to a small white house with a gray wraparound porch, just as Earl had said. Chase reached in the back for a small box marked "Witkowski" and turned to Earl asking, "Do I collect money or just give it to her?"

Earl responded, "No, no, we bill Norma once a month. Just give her her bread and such." With that Chase nodded in agreement and started up the dirt path that led to the porch. Just then Earl remembered something, shouting, "She may ask you for a favor . . . Chase?" It was too late; the van's windows were shut tight because of the cold morning and Chase was too far away to hear him call her name.

Chase took the six steps to the top of the porch and turned right to find that side door Earl had mentioned. Once she did, she gave it a loud knock, as instructed, and waited. Nothing. She knocked a second time and waited. Nothing. Chase got anxious, wondering if her very first delivery was going to be a bust, and she looked back at the van to see if Earl was watching and could help. His head was down as he fiddled with a paperback novel that he had stuffed in his jacket pocket, like some receipt he'd saved from the store.

"Shoot, where is she?" Chase said to herself. With that she gave it one more very loud bang, slapping her knuckles hard enough that it actually hurt.

A second later she heard a distant, "Coming." Another thirty seconds went by before an elderly woman in a white robe slowly shuffled across the kitchen floor to the door. Being blind, she wore dark sunglasses even though she was inside where the light was already dim. "Can I help you?" she said to the darkness.

"Yes, hi, I'm Chase from Aunt Nolly's bakery with your delivery."

Norma Witkowski took a deep breath and said, "Ah, I should have known it just by the smell. Did she send the rolls?" Chase looked down at the box but couldn't tell what was in there. She said, "Um, ma'am, I didn't pack it up, but I'm sure she sent whatever you ordered."

Norma opened the door and said, "Well, come on in. Where's Earl?"

Chase pointed as if she was talking to someone who could see when she said, "He's down there in the truck. I'm Chase, the delivery girl. He drives, I bring the good stuff."

Norma took the box from her hands and placed it on the kitchen counter, feeling her way through several items until she stopped and said,

"Bingo." She then turned to her left and felt slowly for the top of the stove. She had small pieces of electrical tape on the face of the stove showing her where the buttons were, each piece indicating a different function that she had memorized. She started on the piece of tape to the far left and counted over three inches and then pushed firmly with her thumb. Like magic the oven lit up and turned on.

She then took one step right, opened a cabinet, and pulled out a small metal pan. She went back to the box, took out two fresh rolls and placed them in the pan. She then opened the oven and slid them in. She did all this in twenty seconds flat, impressing Chase. "These rolls are amazing when they're hot, but you have to get to Nolly's at six a.m. to get them and this old bird isn't getting up at six a.m." Norma said to Chase.

Chase realized Earl was waiting and probably wondering where she was, but she was curious asking, "I see you have a microwave over in the corner. Why not just zap 'em?"

Norma turned to Chase, almost as if she could see her, and said in a serious tone, "You don't know much about cooking, do you, girl? If you zap 'em they get hot but they also get mushy. The only way to heat bread or rolls is in the oven."

Chase thought for a moment and could see her point, saying, "You're right. It makes 'em crispy." There was a pause when Chase said, "Well, Mrs. Witkowski, we have other deliveries, so I should get going."

Norma said, "All right then, thank you for coming out." Just as Chase started to open the door Norma remembered something. "Wait. I need help with something."

Chase stopped and said, "Okay?"

Norma pointed up at an overhead light she couldn't reach and said, "This light is out. Can you open that drawer next to the fridge, take out a bulb and change this? You'll have to stand on a chair."

This was not part of the job description, but Chase said, "Sure. This drawer?," pointing to the one across the room. She remembered again that the woman was blind, so she smacked her head with her palm, thinking, *Idiot, stop pointing, she can't see.*

As she retrieved a light bulb and dragged a chair over Norma said, "You're probably wondering why I care if the lights work, seeing as I'm blind? Well, my husband is not, and I don't like him coming home to a dark house after driving a dairy truck all day."

Chase climbed up, unscrewed the dead bulb and replaced it with the shiny new one. On the third twist clockwise the bulb lit up in her hand. Chase got down, saw the garbage can in the corner and tossed out the old bulb. Something occurred to her, so she asked, "Did you say dairy truck? Does he deliver for the Foster farm?" she asked.

Norma nodded. "That's right. Best milk in the county." Chase agreed and was finally ready to go when Norma said, "Wait a minute. Did you say your name was Chase? You're that new girl in town who rescued the dog. I heard about you."

Chase smiled, feeling embarrassed and proud at the same time, answering, "Yep, that's me."

She hoped Norma wouldn't ask about her dreams which never really happened when the old woman said, "Good for you dear, saving that puppy. Good for you."

Chase said, "Thank you. Listen, I really should go, unless you need something else."

Norma extended her hand to shake Chase's and said, "Nope, we're all good. Unless you want to stay and eat a roll with me."

In that instant Chase felt sad for the woman, thinking, *she's here all by herself, blind, and probably craves company,* so she said, "How about another time? Maybe we make you my last delivery of the day next time out and I can stay longer."

Norma liked that idea and said, "Tell Earl hello and stay safe, child."

Chase opened the door almost all the way when the writer in her kicked in and her curiosity spoke up. "If you don't mind me asking, Mrs. Witkowski . . ."

"Norma, please call me Norma," she interrupted.

Chase pressed on. "If you don't mind me asking, Norma. If you're blind, how did you know the light bulb was out?"

Norma smiled, because in all her years living this way no one had ever caught on or thought to ask that question. She slowly walked over to a door on the side of the kitchen, opened it, and revealed a closet with cleaning supplies. There was also a mop and a long straw broom. Norma took the broom out and slowly walked over to the center of the room and reached the straw part up until it was touching the light. She held it there about five seconds and then brought it down, pressing the straw against her cheek.

Chase smiled widely and said, "It's hot, isn't it?"

Norma extended the broom over toward Chase now, and she put it up against her own face, saying, "You're a smart cookie, Norma."

Norma smiled and said, "You bet your backside I am. I check the bulb this way once a day."

Chase left, a full ten minutes after she went in. Earl looked up from his book and said, "They got him surrounded, but he'll get out of it, you'll see."

Chase closed the passenger side door, confused, and asked, "They've got who surrounded?"

Earl lifted up the book in his hands. showing her the frayed pages and coffee stain on the cover. "Jack Reacher," he said.

Chase laughed. "Oh, got it. Hey, I'm sorry that took so long."

Earl stuffed the book back in his pocket and fired up the engine again. "What did she have you do, draw a bath? Kill a spider?"

Chase contemplated for a moment how the old blind lady could even know she had a spider in the house, but quickly said, "Light bulb."

Earl put the van in drive and started back down the gravel driveway, wondering aloud, "How the heck does she even know when one is out?"

Chase looked out the window at the tall, thick, snow-covered pine trees that lined these hills like a protective wall when she fibbed and said, "Beats me." It was her secret with Norma. She figured, why give it away?

23
framing Taylor

The final three deliveries were less eventful, just Chase walking a box of goodies up to a door, handing them off, and then jogging back down to Earl. As he pulled away from the last house and headed back toward Manchester, Chase noticed one last small bag with no name on it. "Oops, looks like we have an extra," she said to her faithful driver.

"No, no, that last one is for you," Earl said with a smile.

Chase opened the bag to reveal four more of Aunt Nolly's fresh rolls, the very ones that people drove from far and wide to taste. Chase closed the bag with a vengeance. "Oh no. No way! First the boxes of donuts and Danishes and now this. You guys will have me weighing 300 pounds if you keep this up. I'm sorry, Earl, I can't."

Earl scratched his head as he made the final turn on Fish Tail Lane, the road that led to town, and said, "All right, calm your britches down. Nolly gave 'em to you so they're yours now, which means you're free to give 'em away. How's that?"

Chase put the bag down on the seat between them and said, "Fair enough, and thank you. I should have said that first. Thank you for being so kind, but a girl's gotta fit in her jeans. You know what I'm saying?"

Earl looked over at her, taking his eyes off the road for just a second. "Do you mean a girl's gotta look good for Gavin Bennett?" he asked.

Chase looked out the window and noticed the morning's light snow was still clinging to the tree branches, which had all released their leaves. "Pretty. This snow," she responded, ignoring his question.

To which Earl gave her an exaggerated, "AH HA." His way of saying, *I can see we don't want to talk about boys on this ride this morning.*

They were quiet now, Earl putting on the radio ever so low. It was the oldies station, and a singer named Meatloaf was singing about how "two out of three ain't bad." Earl liked this young lady that Nolly had hired to help out, and she liked him too. He was like the older uncle she never had.

Chase listened to the music and said, "You know I'm a writer, right?" Earl nodded, and she continued. "Being a writer, I'm curious and have to know things. It's not that I'm nosey; it's just wanting to know."

Earl couldn't imagine where this was going when he said, "Okay, go ahead and ask it."

Chase then said, "I've met a number of people over the years with odd names, and they all have a backstory."

Earl jumped in right there. "And you want to know how a woman gets the name Nolly?" he said with a laugh.

Chase said, "I do. If you don't mind."

Earl turned the truck onto Main Street in the town of Manchester and said, "It's not much of a mystery, dear. You see, Nolly and I never had kids. It just wasn't in the cards, but she had nine brothers and sisters. So we got, jeez, I don't know, twenty-five nieces and nephews. The very first one was a boy named Harry, and he had a little trouble with his first words."

Chase was starting to guess where this might be going but didn't interrupt, only saying, "Okay."

Earl continued, "Nolly's real name is Dorothy, but growing up everyone called her Dolly. When little Harry came along he couldn't say Dolly; it came out sounding like . . ."

With that Chase did interrupt. "NOLLY."

Earl nodded. "Yes. And when the next kid came along in the family she called her Aunt Nolly cause that's what the first one called her and so on and so on. It got to a point where everyone started calling her Aunt Nolly."

Chase smiled. "And it just stuck."

Earl nodded and repeated her exact words. "It just stuck."

Chase resumed looking out the window, watching the many shops that lined Main Street float on by. "Makes perfect sense."

As Earl was approaching the two-story building of the small bakery where the day began, Chase saw the innkeeper, Ned Farnsworth, walking down the sidewalk and turning into a store. "STOP," Chase shouted at Earl, nearly giving the poor man a heart attack. "I see who I want to give my fresh rolls to," Chase said to Earl. In one quick motion she unbuckled her seat belt, slid over and gave Earl a kiss on the cheek and said, "This was fun. Let's do it again soon." And without regard for traffic she opened her passenger side door and shouted, "MR. FARNSWORTH!" Too late, he was already in the store. No bother, she just went in right after him.

Before opening the shop door, she looked up at the sign hanging above it and read the words "Oropallo Framing." It was a clear glass door, so she could see all sorts of beautiful artwork hanging from every wall. She gave the door a good tug, and a small cowbell rang above her head. "They sure do like their cowbells around here," she said to herself as she walked in the small shop, glancing around, looking for the nice man who had given her a place to sleep that first night in town at the Sleepy Panther.

The old man wasn't hard to find; he was standing in the back at a counter waiting for something. Chase approached and said, "Mr. Farnsworth, you remember me?"

Ned's eyes were not what they used to be, but Chase was a beautiful young lady and new to town. Ned remembered her instantly, saying, "Chase. Are you following me hoping to get more waffles?"

Chase smiled. "Actually, the opposite. I thought I'd treat you this time." With that she handed him the small white bag.

Ned peeked in and then gave them a whiff. "These aren't Aunt Nolly's, are they?"

Chase nodded proudly, knowing she had done well in choosing who to give them to. "The same," she said.

He pulled the bag close to his chest now, almost like he was giving the rolls a hug. "I'll have them with my soup for lunch. Thank you, Chase."

She didn't know why, but she felt like hugging him just then, so she did.

"Oh my," Ned said, taken off guard. "That's like getting two treats today," he added.

As Chase smiled and was about to go, the door in the back of the framing shop opened and a man appeared holding an 11 by 17 frame that was wrapped up in thick brown paper. The owner, Mike, walked toward the counter and said, "Here ya go, Mr. Farnsworth, it really came out great."

Chase was curious about what was hiding under all that paper, so she lingered to see what the kind innkeeper had framed. He was old and his arthritis was acting up today, so his fingers weren't cooperating as he tried to peel back the masking tape. "Can I help?" Chase asked.

Ned hadn't realized she was still there, but he responded happily, "Yes, please, and thank you."

Chase pulled hard on the tape, and the paper started to come apart. She felt as if she were opening a gift, but it wasn't hers. When the paper was almost off completely, she stepped away and let Ned finish what she'd started. Once the paper was pulled back, it revealed the back of a frame. He picked it up, flipped it over, and there was a photo of his beautiful late daughter, Taylor, standing in a massive field of sunflowers, wearing a flowing white sundress. Her arms were stretched out to the sides, her head tipped back with her eyes closed, and her gorgeous, long red hair was blowing in the wind. It really was a remarkable photograph, capturing just how beautiful and special she was.

"Oh my," Ned said, immediately putting it down on the counter and reaching for a handkerchief he kept tucked in his right back pocket for emergencies. He usually used it for unexpected spills, but right now it was absorbing the tears coming down his wrinkled red cheeks.

Chase wasn't sure what to say as she stared at the perfectly framed image. She just looked at the girl in the sea of yellow and asked the obvious question, "Taylor?"

Ned nodded, collected himself from the emotional avalanche, and cleared his throat. He pointed at the picture and said, "This photo was taken the summer before we lost her. There's a field off route 313 in Arlington—that's a couple towns over. That field is filled with sunflowers, and they bloom for about eight days, that's it. People drive from all over just to photograph the flowers. I took Taylor over, early that August, and I remember she handed me her phone, slipped off her sandals, and walked out into the middle of the flowers."

Chase looked at the photo and could imagine it all as if it were happening now in front of her. Ned continued, "It was hot that summer, mostly ninety-degree days, but that day it wasn't as brutal. We took a drive over. As she stood in the field a strong wind raced down from the mountains and made the flowers sway and her long hair dance. She closed her eyes and just took in the moment. I had her phone in my hand, so I quickly opened the camera and snapped one perfect picture. This picture." He picked the framed photo up again and brought it closer to his tear-filled eyes.

"Well, it looks fantastic, and the chunky black frame makes it look even better," she said.

Mike Oropallo, the owner and man who did all the framing himself, heard them and said, "Thank you, miss. I used to do some framing work for his daughter's paintings, so seeing her again . . ." The shopkeeper felt himself getting emotional, his voice starting to crack. He cleared his throat and said, "Seeing her again was wonderful."

Ned started to put the paper back around it and reattach the tape when he asked, "How much do I owe you, Mike?"

Mr. Oropallo just extended his arm as if looking for a handshake. Ned took his hand and the two locked palms and went up and down twice. "There's no charge. That's for Taylor," he said. "And don't argue with me because I'm done talking about it," he added with a firm tone, followed by a wink.

Ned brought the framed photo of Taylor up against his chest, hugged it, and said a simple, "Thank you."

Chase watched the exchange silently and said, "I'll walk you out. In fact, I'll walk you home if you want company." Ned nodded in agreement, and the two left the store, a cold December breeze reminding them it was no longer sunflower season.

As they slowly strolled the four blocks from the framing shop to the Sleepy Panther Inn Ned surprised Chase when he said, "I should thank you for this. You're the reason I'm holding this picture right now."

Chase looked back, confused, and said, "Me?"

Ned waved hello to a couple coming out of the butcher shop to the right of them as he explained, "Since Taylor died, I've done a terrible thing. I've avoided looking at her picture. Oh, sure, I hung her artwork around the house, you saw that, but did you notice there were no pictures of Taylor?"

Chase thought for a moment and said, "Now that you mention it, I guess I didn't see any."

Ned continued, "We loved her dearly, and it was just too hard seeing her face every day. But then you came a month or so ago and rented that room. I guess hearing the light footsteps of a young lady in Taylor's room again got me thinking about how stupid I've been."

Chase interrupted, "I don't think it's stupid trying to spare yourself hurt."

Ned agreed, saying, "No, for a time, but it's been several years now and, well, it's time Taylor returned to the house, if you know what I mean."

Chase gave him a loving smile and said, "I think I do."

As the Sleepy Panther came into view Ned finished his talk. "Anyway, I found a few of the photos we already had framed, but then I remembered the picture I took of her in the bright yellow sunflower field and how happy she was that day. I thought to myself, this is how I want to remember my little girl, arms stretched out, eyes closed and looking up toward the heavens."

They reached the front steps of the inn when Chase said, "Well, I'm really glad you did that, then, and I'm happy I helped in some small way."

Ned put the photo down, leaning it against the porch railing, freeing up his arms to give Chase a fatherly hug. As he embraced her he said, "You remind me of her. You have that wild, artistic spirit in you. I see it."

Chase liked the way that sounded. As the hug ended, she said, "I'm honored you'd say that. Thank you, Mr. Farnsworth. Ned, I mean."

The old man took his new treasure into the house, and Chase could hear him calling out "Abigail," his wife's name. She paused for a moment and thought to herself, *So much has happened in this wonderful town, and Taylor Farnsworth seems to connect to much of it.* She felt the desire to get home and open her laptop. It was time to start writing her story.

24

bring a staple gun, please

Chase didn't even remember walking back to the old church she was renting and grabbing her laptop, which was waiting patiently for her on the bed. Her mind was swimming with ideas now, and she was eager to get started. She flipped it open, looked over at Scooter, and said, "Here we go."

After opening a blank Word document, Chase typed, "It didn't seem possible, but Manchester, Vermont, was even more beautiful in person than the calendar page that was tacked above my bed back home in Seattle for a dozen years. It's rare to build something up in your mind and then have it exceed expectations."

She looked at the dog and said, "Solid start, I think." As she pondered what should happen next, her phone, which was deliberately set on silent, started vibrating on the nightstand, doing the *pick me up I'm really important* dance that cell phones do when you're right in the middle of something. "Really?" she said to herself as she glanced over to see who was interrupting her work. The phone said two words—Owen Realtor.

She liked Owen and didn't want to ignore his call. She pushed the computer off her lap and pressed the green button to accept the call, putting it on speaker so she didn't have to change her position, which was legs crossed, or as the kids called it when she was little, *crisscross apple sauce.*

"Hello, Owen," she said, loud and clear.

His warm, familiar voice echoed back, "Hey, are you busy?"

Chase looked down at the computer and over to Scooter, who was curled up like a comma, his favorite position, and said, "Um, a little, what's up?"

Owen's voice shifted to apologetic. "Oh, I'm sorry then, don't worry about it."

Chase got up now, grabbing the phone so she could speak directly to him and less to the whole room. "Owen, what's up?"

There was an awkward pause, and then Owen finally said, "I was going to ask two little favors."

Chase paced across the bedroom floor, glancing out the window at the fresh snow on the grass, and said, "Sure, what do you need?"

Owen said, "I have to hang some posters around the town and wanted to know if you could help."

Chase interrupted, "Don't tell me another dog is missing?"

Owen laughed. "No, no, nothing like that. It's the winter carnival. The posters advertise it and the carnival is Saturday, so we need to get them up today."

Chase thought five days' notice sounded a bit short to advertise something, but she ignored the impulse to ask. Instead, she said, "And the second favor?"

Owen's voice was more cheerful now. "Tommy has been bugging me to see your dog again. I figured he could walk your dog and play with him while you and I hang posters. It should only take an hour."

Chase looked over at Scooter and asked, "You want to take a walk with Tommy?" Scooter knew the word "walk" very well, and he jumped up and ran toward the side door where Chase kept his leash. She then said back into the phone, "Well, Scooter is a definite yes, so I guess we're in. Where do you want to meet?"

Owen was happy to have the help, answering, "Awesome, thank you. A group of us on the committee are meeting at the town square. Do you know where that is, where the big statue is with the benches?"

Chase remembered the day she joined the posse there and went searching for the missing dog and said, "I sure do. See you there in a half hour."

She was about to hang up when he said, "Oh, Chase? I don't know if you have one, but bring a staple gun, please." Chase agreed, and after hanging up the phone she realized she didn't even have a hammer and nail, let alone a staple gun. She bent down to pet Scooter and started thinking, then realized who might. Chase grabbed up her phone again, scrolled through her recent calls, and hit "send."

When Gavin was working on farm equipment in the barn, he usually had the radio turned up loud to 102.7 WEQX, a local station that played alternative rock. Despite being a farmer, he had never quite gotten into country music like so many of the locals. Although, as he displayed in the diner the night he met Chase, he wasn't afraid to sing a little Toby Keith when it suited him.

The music was loud. When Chase called he couldn't hear the phone ring. Lucky for her the cell was sitting on a workbench facing Gavin, so he saw it light up and her five-letter name sprawl across the screen.

"Hey, beautiful," he answered.

Chase really liked this man and felt they were close to taking things to a whole other level, but this call wasn't for a date, so in her most formal voice she said, "Hello, Mr. Bennett. I appreciate you calling me "beautiful," but this is a business call."

He could hear her giggling as she tried to pull this off without laughing. "Oh, well, excuse me, Miss Harrington; to what do I owe the pleasure of this welcome interruption from my tedious labors?"

Chase laughed at the way he played along, then said, "Okay, you can knock it off. Owen just called me looking for help hanging posters for the winter carnival thingy and he told me to bring a staple gun, but I don't have one. I don't suppose . . ." She didn't finish her request.

Gavin returned to his serious tone. "So, you want me to stop what I'm doing and drive all the way into town to give you my one and only prized staple gun?"

Chase bit her bottom lip thinking how much she liked his deep warm voice, especially when he took on that manly tone with her. "If you don't mind," she said a bit tentatively, knowing it was a big ask.

Gavin lightened up instantly and responded, "Of course. I have to go to the CVS in town and pick up my dad's cholesterol medicine anyway, so I can bring it to you then." Gavin looked at his watch and said, "In fact, I think I'm done for the day anyway. Do you want some help with the posters?"

Chase shot back instantly, "YES, I'd love that."

They agreed to meet at town square in twenty-five minutes, giving him just enough time to splash some water on his face and find some cologne to cover up the smell of grit and grease. What Gavin didn't know was Chase liked that part of him, the hands-on farmer unafraid to get down in the muck to get a job done. She thought to herself, there were different *Gavins* depending on what needed doing, and a part of her liked all of them.

A short time later Chase and Scooter arrived at the park to find Owen was already there. She then heard a female voice yell to her, "Hey, Chase, over here." It was Brenda from the diner, the nice waitress she'd met a time or two when she went in. Brenda had just finished the morning shift and had decided to help with the posters, but not for reasons Chase suspected.

"Hey Brenda, how you doing? You here to help too?"

Brenda moved closer to Chase and immediately took her by the elbow, pulling her to the side away from the others. "Can I ask you a question? I don't want you to think it's weird, 'cause if it's weird I can just not ask it."

Chase was confused but smiling. "You can ask anything you'd like."

Brenda glanced over at Owen and Tommy, who were standing near a folding table getting things organized, and said, "Do you like Owen? I ask because I saw you two together a couple of times, and it may have just been business, but sometimes business becomes more than business and you're so pretty and he's so . . . God . . . well, you can see how he is." Chase thought Brenda looked like a teenager describing a hot fudge sundae when she spoke about Owen. Before she could answer her question, Brenda continued. "But then again, I've seen you with Gavin and I heard through the grapevine you two had a date by the stream and there may have been a kiss, but nobody has been able to confirm that and I just . . ." She paused now, collecting her thoughts so the next thing came out just right. "I just have always liked Owen, but if you like him too or if it's *more than friends* I'll just go back to being silly Brad with the goofy name tag that nobody notices and, ya know, leave it be."

Brenda looked up with her big doe eyes waiting for a response, and Chase took both of her tiny shoulders in her arms, putting herself almost nose to nose with Brenda, saying, "Owen is awesome and my friend, but nothing more. I do like Gavin and I did kiss him, and I plan on kissing him again. You are not *silly Brad*, you are *beautiful Brenda*, and Owen would be lucky to get a girl as nice and cute as you, whatever your name tag says."

Brenda giggled loudly and hugged Chase, almost taking her off her feet. Chase then added, "And I think if we're going to hang these posters all over town, we should do it in teams of two. One person to hold the stack and hand them to the other person who then staples them up. I think you should partner up with Owen."

She then took her by the hand and led her over to the group gathered by the table. Gavin had just arrived, staple gun in hand as promised, and Chase announced to everyone, "I think we need teams of two. I'm with Gavin. Owen, you're with Brenda."

Owen looked up at the pretty waitress who had poured his coffee about a thousand times and noticed she wasn't in her usual uniform or apron. She was wearing blue jeans and a pretty pink winter coat with fake fur around the hood that was zipped up tight, revealing her very nice figure. Owen took a moment to look at her and glanced back over to Chase, wondering why she was making this public announcement of who was working with whom. Chase gave him a wink with her right eye so only Owen could see it, and he turned his attention back to Brenda and said, "Sounds good to me. Brenda, you're with me."

Brenda looked down, blushing instantly, and then glanced over to Chase, waiting to catch her eyes. When she did, Brenda mouthed the words, THANK YOU. And Chase smiled and nodded right back.

They quickly spread out around the town, stapling the announcement of the winter carnival on every telephone pole and bulletin board they could find. As Tommy walked Scooter, Chase took a moment to notice how handsome Gavin looked in a black peacoat that was buttoned up snug, his collar turned up, making him look even more debonair. "Nice jacket, Mr. Bennett," she said with a smile, running her fingers down his arm until they momentarily locked hands.

Gavin looked down at himself and said, "Tommy Hilfiger, I think. Glad you approve." She did a lot more than approve; she was starting to adore this man more every time she was around him.

As they continued to walk and staple, and the stack of posters in her hand got smaller, Chase asked, "So what happens at a winter carnival?"

Gavin stopped to think and said, "Picture a regular carnival, only on ice."

Chase responded with a surprised, "Ice?"

Gavin continued, "Yeah, every year for as long as I can remember the whole town gathers on the second Saturday in December and has a carnival on Equinox Pond, just outside the town."

Chase had never done a thing on ice, not even skating, so she asked, "You mean like games, food, rides, regular carnival stuff?"

Gavin stapled the last poster to a wooden pole near the barber shop. "Exactly. Not big rides like you'd see at an amusement park, but snowmobile rides for the kids, fried dough, games of chance, stuff like that."

Chase was amazed at the prospect of moving an entire carnival out on a lake and asked one last question. "And it's frozen?"

Gavin gave her a sarcastic look now. "No, we all take turns walking on water. YES, it's frozen. Lakes around here are frozen solid by now."

Chase nodded in agreement, and the two of them started walking back toward the town square to meet up with the others and see how they made out. Since there were no posters left, Chase's hand fell to her side and lingered there, hoping for something to happen. Not three paces into their stroll back it did. Gavin's hand came down and locked fingers with hers. Chase could only think to herself, "Holy guacamole, I think I have a boyfriend."

25

the second window

For the next two days Chase's life was perfect. Each day started with a healthy breakfast and a run. Then she'd deliver baked goods for an hour with good old Earl, and afternoons she spent writing and walking Scooter. Each day seemed to get a little bit colder, while her relationship with Gavin only got warmer. They had dinner at a cozy little restaurant called the "Creekside" in nearby Shaftsbury, Vermont; it was aptly named because every table had a view of a beautiful stream that ran the entire length of the restaurant. It reminded her of their first date, having wine and cheese by the stream near Manchester. Their amazing meal was followed by dessert at a place on Route 7A called "The Chocolate Barn." Every possible thing you could imagine eating, they offered, dipped in the most delicious chocolate. Not wanting to undo all her hard work to stay fit, Chase split some chocolate dipped pineapple with Gavin. They ate it parked in the center of a nearby covered bridge. She mentioned to Gavin that she'd only seen those types of bridges in old movies and always wondered if they were real. He told her everything you could imagine could be real if you wanted it enough.

Life was perfect and uncomplicated until Thursday night, just thirty-six hours before the winter carnival.

Chase hadn't noticed, but she'd stopped using the front entrance to the old church she was living in. It was often the most direct path into the living area and certainly the closest to the street. Yet most days she parked on the side of the house and used the kitchen entrance by the garage. Perhaps she liked the extra steps for the Fitbit she wore on her right wrist, but the truth was more complicated, as it almost always is in life.

The truth was she was avoiding those four church windows. Not because they weren't beautiful—they certainly were. The first showed Jesus preaching. The second portrayed the apostles in a boat on a stormy lake while Jesus walked on water. The third revealed the moment the people were going to stone a woman who had sinned. And the last showed Jesus ascending to heaven. The Tiffany glass and images were remarkable works of art, but that first window had shown her that they were also something more—something that defied explanation.

Chase was convinced people would call her crazy if she ever revealed what happened with that first window—the dog and the well—but she knew what she had seen and nothing would change that. Still, she didn't need to walk by those windows six times a day and be reminded of it. Normally if you wanted to avoid an area you'd close it off completely, but it was cool in that part of the building, and Scooter often got hot and liked to sleep in there. So, what was once a church for hundreds was now a house of worship with a congregation of one, a parishioner who liked to drink from puddles after it rained.

After three days of blissful, perfect, normal life Thursday came, and Chase fell into a deep sleep. Shortly after four a.m. she heard it, faint at first and then cutting through her like a chainsaw on the brain. It was Scooter barking relentlessly off in the distance. Chase didn't bother searching for her slippers, so the cold hardwood floors felt sharp under her feet, helping her wake up more quickly. Her fast steps snaked her through the building as she called out loudly, "SCOOTER!" There was a flashlight on a long narrow table in the hallway where she often kept her car keys, so she swooped it up in her hand without breaking her pace.

Her heart shot up into her throat, because she knew what was happening even before she got there. This was playing out exactly as before: her puppy was in the church, carrying on like an animal out of control. Chase rarely prayed, but it didn't keep her from announcing to the empty church, "Please,

God, let there be a mouse or something this time." When she stepped into the large empty room, she saw she wasn't that lucky.

It was Scooter sitting up and frozen like a statue, staring up at the second window in the old church—the scene where the boat is about to capsize on the stormy sea and Jesus is coaxing one of the men to step out on the water and trust him. "Scooter, stop, please," she implored her dog. He slowed down his bark long enough to look over at her and then back at the large window high above him. It was as if he were saying to his mommy, "Look, don't you see it?"

Chase obeyed, stepping directly next to her dog, turning on the light and shining the beam up to the glass. At first it looked exactly as always to her. There were the men on the boat, faces painstruck. Jesus was out on the water as always; nothing seemed amiss. "Bark, bark, bark," the dog continued, like the ticking of a loud clock, when Chase finally saw it. Jesus wasn't looking at the men in the boat; he was motioning with his right hand extended, almost pointing to an area far in the background of the image. Chase grabbed the chair she had left in the corner of the church, stepped up, and put the narrow light exactly in that location of the church window.

The water of the lake didn't look like water at all; it was ice covered in snow. And in that place Jesus seemed to be pointing to where there was a hole in the ice and a woman in the frigid water clinging to the edge. So much of her body was in the lake you could only see her shoulders, face, and hands. Her expression was one of terror. Behind her was something that Chase couldn't quite make out. It was some kind of machine that was green and yellow, mostly submerged in the dark, cold hole in the lake. Chase squinted her eyes to make out some writing on the side of the thing that was in the water. Most of the word was hidden, but it looked like the word CAT partially sticking out of the lake.

It didn't make sense to her, any of it, but she looked down at Scooter and said, "I see it, boy. I see it." Chase hopped off the chair and ran as best she could through the old musty church back to her bedroom to retrieve her smartphone. There was no way she wasn't going to get a picture of this as proof that she wasn't insane.

On the way back, with her phone clenched tightly in her fist, she slammed her left knee on a doorway making a turn too fast. "Darn it," she said, biting down on the pain but refusing to slow down. Despite her daily runs she was almost out of breath when she got back to the church to get this craziness down on film.

She raised the light up, opened the camera app and zoomed in to capture the entire window. She'd take a wide shot first and then zoom in on the area where the woman had gone through the ice. Then she planned to take detailed photos of every inch of the stained glass window in case there was something she was missing. As she focused her eyes on the image, now shining brightly in her phone, she let out a painful sigh that almost led to her crying. Chase didn't step down from the chair as much as collapse from it, crashing into a heap on the floor next to Scooter, who, she realized, had stopped barking.

"You've got to be kidding me," she said out loud, with anger in her voice. "Not again." Without moving from her seat on the cold church floor she raised the beam of light back up to the second window and there was Jesus on the water, the men in the boat and nothing else. The ice, the hole, the woman in distress all off in the distance? They were all gone. The window was exactly as it always was.

She stood up, a young woman no more than 135 pounds, standing alone in the heart of the old building, and let out a scream people would have heard ten blocks away had anyone been up and about at four a.m. "WHY IS THIS HAPPENING TO ME?" She yelled this so loud her words echoed back to her from the deep, dark corners of the old stone church. Then, in a softer voice, she asked, "Why? I don't understand this." She glanced back up at the window, and then the other three, and found them all exactly as they were the day she moved in.

Chase slowly left the area, closing the door tight behind her. She knew she wouldn't sleep now, but she couldn't start waking people up in the middle of the night. Instead she'd sit by the fireplace with a cup of tea and wait for the sun to rise. Then she had three phone calls to make and a difficult conversation ahead of her. She knew there was a real possibility when she was done talking: Chase might find need to pack her bags and leave Manchester forever.

26

just do me this favor

Chase reasoned that seven a.m. was likely the time that a farmer, a Realtor, and a sheriff would all be up and awake. Her first call went to Gavin, the second to Owen, and the last to Erastus Harlan. She had plenty of time to rehearse what to say in her head, so she kept it direct, short, and bordering on grave. "Hello, I'm sorry to bother you so early. This is Chase Harrington. Something has happened, and I need you to meet me at nine a.m. here at the old building where I'm staying. Use the front entrance as if the church were still open and you were coming to Mass. This is important. Nine a.m." With that she hung up, offering no explanation to their repeated questions. Gavin especially was concerned, because he was very fond of Chase and could hear something, almost fear, in her voice.

The three men all arrived early, which didn't surprise Chase in the least. All were good men, serious men, and they all respected this new woman who had quickly warmed up to their quiet country town. Most outsiders took years to truly blend in and belong, but for Chase it seemed effortless. That advice from her former teacher, taking a job to get to know the people here, was brilliant and helpful. Yet it was more than the job; she felt a strange connection to this place and its people, and they to her.

The three men greeted each other outside the church on the bumpy gray cobblestone sidewalk. Harlan began, "Gavin. Owen. You two know what this is about?"

Gavin replied, "No clue, only that she sounded upset. I didn't even realize you two were coming. I'm assuming you didn't know I'd be here either?"

Owen was in a black parka with a matching knit cap on. He pulled hard down on the hat, protecting his ears from the morning cold air, and said, "No. I didn't know. I just knew she needed me here. I guess she needs all of us. And you're right, Gavin, she did sound upset."

Harlan, by far the senior of the three men, said, "Let's see what this is about."

Chase heard voices outside, so there was no need to bang on the large wooden door with the wrought iron lion knocker. She opened it first and said, "Thank you so much for coming. Please come in, gentlemen."

The morning light pouring in from the east gave the empty church an eerie kind of half illumination. Chase had three chairs lined up as if she were going to teach a Bible study class, all of them facing the side of the church with the first two windows that had been causing her so many sleepless nights.

"Sit, please. And before you are tempted to speak or ask questions, let me say what I need to say, knowing full well that I know what I'm about to tell you sounds insane."

All three men liked Chase in their own way, and all were genuinely concerned for her as they unzipped their jackets, removed their hats, and sat down as instructed.

"For starters," she began, "I didn't have a dream that a dog fell into a well out at the Foster Dairy farm. A couple of days after I moved into this old church, that window to your right, the first window there, changed."

Owen couldn't help himself, ignoring her instructions, when he said without thinking, "Changed? Changed how?"

"Take a look at the image. Take a good look." All three men did and then their eyes went back to Chase as she continued. "I'm guessing that window looks exactly as it did the day they put it in this church more than a hundred years ago. The same way it did every time you three saw it coming in here as kids for Mass or weddings or funerals."

All three looked back at the window and nodded in agreement when Gavin added, "I never looked at it much, I'll be honest. I mean, who stops to stare at a window? But yeah, Chase, it looks like the window it has always been."

"Exactly," Chase said. "That's how it looked when I moved in, and that's how it has looked ninety-nine percent of the time."

Harlan chimed in, "And the other one percent?"

Chase paced the floor for a moment not saying anything, knowing she only had one chance to drop this bomb on them. Finally stopping and saying, "Please know, I know what I'm about to tell you sounds nuts. I get that, and if I were you I'd think this lady who came from someplace else was cuckoo."

Gavin, in a trusting tone, said, "Just tell us what happened."

Finally, she did. "One night, for a short time, that window changed. Most of it stayed the same, but up in the background a well appeared, like the one I drew on the sketch pad and texted you, Owen, do you remember?"

Owen nodded in agreement, not sure what to say. "The well appeared, and I thought it must have always been there and I had just missed it. Then I went for a run, and when I came back I looked again, and that's when I saw a small brown leather dog collar sitting on top of the well. I know for absolute certain that wasn't there before my run that day."

Gavin interrupted now. "And that's when you called me asking for a ride to the dairy farm—this was that night?"

Chase was trying to reign in her emotions now. "YES, YES, that very night." She looked at Sheriff Harlan, who was listening to all this silently. "I knew that dog was missing. I even helped look for the poor thing with the others in town. Then I come home and see a well that wasn't there before, and a collar appears, and my mind starts racing."

Harlan finally spoke. "And you thought, I don't understand what I'm seeing, but I have to tell someone. I have to at least look."

Chase was overcome with relief as she felt they were getting it. "Yes, Harlan. Exactly right."

Owen then asked, "Please don't take this the wrong way, Chase, but are you sure you weren't dreaming? You said it was a dream—maybe it was. Dreams can feel real sometimes."

Chase stepped closer, leaning down right in front of Owen's face. "Look in my eyes. I was not dreaming. Absolutely certain. I was awake as I am now."

Gavin chimed in, "Why didn't you just tell us what happened? Why make up a story?"

Chase shot back in a sarcastic tone, "Oh, and you guys would have believed me." She continued in a mocking tone to drive home her point, "Hey, everybody in Manchester. Hi, I'm Chase and the window in the old church I'm renting is sending me secret messages. You want to come see? Oops, sorry, it just changed back. I guess you'll just have to trust me."

Gavin chuckled at her tone and said, "I'm sorry, I'm sorry. You're right. A dream did sound more . . ."

"Plausible," Chase said, finishing his thought.

Gavin looked at her with those deep blue eyes trying to reassure her that he didn't think she was crazy. "Yes, that's the word."

Owen added, "Being a stranger you were probably right to keep your mouth shut or change the story that way. Hey, at least you said something, and you found the dog."

Chase was pacing again, uncertain of how to tell them the next part. Harlan saved her the trouble. For an old small town lawman he was smarter than he looked and good at sizing up situations quickly. As Chase struggled for how to continue, Harlan stood up and said, "So the seven a.m. call in a panic this morning. You didn't suddenly wake up today and decide you had to tell the three of us about the window and missing dog, did you?"

Chase locked eyes with the sheriff now, both of them sharing a serious look; she could tell he had it already figured out. She said, "No, I didn't just decide today was the day to tell you." The sheriff nodded in agreement, as if he understood what was happening.

Gavin looked at the two of them and said, "What are Owen and I missing? Chase?"

Harlan looked up at the windows on the church walls and then back to the three of them and said, "It happened again, didn't it? You saw something last night?"

Chase's eyes filled with tears, because for the first time since this window nonsense began, she didn't feel alone with a secret. "Yes, it happened again in the middle of the night with that window." She was pointing at the second window with the apostles in the boat on the stormy sea.

All three men stared intensely at the image, when Owen asked what they were all wondering. "And? What changed this time?"

Chase let out a deep breath and said, "Everything you see there now was exactly as it is, except in the background. Off in that top right corner the lake was frozen and there was a hole in the ice. A woman I don't know had fallen through and was clinging to the side, terrified."

All three men looked up at the window imagining exactly what she was saying. Gavin said, "Was that all?"

Chase continued. "No, behind her in the water was some kind of machine that was mostly submerged and sinking."

Sheriff Harlan spoke as if he was questioning a suspect. "Describe it, in detail."

Chase closed her pretty eyes, her long lashes coming down like a closed window, focused on the memory, and then said, "As best I can remember it was green and yellow, with a little bit of black on top, and there was writing along the side. Most of the words were under water, but I could make out three letters: C A T."

Gavin said what the other men already knew from growing up in rural Vermont where winter storms sometimes dump two feet of snow and people need something besides a car to get around. "A snowmobile. That sounds like a snowmobile."

Harlan agreed. "Yes, an Arctic Cat snowmobile. Does anyone have one that's green and yellow with a black seat?"

Owen lit up instantly. "My neighbor Nikki Cheshire does."

Chase walked in a circle thinking hard and then said, "You said people will be on the lake this Saturday for the winter carnival. Does she usually drive her snowmobile during that? Your neighbor Nikki?"

Owen nodded, adding, "Not only does she drive it, she usually gives Tommy rides around the lake."

Chase got very emotional in that moment when she said, "Owen, there was no boy in that picture, just the woman hanging on for her life."

Owen walked away from the group, now waving his hand at them. "Oh, this is nonsense, this is crazy. Are you telling me something is going to happen to my Tommy?"

The other two men didn't speak, only looking at Chase and waiting. "I don't know what I'm saying or why I'm seeing these things in these windows, Owen. I just know I wasn't dreaming and I saw it and now I'm scared."

Owen came back at her with logic, saying, "Wait, wait. They go out there and drill down in the lake to make certain it's frozen and nothing and nobody can fall through. Sheriff, how thick is that ice right now?"

Harlan said, "They tested it Tuesday and it was nearly a foot thick. You're right, Owen; a snowmobile couldn't fall through that ice right now even if it had a minivan riding on the back."

Gavin listened but felt himself taking Chase's side in this. "Okay, fine, the ice is too thick, but let's believe for a second what Chase is telling us is true, what she saw. Let's remember the dog was down the well. Do we really want to ignore this and say nothing?"

Chase looked at the three men hopefully when the sheriff said, "We can't cancel the carnival, Gavin, but we can go out there today and double-check the ice, just to be sure." Harlan continued thinking silently, then looked at Owen and added, "And maybe just this year you keep Tommy off the snowmobiles."

Owen let out a sigh. "Ah, man, he really looks forward to those rides, especially when he hits that open ice and goes fast."

Chase took Owen's hands in hers and said, "Just do me this favor . . . no riding for Tommy on any snowmobiles tomorrow. Please." Owen saw how upset Chase was and how convinced she was of what she'd seen, so he relented, saying, "You have my word."

The four of them agreed to keep to themselves what Chase had seen. Gavin and Harlan headed out for the lake to make certain the ice was more than thick enough to withstand the weight of the carnival goers, and Owen set out for home, knowing he had to deliver some bad news to Tommy. Still, he thought, losing Grace was more than enough pain for a lifetime. He wasn't convinced Chase was right, but he wouldn't play games with his son's life.

What the four of them didn't know was that there were two other teenage boys they should have been concerned with. Those boys had a little mischief planned for the night before the carnival that would put the whole town in danger.

27
the stupidest idea

Everyone who lived within a country mile of Manchester, Vermont, would tell you the Fletcher twins should have been born with a warning label attached. The two fifteen-year-old boys were nothing but mischief from the moment they left the crib and could get their hands on anything of danger. Guns, knives, gasoline, a go-cart without brakes; if it could cause mayhem, they were attracted to it and not afraid to cause trouble for their own amusement. The family lived too far outside the town to get cable TV, and the grandmother who raised them wasn't about to spring for satellite or pay for Netflix. So, the twins found other means of entertainment.

They had recently been instructed to clean out an old shed on the backside of their property, one that had been padlocked shut for as long as they were alive. It once belonged to a great-uncle who went to Vietnam before they were born and never did return. Their grandmother was tired of looking at the ugly, ramshackle relic.

Bolt cutters made quick work of the rusty lock, and you could almost see and hear the ghosts of the past rush out of the musty structure when they pried open the thick wooden double-latched door.

"Nothing but junk, what did I tell you?" said Hamilton Fletcher to his younger brother, Harry. The sunlight poured into a space that hadn't seen the sun in more than twenty years, revealing a half dozen useless bikes, a little red wagon that was missing the back wheels, and a large steel toolbox that felt nearly empty when Harry lifted it up from the clinging cobwebs.

He gave the chest a good shake, and heard something rattling around in there.

"Open it," Hamilton said impatiently, and when he did the boys said in unison, "WOW." Inside the steel box were what looked like six small sticks of dynamite. Harry immediately picked one up and raised it up to the light to read the side. In faded black lettering it said AMERICAN CYNANAMID COMPANY M-80 MILITARY GRADE.

The boys carried the box of trouble out of the shed and hid it under the back porch of their home. After clearing out the rest of the junk in the eyesore of a structure, as instructed, they returned to their grandmother to show her their hard work and collect the ten-dollar bill she promised each of them.

Once she returned to her recliner and drifted off for her afternoon nap, the boys grabbed up her smartphone and Googled the exact wording on the explosives they found. A Wikipedia page told them they had struck gold, because now in their possession were some vintage sure-to-wake-the-dead boom sticks.

Hamilton read out loud to Harry, "These M-80s are far more dangerous than the ones which were sold to the general public. The military used them in the 1960s to simulate real combat situations while training the troops and if mishandled they can be extremely dangerous."

Most children would stop dead in their tracks knowing they were now the proud owners of something that could literally blow their hands off, but Harry and Hamilton simply smiled at each other and said in unison, "Awesome."

Hamilton, being the oldest by a full two minutes at birth, always seemed to get the stupidest ideas, so it was no surprise when he said, "Guess what we're going to do tonight when everyone's asleep?" Harry looked back, uncertain of what to guess, so Hamilton told him, "Ice fishing, dynamite style."

The lakes of Vermont were teeming with large-mouthed bass and trout of every stripe and size, but fishing in mid-December was impossible unless you were willing to cut a hole in the ice and drop in a line. The boys borrowed their neighbor's steel auger, a device that is used to drill a hole in any thickness of ice, and waited until well after dark to sneak out the back door and make a beeline for Equinox Pond, the very site of the next day's winter carnival.

Despite being called a pond, the body of water where the town would gather in a dozen hours was large enough to be considered a lake. There was no security to speak of, even though tents and tables had already been set up, the thinking being, who is going to go out on a lake in the pitch-black when it's three degrees outside and steal a folding chair? They slowly walked out to a spot far away from the picnic area where people would gather, because they didn't want someone seeing a hole in the ice the next morning and knowing they'd been there.

Hamilton and Harry were armed with flashlights and a knapsack that housed the auger, the explosives, several stones, duct tape, and one blue Bic lighter. The idea behind fishing with dynamite was as simple as it was horrific. You cut a hole in the ice, tape the stick of dynamite to a heavy stone so it will sink, light the fuse, drop it in, and KABOOM!

The ice was nearly a foot thick, so they took turns working the hand-cranked auger, making their way deeper and deeper. After a solid five minutes of turning, the sharp end of the device finally punched through, and they pushed out the round slab of ice they'd just cut free. Harry taped the first M-80 to a stone, circling it with sticky tape a half dozen times so it couldn't break free.

"Hey, won't the burning wick or fuse go out once it hits the water?" Harry asked.

Hamilton smiled and said, "Nope, not these. Because they're military grade they should keep burning. Thank you, Wikipedia," he added with sarcasm at the end.

Harry held the make-shift bomb and fish-killing device directly above the hole, Hamilton lit the fuse, and Harry dropped it like an elevator with no brakes. "Splash" was all they heard at first, both of them not sure what exactly to do at that moment.

"Maybe we should step back from the hole a bit," Harry advised. Hamilton didn't need to hear the suggestion twice, as both boys backed way up from the scene of the crime. Both were counting to ten in their heads, but when nothing happened sadness fell over them. Together, as twins often do, they mirrored each other's movements as they slowly crept back toward the hole in the ice, certain something had gone wrong.

"Maybe the fuse went out after all," Harry said.

Hamilton responded, "Maybe they're so old they just don't wor . . ."

BOOM! The dynamite went off before Hamilton could finish that thought. A large gush of water shot up out of the hole, splashing both of them directly in the face. It was freezing cold, causing both to shout out, almost in pain at the abruptness of it. The icy water literally took their breath away.

When they collected themselves, they both darted back toward the hole, bending right over it and shining their flashlights deep into the abyss. "Do you see any fish?" Harry asked his brother.

"Nope," Hamilton replied, "I see nothing but cold water."

Both stood up, now wondering if they were somehow doing this wrong, when Harry looked at his brother and said, "Again?"

Hamilton didn't hesitate when he responded, "Again!"

They repeated this ridiculous and unfair act of angling over and over again until all of the dynamite was gone. Each time they were certain not to repeat getting splashed with the freezing water, and each time looking down with disappointment to see they hadn't killed a single fish. What the pair of Einsteins didn't know was that fish tend to go deep into the lake when it gets this cold, so all they were doing was shooting water out of a hole in the middle of the night like a whale blowing his spout.

Well, that's not all they did. What the terrible twins known as Hamilton and Harry Fletcher didn't realize was that every time they set off an explosive under the ice they were causing it to crack in that one area. Even ice that thick has its limits. Lucky for them they only had six chances to bomb the fish who weren't there and get this wrong, because had they set off another two or three charges of that magnitude, the ice under their size nine work boots would most certainly have given way, dropping them into an early grave.

The boys gathered up any remnants of their visit and turned their flashlights toward the closest shoreline so they could make their way home. As they cleared the frozen lake's edge and headed for the dirt path that would eventually take them through the woods and home, Harry said, "I can't believe we wasted them on nothing."

Hamilton, always one to tease his brother if given a chance, responded, "At least you got a bath. You were starting to stink."

HA, HA, very funny," Harry said, as they pushed through the tree line and the dark forest swallowed them whole. Both boys would sleep soundly in their warm beds that night, having no clue what they'd just done.

28
an icy drop

If there was one day a year where you could roll a bowling ball down the middle of Main Street in Manchester and not hit a soul, it was the second Saturday of December. That day was set aside for the annual tradition known as the winter carnival. Every shop and restaurant closed that day as if it were a holiday, and everyone made their way to Equinox Pond for fun and friendship.

Colgan Murphy, from the Empty Plate Diner, played a fiddle, and several others from the town brought instruments, including Roddie Valenti, who had a nice singing voice and wasn't half bad on guitar. There were games of chance, the kind where you throw a dart at a wall full of balloons and everyone is guaranteed a prize, and more fried food than a town could eat in a month. A wagon filled with soft hay and pulled by two horses took children on a short ride around the carnival, and anyone who owned a snowmobile brought those too.

Chase arrived, wearing a tight red parka that hugged her curves and made every head turn, her hands tucked warmly inside a pair of Ugg leather shearling gloves. It was her right hand most people were focusing on, because it was locked tightly around Gavin Bennett's strong fingers, the two of them announcing to the world with this simple gesture that they were indeed a couple.

Owen was there too with his son, Tommy, and Brenda the waitress from the diner greeted them by the tent that was selling powdered sugar fried dough. These two, Brenda and Owen, were clearly taking it slow, but something was warming up along with the vat of bubbling grease.

"Owen, Brenda, how are you two?" Chase asked with a mischievous smile, happy indeed to see them spending more time together.

Brenda giggled like a schoolgirl with a crush, and Owen blushed a bit, looking down toward the fresh half-inch of snow that had fallen on the frozen lake as they all slept. "We're good, Chase. Did you get any sleep?" Brenda thought this was an odd question to ask, but Chase knew exactly why Owen was wondering, given their conversation the day before and the goings on at the old church with the stained glass window.

Chase glanced back at Owen and offered up a one-word answer. "Some."

Gavin was listening to all of this and, trying hard not to give anything away to the others around them, said to Owen, "Did you have that talk with, ya know? About not riding today." He was referring to Owen telling Tommy he couldn't get on the snowmobile given the window's troubling premonition.

Owen looked at Tommy and back at Gavin and said, "I did. No snowmobile today." Tommy heard what his father said and was told the decision was final earlier that morning. That didn't keep him from kicking at a piece of ice to his side in a display of adolescent protest.

The day rolled on uneventfully, and while Tommy was forbidden from riding on his neighbor Nikki Cheshire's snowmobile, that didn't keep dozens of others from revving their engines and circling the pond. They went so many times around in a counter-clockwise motion that they seemed to etch out a track in the snow, making it look like a frozen Daytona 500. The ice was holding up just as they knew it would, and Gavin, Chase, and Owen were all starting to feel a bit foolish for worrying so much. Still, Chase was happy Owen had listened and kept his son off the sled.

Later that day, with about an hour of sunlight left, the songs had been sung, the food eaten, and the kind of tired you only get on a cold winter day was starting to settle into everyone's bones. Chase and Gavin were sipping homemade raspberry wine and talking about warmer weather and their favorite beaches and how they'd have to visit them someday. Sheriff Harlan was there as well, but he steered clear of the alcohol. Despite this being a festive occasion, he was in uniform and riding his snowmobile slowly through the carnival grounds, making certain everyone was behaving. They always did; Manchester was not the kind of place where people got drunk and caused trouble.

Foster's Dairy farm had a small tent set up with a game all the kids loved to play. For one thin dime you could try to toss a softball into the top of an old-fashioned milk can. Only two people had been successful all day, earning themselves a large stuffed animal, a tiger. One of them was Norma Witkowski, the blind woman who Chase delivered baked goods to once a week. How someone who couldn't see pulled off that trick was amazing, but somehow Chase wasn't surprised by what she could do. Norma was smart and surprisingly lucky, a nice way to go through life.

Tommy had just wrapped up his latest failed attempt at tossing the ball at the milk cans when he set his sights on a new prize, working on his father to deliver it. "Please, Dad, please." He knew the carnival was fast approaching an end, and he still wanted just one ride on the snowmobile. "Everyone has gotten a ride but me; it's not fair," he said with a hurt voice. Owen had promised the others he'd keep Tommy away from the snowmobiles, but his son was right, everyone had been riding on the ice all day and nothing bad had happened. It was impossible for something to happen because you could drive a Buick on this lake and still not break through.

Owen rubbed his face with both hands, let out a kind of growl, and said, "Okay, okay, one ride."

With that Tommy ran over to Nikki Cheshire, who was finishing off a fried sausage, and said, "My dad says it's okay. So, can I have a ride now, please?"

Owen's neighbor had been told firmly earlier that day she was not to let Tommy so much as sit on the sled, even if the engine was off, so she looked over toward Owen for some kind of confirmation to what she was hearing. Owen nodded, raising his arm and holding up one finger. "It's all right. You can take him around one time. But just one."

Cheshire pushed the ignition and the snowmobile rumbled to life. She handed Tommy a helmet, helped him click the chin strap, and then slowly started to drive away from the crowd and toward the racing track the others had created on the frozen lake. Tommy locked his hands together around his neighbor's waist and started laughing and getting excited even though they were barely moving.

Once they were a safe distance from the tents Nikki gave the sled more gas, and suddenly they really were picking up speed. Chase had her back to the lake and the track the snowmobiles were using, and was sharing a story with Gavin about how she wanted to someday take a whale watch from a place she'd read about in Massachusetts called Gloucester. "It's the same place those guys from *A Perfect Storm* sailed out of," she explained.

Gavin loved her voice and could go on listening all day, but then something in the distance caught his eye. Over Chase's right shoulder, about a half a football field away, Gavin saw a green and yellow snowmobile motoring along at about twenty miles per hour with a woman in the front and what looked like a child in the back. The boy was in an orange parka with his hood hanging down the back, flapping in the breeze. Gavin instantly closed his eyes and started scanning his memory from earlier in the day when he had greeted Owen and his son. "What was he wearing?" he said under his breath.

Chase stopped talking and said, "What was who wearing?"

"TOMMY," Gavin shot back, startling her. "What color jacket was he wearing earlier today when we saw him?"

Chase paused a second then said, "Orange, I think. Yes, definitely orange. Why?"

Without saying another word Gavin took off running like he'd been shot out of a cannon, nearly knocking Chase to the ice. She turned in confusion, not certain what was going on, but her gaze went from her boyfriend running away to the direction he seemed to be heading toward, fast.

Gavin was smart enough not to run where the snowmobile was, but where it would be going. His plan was to cut it off, but with each long stride in the snow and ice the sled seemed to be getting faster. Chase finally saw why he had darted away and who was on the back of the snowmobile and said, "OH, JESUS." She looked around, panicked now, and screamed, "OWEN?" Her eyes scanned the dozens of people standing around, oblivious to what was happening, and she couldn't find him. Just then she saw Sheriff Harlan leaning on his own snowmobile talking to some townspeople when she yelled, "SHERIFF." He immediately looked over, knowing whoever was calling his name sounded upset. His eyes met Chase's and she pointed toward the lake and said, "Tommy's on a sled."

Harlan didn't hesitate, swinging his right leg over the device and igniting the engine in one swift motion. As he punched the throttle and started moving, he could see up ahead of him was another adult running like he was being chased by the devil himself, making a direct line for the snowmobile carrying the child.

Gavin was in incredibly good shape, working on that farm every day, and he closed the distance between them fast. Unfortunately, the driver wasn't aware anyone was chasing after her, so she kept going faster and faster as Tommy laughed and cheered. Chase was certain Gavin wouldn't get there in time, and the truth was he didn't; not really.

Just when it seemed the sled would slip away, Gavin instinctively did the only thing he could to save the boy; he dove like an outfielder in a baseball game trying to catch a fly ball. His outstretched hands reached as far as they could, and his fingers closed down tightly on the only thing he could grasp, Tommy's orange hood that was whipping in the wind. As the snowmobile sped away, Gavin's grip yanked Tommy hard right off the back of the sled, slamming him down hard on the ice. The child instantly started crying.

Many in the crowd let out a loud gasp, having witnessed what appeared to be this reckless act by Gavin. Owen heard them and turned his head from where he was standing to see what all the commotion was about, only to see his child laid out flat as a pancake on the cold ice, sobbing.

Owen was the one running now trying to get to Tommy. His mind was racing, and the only explanation he could conjure was that Tommy had somehow fallen off the back of the sled.

Owen skidded into the ice next to Tommy, coming down hard on both his knees. "Is he all right? Is he hurt?" Owen asked.

Gavin looked up, barely able to talk he was so out of breath, and said, "Yes, he's fine. Just shaken up."

Owen sat Tommy up and gave him a firm hug asking, "Did you fall, buddy?" Tommy broke the embrace and with tears in his eyes glared at Gavin and said, "No, he pushed me."

Time stood still now for Owen as he tried to understand what his son was saying. Finally, he said, "Pushed you? He pushed you?"

Owen's eyes turned to Gavin searching for an explanation, when Gavin said, "Yes, I dove and pulled him off. I'm sorry it was so rough, but I know you didn't want him riding today."

Part of Owen understood why Gavin would spring to action and want to help, but what he described happening sounded more reckless than helpful. "So, you decided to yank him off the moving sled by his hood? Are you insane, Gavin? You could have broken his neck."

Gavin thought in that instant Owen was going to haul off and slug him right in the face, seeing the rage the father had in his eyes over what had just happened to his son. Just then, Chase ran over, putting her small, thin body between the two men. "Owen, don't. Tommy is all right. He was just trying to save him."

Owen helped Tommy to his feet now, feeling the anger only rising from his stomach to chest. "Oh yeah, help him right to the emergency room."

Gavin looked down, feeling ashamed and sorry his friend was so upset with him. "I'm sorry if I overreacted. I'm sorry." There was nothing more he could say.

As Owen put his arm around Tommy's shoulder preparing to walk him back to the shore, they heard a scream. Off in the distance, halfway across the lake, there was a woman pointing and yelling, "Help her."

Everyone at the carnival looked west, and a quarter mile away they saw a snowmobile had somehow fallen through the ice.

When Nikki Cheshire hit the throttle to pull away from the crowd thirty seconds earlier, the vibration on her sled was so strong she didn't even feel it when Gavin yanked Tommy off the back. She turned onto the track the others were using to go in circles all day, and seeing there was only one sled up ahead of her, she hit the gas hard. She was going nearly forty miles per hour when a young married couple on the sled in front of her stalled and stopped dead in the middle of the track.

Going that fast, Nikki only had three choices: hit them full on, veer left, or veer right. In the blink of an eye she jerked the handlebar to the right, sending her snowmobile a good thirty feet off the track onto a section of ice that up until that moment hadn't been ridden on.

Because of the light snow overnight Nikki couldn't see or know that there was a hole in the ice where she had just driven, a hole that was only partially refrozen. She also had no way of knowing that because two idiot teenagers had been setting off small sticks of dynamite in that very spot only a few hours earlier, the rest of the ice around the hole had been compromised. Her 500-pound sled hit the weak spot and dropped through the ice in a split second, the thirty-six-degree lake water hitting Nikki's skin like a thousand sharp knives.

Owen, Gavin, Chase, and all the others at the carnival felt powerless to help as they saw Nikki Cheshire claw her hands on the edge of the ice trying in vain to pull herself up. Her yellow and green snowmobile with the words ARCTIC CAT slowly slipped into the murky water beneath her. Soon you could only see the word CAT peeking out of the watery tomb. Gavin looked from the horror on the ice back to Chase's eyes, neither able to speak, but both knowing this was exactly what the window at the church had foretold.

Just when it seemed all hope was lost, a second snowmobile appeared and closed in quickly on the hole in the ice and the woman hanging on for dear life. It was Sheriff Harlan, riding fast on his red Polaris sled. Careful not to get too close lest the ice crack under him, Harlan opened a side saddle bag on the sled and produced a rope with a lasso already tied and ready to be thrown as if he were at the rodeo.

"NIKKI," he shouted, the sheriff swinging the lasso in a circular motion several times above his head before letting it go and having the rope fall gently into the hole that Nikki Cheshire was fighting to clear. "Loop it over your head and under your arms and tighten it," Harlan said. Despite being freezing and closing in fast on hypothermia, Nikki did as instructed and gave Harlan a thumbs-up sign. Harlan looped his end twice around the metal bar on the sled and slowly squeezed the throttle, pulling the woman out of the icy grave.

An EMS crew that was there on standby quickly got Nikki Cheshire to the warming tent and got her changed into dry clothes. Harlan made his way back to the crowd and received a standing ovation from, it seemed, everyone in town. Despite being a hero, that wasn't what was on his mind at the moment. He found his way to Chase, Owen, and Gavin, and all four just stared at each other in disbelief.

Owen said to Chase, "Well, now we know why you told us that first window you saw was a dream." He paused, looked over at the townspeople he'd known all his life, and added, "Nobody would believe you."

Gavin then said, "Heck, I just saw it and I'm not sure I believe it."

Chase felt grateful that she wasn't alone in whatever it was that was happening here, but she was also curious about something. "Sheriff?" she asked. "When I told you about the second window, you seemed the most skeptical of everyone."

Harlan nodded in full agreement. "Yes, yes I was."

Gavin saw where Chase was going with this, asking for her, "So why did you have a rope and lasso already tied and ready to go on your sled?"

Harlan saw all three raise their eyebrows at him now and smile in unison. The old sheriff responded, "Hey, we already had a dog in a well. I didn't need a Cheshire in a lake." They all shared a laugh and agreed, for now at least, to keep what had just happened to themselves.

Later that evening, all four would lie awake in the safety of their warm beds, wondering the same thing: What might possibly happen with the two windows left?

29

the sad panther

The day after the winter carnival, downtown Manchester was the exact opposite of the day before. Where before you could look far and wide and not see a soul in the streets, shops, or cafés on Saturday, Sunday it was a beehive of activity. This was the day everyone brought out their Christmas lights and decorations and turned the small town into a Norman Rockwell painting. The smell of eggnog and fresh pine boughs hung in the air like an intoxicating perfume, telling locals and visitors alike that the Christmas season had indeed arrived in Vermont.

Chase and the others agreed to keep their mouths shut about the second window in the church and the premonition about Nikki Cheshire's unanticipated ice bath. No, today was strictly for decking the halls and getting in the holiday spirit.

Chase started her day as always, with egg whites and whole wheat toast, and a two-mile run through downtown and looping around by the old train station and then back home again. After dusting around the house and doing her best to avoid going into the part of the building where the windows seem to be talking to her, Chase heard a knock on the door and saw a handsome, welcome face on the other side.

"Gavin," she said, planting a healthy wet kiss on his soft lips, locking her hands in his and pulling him into the kitchen. He was about to grab a seat and ask for a cup of coffee when Scooter barked and scratched at the foot of the door. "Oh geez, I promised him a walk," Chase said to her new boyfriend. She liked the sound of that in her head: boyfriend. She hadn't had a serious relationship in years and thought to herself in that instant, *I've got a guy who can grow the food to feed us, slay a lion if one attacked us, and can probably quote Shakespeare in the process.* The thought made her giggle with joy.

"What's so funny, pretty lady?" he asked.

Chase shot him a side glance with seductive eyes and said in a sexy voice, "I'll never tell." He scooped her up in his arms like she weighed five pounds and plopped her down on the kitchen island. He was about to move in for a second kiss when Scooter barked again. Gavin turned to look at the pup and said, "You're killing me, smalls."

Chase smiled and said, "Smalls?"

Gavin gave a surprised look, asking, "Don't tell me you never saw the movie *The Sandlot?*"

Chase was genuinely at a loss. "Um, no. Is that bad?"

Gavin lifted her down from the countertop and gave her another quick peck on the lips. He turned to grab Scooter's leash, which hung off a hook by the door, and said "Oh, we are seriously going to rent a movie soon."

Chase asked innocently, "*The Sandbox?*"

Gavin smacked his open palm on his forehead and said, "Oh good grief, not box—lot. SAND LOT."

Chase repeated it correctly saying, "Sandlot. And I'll find out who Smalls is and why he's killing some guy?"

Gavin couldn't take her cuteness any longer and said, "I really think I love you." With that he clipped the leash on Scooter's collar and opened the door, stepping out into the bracing cold.

"Wait, what? Did he just say he loved me?" Chase asked the empty kitchen. She then thought, you don't just say something like that and then walk out of the room. "He's kidding. He must be kidding, right?" Again, none of the appliances residing on the counters of the empty kitchen offered up an opinion one way or the other to her question about Gavin's love.

The door suddenly swung back open and Gavin's gorgeous face popped back in, "Are we coming, princess? The dog is waiting." She could have smacked him right then and there, dropping the L word and dashing out. Oh, they'd be discussing this in detail later, but right now Scooter did need his walk.

They held hands as they slowly sauntered along through the town. Everywhere they looked, lights were being strung around poles or trees, and beautiful wreaths with bright red bows dotted almost every shop door and home.

Chase thought back to the calendar page of Manchester that had hung on her bedroom wall all those years and the joy and hope it had given her that such a world existed. Now here she was, holding the hand of a big, strong farmer, watching it come to life right before her very eyes.

They walked the one-mile stretch of Main Street, waving hello to everyone they saw, turning around at Monument Square, and making their way back. Every single building was lit up in holiday cheer except for one. It was a place she knew well, one she had found comfort and kindness in on her very first night in town. It was the Sleepy Panther Inn. As pretty as the building was, it looked kind of sad to her.

Gavin saw Chase give a somber look as they slowly walked past the inn and then glance up at the ungarnished windows and barren front porch. It looked exactly as it had looked when she'd arrived in November, the same way it would look in July or any other month. Reading her mind, Gavin said, "They don't really celebrate Christmas since the accident."

Chase stopped now, his words striking her like a cold punch to the heart. "That's sad," she said. She kept staring up at the inn and at the second-floor window of Taylor's old room, the one Chase had slept in and where she'd found all those beautiful paintings hiding on the closet floor.

"Chase?" Gavin asked, wondering why she wasn't speaking.

She then said firmly, "It's sad and not right."

Chase turned to Gavin with a new energy he hadn't seen before in her. "Do me a favor and take Scooter home. If you want that cup of coffee, help yourself. I'm going to be a little while." Gavin was confused and was about to ask what was going on when Chase said, "Please." There was something in her eyes that told him not to question it, just do as she asked. He left with Scooter, and Chase climbed up the front steps of the Sleepy Panther Inn.

A hard knock on the door brought Ned Farnsworth straight away. Before it was even open, Ned could see her through the glass and the thin curtains and said, "Chase? How are you, dear?"

Chase began, "May I come in, sir?"

Ned opened the door and said, "'Sir,' is it now? Such formality for friends."

Chase looked at the old man and said, "We are friends, and that's why I'm here. I don't want to overstep my bounds, but why are you the only house in town not decorated?"

Ned took a seat on an antique wooden chair near the staircase and said, "Oh, that."

Chase didn't wait for any further response, saying, "I know it's none of my business, but everything you've told me about your daughter, Taylor, was that she was full of life. True?"

Ned's arthritic hands fumbled with a handkerchief he kept in his back pocket and said, "She was."

Chase then asked, "Then how is this honoring her memory by not celebrating Christmas? I think if she were here, she'd want you to. Don't you?"

Ned got up and paced in a small circle, thinking. Part of him wanted to tell Chase she couldn't possibly understand his pain and loss and she should mind her own beeswax. But a deeper part of him knew the pretty young stranger who he had quickly grown fond of was also right.

He returned to his chair, sat back hard on it, almost collapsing into the seat and letting out a large gasp of air. His eyes were filled with salty water now, as he looked up at Chase and said, "She'd be furious with me."

Chase knew it was the truth Ned was speaking, and it was hard for him to say it out loud. She kept quiet a moment, and then the old innkeeper said, "The truth is Taylor always helped me with the decorations. It was kind of our thing to do together. I couldn't bear the thought of bringing the boxes down from the attic and doing it without her."

Chase lowered herself to one knee, bringing her closer to Ned's eye level and said, "I'm not your daughter, but I'd be happy to help. Maybe we can do it for her."

Ned sighed a bit, and then extended his hand to help Chase up to her feet. "I think she'd like that, and I think you're right." Ned looked around at the beautiful inn that hadn't seen a Christmas light, candle, or ornament since the crash that had claimed Taylor's life, adding, "It's time."

For the next hour Chase and Ned Farnsworth decorated the porch, the windows, the staircase, and the fireplace, turning the Sad Panther into The Sleepy Panther of days gone by. They both walked outside and went down to the curb so they could see how it looked for everyone passing by. "You like?" Chase asked him.

Ned smiled and said, "It's perfect. Thank you, Taylor." Chase remembered that he had accidentally called her that the first morning he made her breakfast at the inn. She didn't dare correct him.

Instead she felt herself getting emotional, turning away so the old man wouldn't know. Her phone buzzed in her pocket, and she opened it to find a text from Gavin. Four words followed by a question mark: "You decorated didn't you?"

Instead of replying, Chase snapped a photo of the outside of the house and hit "send."

Gavin replied with the emoji of a heart. She gave Ned Farnsworth a hug goodbye and started the walk home, thinking, "Maybe he wasn't kidding about loving me, after all."

30
confessions of a pizza party

A couple of hours after Chase left the now beautifully decorated
Sleepy Panther Inn her phone rang, revealing a number she didn't
recognize. She normally wouldn't answer a call not knowing who was on
the other end, but it had an 802 area code, which indicated it was a phone
in Vermont.

"Hello," she said.

"Hey Chase, I'm sorry to bother you like this after you just did me
such a nice favor." She knew the voice instantly; it was Ned Farnsworth
from the inn. "I wanted to call you, but I didn't have the number, so I
called your Realtor friend, Owen, and he gave it to me."

Not bothered at all, Chase asked, "How can I help you, Mr.
Farnsworth?"

Ned was smiling and sounding chipper when he said, "My wife,
Abigail, and I are so excited about the house, how nice it looks, we decided
to have a last-minute pizza party right here at the inn. I've already invited
the sheriff and Colgan and Shayla from the diner, and I think you know
Maria Millington, the lady who lost her dog, and gosh, we called around
a dozen people. I'd love it if you could come."

Chase was so happy to see the sad old man finally sounding cheerful
and said, "I wouldn't miss it for the world. Can I invite a couple of people?"

Ned responded, "Well, I already told Owen to bring his boy, but you should definitely invite that farmer fella who was here the other day asking you out on a date. You still seeing him?" Chase confirmed they were now boyfriend and girlfriend, in a Manchester kind of way, meaning they were taking it slow and respectful.

"Everyone is coming at seven sharp, and I'm ordering all the pizza in Bennington County," he added with a hearty laugh.

"We'll see you at seven," she said, before hanging up and immediately calling Gavin.

As pretty as Manchester looked in the day, at night when all the Christmas lights came on, it was downright magical. Driving down Main Street one couldn't help feeling as if they were living in some fairy-tale romance novel. Crisp white bulbs dancing in the air, wrapped around poles, trees, and fence posts, and bright red bows were everywhere you looked. It was as if the city itself was a present, and everyone took part in wrapping it for Christmas morning.

One by one the friends of the Farnsworth family arrived at the inn. There were candles in all the windows, and you could hear soft music playing all the way down to the sidewalk as you made your approach. The scent of fresh pine filled the air, courtesy of the boughs Chase and Ned had strung all over the porch and above the front door. The peeling paint that Ned had promised himself he'd scrape and repaint by Halloween was still there, but it only added to the charm of the place.

Abigail placed some chips and dip out on the tables near the large fireplace in the den, and cheese and crackers greeted guests if they wandered into the kitchen. It was something to hold people over until the half-dozen pizzas arrived. Chase was chatting with Brenda, the waitress from the diner, asking how things were going with Owen, and she blushed and said, "He's so incredibly sweet. It's hard trying to replace someone like his wife, Grace, though."

Chase squeezed her hand and said, "Hey, you don't have to. Just be you. It's you he likes. Brad the waiter." They both laughed, then Brenda put down her drink and gave Chase a hug, whispering "thank you" into her ear.

"Young lady?" a voice boomed behind them. It was Ned. "There's someone you should meet. This is Father James O'Brien; he used to live in your church."

Chase looked confused as she shook his hand, and the priest said, "St. Pius. I was the pastor at St. Pius, the old one, before we built a new church on the edge of town, Route 7 right before you hit Dorset."

Chase finally got it, saying, "OH, OH, right, I'm sorry. You said 'my church' and I got confused. I didn't know I owned a church." With that they all shared a laugh. "So you were the pastor in the St. Pius I'm in now?"

The priest shook his head to correct her. "Well, technically you're not in a church anymore. It's just a beautiful old building now. The church is where the altar is and where we celebrate Mass, you understand."

Chase nodded. "I do."

As the conversation lagged and the priest was about to move on to chat with other guests, Chase said, "Father James, is it? Do you mind if we chat in private for a second?"

The priest, always one with a sense of humor said, "Well I take confessions Saturday afternoon at three, but if it's a quick one." Chase took him by the arm, guiding him over near the window away from prying ears and then froze, uncertain how to proceed.

Finally, the priest said, "Did you have a question, dear?"

Chase threw her hands in the air like someone who just lost the lottery by one number and said, "Oh to heck with it, I'm just going to ask it. Father, when you were pastor at the old church, did anything strange ever happen?"

Father O'Brien gave her a befuddled look and said, "Strange? Strange how?"

Chase wasn't sure how far to go with this. "Oh, I don't know, you see anything weird there, like say, with the Tiffany windows?"

The priest was lost now, uncertain what she meant. "Um, honestly, I can't say I did. They're certainly beautiful."

Chase should have quit while she was behind, but she pressed on. "So, you never saw one thing in a window and then later saw something else?"

The priest considered her words for a moment and then smiled as if finally understanding, and said, "Oh, I see what you're asking. You mean, can a person admire a window and then later come back to that same window and have a better understanding of God's plan?"

Chase shook her head. "Um, no, that's not what I mean. You know what, Father, never mind. I appreciate your time."

Father O'Brien smiled and said, "Well, glad I could help."

Sheriff Harlan was watching the private conversation from across the room and knew what Chase must have been asking the priest, without even hearing a word. He gave Chase a look that said, "Well? Any luck?" Chase made a funny face like she was in pain and shook her head NO right back at the sheriff. Her expression made the sheriff laugh.

Gavin arrived with his father and immediately crossed the sea of people to get to Chase and gave her a big hug and kiss. Everyone in the room was watching them, even though they pretended otherwise. Just then there was a clanging sound. It was Ned, standing up on the third step of the staircase so everyone could see him, banging a metal fork against a crystal glass. "Can I have everybody's attention? I just wanted to thank everyone for dropping everything and coming over for pizza. Which, by my watch, should be here any minute. Abigail and I haven't had much reason to celebrate lately, but this is nice. Just . . . well . . . thank you." You could hear the old man's voice starting to crack, so he finished his speech quickly before his emotions got away from him.

Everyone was in the den now where plates and napkins were laid out for dinner, and a loud knock hit the front door. "That's dinner," Abigail announced.

Gavin without hesitation said, "Listen, Dad and I had a good fall season at the farm, so the pizza is on me." Ned and his wife smiled and nodded out of respect for the gesture, and Gavin walked quickly toward the door saying to Chase, "Come help me with all this food."

They opened the door and found the delivery man had the pizza boxes stacked neatly on the porch railing. As Gavin took them all in his big strong arms he said to Chase, "My wallet is in my back pocket." She took it out and pulled out a fist full of cash, a half dozen twenties lined up and waiting.

"That's sixty-eight dollars even," the delivery man said. Chase smiled when she noticed the man's shirt said Dante's Inferno Pizza above the breast pocket.

"Cute name," she said pointing toward the company logo.

"We try," the man said back politely.

"Just give him eighty dollars," Gavin said, as he strained to balance the weight of six large pizzas, most of them covered in some kind of yummy topping.

They took the pies into the house and straight into the den, placing them on the tables that lined the far wall, opposite the fireplace. As everyone jockeyed for position, Chase realized she was still holding Gavin's wallet, and it was slightly open, revealing several credit cards tucked into their slots and a half-dozen small pictures. The top one was of Gavin and his dad standing proudly next to their tractor, the vast beautiful farm in the background. The next photo was a black and white of a beautiful woman taken some time ago, no doubt his mom. She realized in that instant she was snooping in her boyfriend's wallet, which was not nice at all, and she was about to close it up and hand it back when a splash of bright yellow caught her eye.

The third picture in the half-dozen photos that Gavin carried around with him was a bright yellow field of flowers with a pretty young girl standing in the middle of it, her arms stretched out and silky red hair dancing in the wind. Chase swallowed hard and almost felt sick at that moment. "I know this photo," she said out loud, loud enough for others to hear. She turned and her eyes scanned the room searching for Gavin's. Once she found them, she said, "This is Taylor Farnsworth. Why do you have a photo of Taylor in your wallet?"

Ned Farnsworth put down a bottle of Sam Adams Winter Lager he'd been drinking and pushed past a couple of his neighbors to put himself directly into this conversation now. "Why do you have a photo of my daughter?"

Gavin took a deep breath, feeling like he was in the confessional at Father O'Brien's church, and began. "First thing you should know is we were friends. That's all. That's as far as it got." Chase instantly felt better about whatever he was planning to say next.

Gavin turned to Ned, now meeting his eyes and continued. "We were friends in high school but not very close. I was a jock and . . ." He stopped himself, looking over toward Owen and Brenda now because they knew him back then, as he continued. "If we're being honest, I was kind of an arrogant jerk back then and Taylor was the artist type." Everyone at the party was listening now, Abigail turning the music off so Gavin's words wouldn't have competition to be heard.

"And artists and jocks don't hang out. After graduation I went to college and lost track of pretty much everyone here in Manchester. When I got back and started working with Dad on the farm full-time, I started to reconnect with people."

Chase interrupted, "And one of them was Taylor?"

Gavin smiled, with softness in his eyes. "Yes, one of them was your Taylor," he said, looking at Ned and Abigail. "We never even technically had a date. We started chatting on Facebook and I bumped into her once at the diner by accident and we ended up sitting together on the stools at the counter and talked for nearly three hours."

Shayla Murphy, standing next to her husband, Colgan, said, "I think I remember that day. I must have poured you both five cups of coffee."

Gavin walked over to Chase, now concerned how all this might be hitting her and said, "But we weren't boyfriend and girlfriend like us. It hadn't gotten that far."

Brenda asked, "Why not?"

Gavin's expression changed, and he looked like a wounded child now, biting down hard on his bottom lip, not saying a word. Colgan Murphy spoke for him, "The accident?" Gavin just nodded, looking down almost in shame.

Chase finally got it now. "She was the girl. Back when you were at my house talking to Owen, he asked you why you never got serious with anyone and you told him there was one girl you really liked but she went away. She left town, you said. That was Taylor?"

Gavin met Chase's eyes and confirmed it. "Yes, that was Taylor."

Owen spoke then. "But I don't understand. Why didn't you tell anyone?

If you knew and liked her you must have been devastated when you lost her."

Gavin had tears in his eyes now as he looked toward Ned and Abigail Farnsworth, and said, "Shame. That's why I never said a word. Shame. I had to work late on the farm the day of the tree lighting and bonfire because we had a calf being born. I was supposed to meet Taylor up on the mountain but told her I had to stay on the farm. We agreed to meet in town after I was done."

Ned said, "And that's why she left early that night. She was going to meet you?"

Gavin looked at the Farnsworths and said, "I'm so sorry."

Gavin's father spoke up. "It's my fault, Gavin. I knew you wanted to go to the bonfire and I told you I could handle the calf. When you insisted on staying I should have shoved you out the door."

Ned spoke again. "Are you two crazy? I'm the one to blame for this. I saw it was starting to snow and I told her to take my truck, not that little sports car she sped around in. I should have made her take the truck."

No one said anything for a moment when a familiar voice offered an opinion. "Do you hear yourselves?" It was Father O'Brien. "Stop. Please stop." He looked toward Gavin and his father first. "You stayed with your father to help with the birth of a calf because that's what good sons do; they help their fathers when needed. And you, sir, think you were going to tell your twenty-something-year-old son he has to leave when he knows you need him? Not a—no way."

The priest then turned to Ned and Abigail. "And Ned, I knew and loved your daughter and she did exactly what she wanted to do. Always. She was a true artist, down to her soul. She drove her car because she loved her car and didn't feel comfortable in that big truck. She could barely see over the dashboard, for goodness' sake."

The priest then looked at everyone in the room and said, "This is no one's fault. It was an accident, nothing more. An icy road on a dark night. And all of you need to stop blaming yourselves for it. Do you think that's what Taylor would want?"

Ned and Abigail hugged each other and realized the priest was right. Gavin's father put his hand on his son's shoulder and said, "I'm so sorry you've been carrying this around with you all these years."

Chase was standing alone, taking it all in when Gavin turned to her and said, "Are we okay? Please tell me we're okay?"

Chase really did love this man and felt a genuine hurt for his loss. Still, she couldn't help herself asking, "Just tell me you two didn't have a picnic by the stream and do that lightning bug trick, 'cause that would tick me off."

Gavin laughed loudly and hugged his girl saying, "No, we did not. Like I said, I did like her, but we had just started to really get to know each other when . . ." He stopped that sentence short. Chase finished it, "When you lost her."

Ned suddenly appeared to their left and extended his right hand toward Gavin's to shake it. "She wouldn't tell me who the new boy was she met but I knew she liked him. She would only tell me *he's a good, solid guy, Dad*. Those were her exact words. For whatever joy you gave her in those final days, I'm grateful, son."

Gavin found himself wanting to cry, to grab the old man and hug him. Instead he tightened his grip on the long-overdue handshake and said, "And she loved you and your family very much. That I knew for certain, sir."

"Ned. Call me Ned," the innkeeper responded, pulling in Gavin for a hug anyway.

As the friends and neighbors turned their attention back to the food and refreshments, Chase looked around at these townspeople and thought it felt like a nine-hundred-pound weight had just been lifted off their shoulders. What she didn't know was that while she and the others were caught up in the "confessions of a pizza party," her dog, Scooter, was having his own excitement going on back at the old church. The pup was standing in front of the closed and locked door, barking loudly. On the other side of that door was a large empty space with four panes of Tiffany glass. He needed to reach the third window.

31
the third window

Chase parked her Mustang on the side of the vacant church she called home and used the side entrance that led to the kitchen. She was barely three steps toward the door when she heard her dog barking like a madman. She assumed in that instant that she'd left him too long and the poor guy had to get outside and do his business, but when she went to turn the doorknob and looked in through the glass, she saw Scooter wasn't on the other side eagerly looking up. She opened it and realized the loud barking was coming from around the corner, in the hallway that led to the part of the building with the Tiffany windows.

Chase stopped for a moment and let out a loud sigh. "What in God's name now?" she muttered to herself. Then, she quickly pushed aside the negative attitude and decided to be smart this time. She grabbed a small folding chair in the hallway, the flashlight, and her cell phone. There would be no doubt; if something was happening with the windows again, she'd get a photo of it this time.

"Hush, Scooter, hush," she said, as she used her leg to gently push him out of the way. She opened the thick wooden door and the dog shot past her, vanishing into the darkness that lay ahead. Chase turned on the light, which did a decent job of illuminating the empty space, and watched to see where Scooter went this time. It was no surprise, especially to Chase, when the pup dashed off to the right side of the building and started barking up at the third window.

Chase took her time approaching, feeling that whatever was happening now it would wait for her. Forty paces later her feet stopped directly in front of the third window. It was the one where the people were planning to stone a woman who had sinned. Chase had spent almost no time in church growing up, but even she knew the phrase, "Let him among you who is without sin, cast the first stone." If she remembered the story correctly, one by one the people dropped the rocks they were holding and walked away.

Chase looked up, and the window appeared to be exactly as it always had. There was the crowd holding their rocks and there was the woman, the sinner, standing with her head hanging down in shame. Chase then remembered that with the first two windows the changes happened, not in the foreground, but hidden in the background. So, she put the sharp beam from her flashlight up to the window and slowly moved it over every inch, looking for something that wasn't there before. This went on for a good minute when Chase announced to the empty church, "I don't see it."

Scooter had not stopped barking, and now he was spinning himself in a circle over and over again, almost as if he were saying, "It's there, it's right there, look, look, look!"

Chase did look again, especially in the corners of the window, but again she saw nothing out of the ordinary. Then she cast her gaze more closely on the main images, the people holding the stones and the woman awaiting her punishment. It was then she saw what Scooter was dancing on about; the people weren't holding rocks anymore; they were holding something else. Chase got on the chair to look more closely and said, "You're kidding me?" The rocks were ornaments, the kind you hang on a Christmas tree. Red, yellow, blue, pink, every color in the crayon box.

A dozen or so adults were holding the ornaments, and down on the end was something she hadn't noticed before. The last person among them was a child, a boy in his early teens. She looked him up and down and saw he was holding something as well, but it was different from the others. He had what looked like a sparkling silver star in his hand, the kind you'd put on the top of a Christmas tree.

Chase continued looking for other changes and turned her attention to the woman hanging her head in shame. She noticed her hair was long and red and could have sworn it used to be brown. She wore the same clothing as before, only now she seemed to have a T-shirt on with an image on the front. Chase didn't remember that from earlier. Chase squinted her eyes to get a better look and saw there was a picture of a little girl on the front of the shirt. She looked kind of sad, her hair was a bit messy, and a black cap of some kind was on her head. She also noticed there were white clouds off in the distance behind her, with a small gray building only partially visible. Chase honestly didn't know what to make of it.

She then remembered her smartphone was in her back pocket. She took it out, opened the camera app, and brought the lens up to the window and looked into the phone to see the image before snapping the picture. She was finally going to get this nonsense on film and show everyone she wasn't crazy.

"Seriously?" she said with anger. The image her phone was showing her was the window in its original state. The people were holding rocks, the woman had brown hair, the child was not there. When she looked up at the window with her own eyes she saw the changes, but when she pointed the phone's lens at the window they didn't exist. Just to satisfy what she already knew, Chase snapped two photos of the window with the phone. When she pulled them up to view them, she saw the window as it always was, not what Chase knew she was seeing right now.

"I give up," she said in a loud voice to the empty air above her. Then she clenched her tiny fists and shouted, "I said, I GIVE UP. WHY ARE YOU DOING THIS TO ME?" The silence of the cold December night was her only answer; well, that, and the echo of her own voice bouncing off the crooked beams that had held the church up for more than a century.

Chase sat down on the folding chair, and suddenly a calm came over her. She glanced down at Scooter, sitting next to her obediently, and said,

"Maybe I'm looking at this all wrong." Scooter wagged his tail, not certain what to do to make his mommy happy; but it wasn't necessary. Chase stood up quickly and said to the dog, "We have to make some calls."

With those words she marched out of the church and back into the kitchen, grabbing a bottle of cold water out of the fridge and parking herself at the island in the center of the room. She thought for a moment and then said, "Ned first." She pulled up the number for the Sleepy Panther Inn on her cell phone and hit "send." Ned answered on the fourth ring, assuming one of his guests who had just left his pizza party was calling because they'd left a pair of gloves or something behind.

"Hello?" he said cheerfully.

"Hi Mr. Farnsworth, this is Chase Harrington. I'm sorry to bother you, but I have a strange question."

Ned took a seat in his recliner and said, "Okay, shoot."

Chase asked directly, "I know this is out in left field, but did your daughter Taylor have a daughter?"

Ned didn't hesitate, responding, "No. No grandkids, not yet, certainly not one from Taylor."

Chase thought a moment and said, "What about a little sister, did you have a child, a girl younger than Taylor and perhaps lost her?"

Again, Ned was quick with a, "No, I have three kids, the ones I told you about. What's this about, Chase?"

Chase thought again and realized she might be overthinking this, and then asked a more obvious question. "I'm sorry, I know this must seem strange, these questions. I have one more, please."

Ned said, "All right."

Chase then asked, "Did Taylor own or wear a shirt with the photo of a little girl on the front?"

Ned scratched his head and said, "I'll be honest, Chase, I didn't pay much attention to what she wore, but Abigail did the laundry around here, so maybe she'd know. ABIGAIL?" he shouted toward the stairs, hoping his wife could hear him from the upstairs bedroom.

"What?" a female voice said in return.

Ned shouted back, "Can you come down here, please?" "She'll be just a second, Chase," he said back into the phone. Chase could hear footsteps coming down the wooden stairs she herself had gone up and down a few times, and then heard Ned again talking to his wife: "It's Chase Harrington, the nice girl who stayed with us. She's asking if Taylor owned a shirt with a picture of a girl on it?"

Abigail took the phone from Ned and said, "Hi, Chase. Can you describe the girl?"

Chase said, "Hang on," as she quickly ran back into the empty church. "Of course," she said to herself as she looked up and saw the window was back to the way it always was. The girl, the ornaments, the kid, the clouds; all gone.

"Chase? Are you there, dear?" Abigail asked into the phone.

Chase said, "Yes, I'm here. Let me think for a second. The girl on the shirt was young, maybe five or six years old, her hair was messy, and she had some kind of cap on. It was just her face, not the whole girl, and she looked sad."

Abigail thought for a moment; it had been so long since she'd seen her daughter with the flowing red hair bounce through this house with her sketch pads and paint brushes in hand. She thought back to all the outfits Taylor loved to wear when it hit her like a freight train. "WAIT," she said loudly. "You said the face of a young girl, looking sad and disheveled, right?"

Chase answered back, "Yes, that's exactly right."

Abigail looked at Ned and said, "Do you remember her senior trip to New York City?" Ned seemed lost, not sure what she was talking about. Abigail turned back to the phone, "Back in her senior year of high school the kids took a trip to Manhattan to see a Broadway show. They saw *Les Misérables*—do you know the show?"

Chase thought for a second and said, "I think so. Yes, I saw the movie with Hugh Jackman and Anne Hathaway; I think she won an Oscar for it."

Abigail continued, "We gave Taylor fifty dollars to buy herself food and a souvenir. She'd never been to New York City before."

Chase was listening closely. "Okay."

Abigail said, "She absolutely loved that show, and instead of using the money for a fancy meal with the other kids she bought herself an expensive T-shirt right there at the theater, and it had the image of a little girl on the front. She said it was the same one on the marquee outside the theater. She even had the poster on her bedroom wall for a while."

Chase immediately opened up Google on her phone and typed in "*Les Miserables* Poster" and up popped a dozen identical images. It was the face she saw on the woman's shirt in the Tiffany window; right down to the stray hairs that lay on the child's forehead.

Abigail's memory stirred now, and she added, "She told me that girl on the T-shirt was an important character in the show. In fact, she sang Taylor's favorite song. Ned, do you remember that song she was always singing around the house?"

Ned stood up; he was starting to remember now too. "It was something about a castle in a cloud."

Abigail smiled. "That's exactly right. I can't remember the words, but it was pretty when Taylor sang it as she was doing chores or taking a walk."

Chase said, "Hold on a second," and walked back into her bedroom, where her laptop sat at the foot of the bed. She quickly opened up YouTube and typed in "Les Mis Castle in Clouds." A split second later a variety of videos popped up with the song, and Chase pressed "play." As the haunting melody began, she held her cell phone up to the computer so Ned and Abigail could hear it.

"Oh my, that's the song. That's Taylor's favorite," Abigail said. She felt her voice quivering and reached for a glass of water to compose herself before speaking again. "Chase, what is this all about?" Chase's mind was racing a mile a minute, but she owed them some kind of explanation.

"Abigail, Ned. I promise I will explain the reason for this call to you tomorrow. I have another call to make right now. Please be patient. I'll explain tomorrow."

The elderly couple was holding hands now, wondering why this memory of the precious daughter they had lost was coming to light and how Chase even knew about any of this. They simply trusted her, saying in unison, "Okay."

Chase rushed to pull up Owen's phone number next in her phone. He answered on the first ring, the trick his late wife had taught him if you wanted to keep real estate clients happy. "Yes, Chase, what's up?"

Chase was as direct with Owen as she had been with the Farnsworths, asking, "When the town used to have a big bonfire and tree lighting, did they put something special on the top of the tree? A ribbon, an angel perhaps?"

Owen thought it was an odd question, but responded, "Yes, but it was a star."

Chase followed up with, "And did they ever let a child put the star on the top of the tree?"

Owen nodded, even though Chase couldn't see him, saying, "Yes, yes, they did. In fact, they took turns with different kids in town. Why are you asking me this?"

Chase said, "I'll get to that in a minute. The last night the town had the tree lighting, the night of Taylor Farnsworth's crash; did your son, Tommy, put the star on the tree?"

Owen was intrigued now by that specific question, replying, "No he didn't, but he was supposed to."

Chase shot back, "What does that mean, 'he was supposed to'?"

Owen then explained, "To put the star on the tree you have to climb up a very tall ladder. It was Tommy's turn, but he was younger then, only about seven or eight, and you know he's on the autism spectrum."

Chase answered back, "Yes, go on."

Owen then said, "He can get excitable sometimes, and the other parents were worried he might fall from up there if he got spooked or whatever. So, at the last minute we had to tell him he couldn't put the star on top."

Chase asked thoughtfully, "How did he take it?"

Owen had to think for a second—it was six years ago. "Um, honestly, he was a bit upset, but we promised him he could do it next year when he was a little older."

Chase chimed in, "Only there never was a next year because of the crash and everything being cancelled, right?"

Owen nodded again. "Yes, he missed his chance. Chase, why are you asking me this?"

Chase said the same thing she told the Farnsworths. "Owen, I have to ask you to be patient with me. I promise I'll explain this tomorrow. I gotta go." With that she hung up and punched in Gavin's name and hit "send" one final time that night.

Gavin answered, "Hey, sweetheart."

Hearing him call her that would normally make Chase's knees buckle a bit, but she was in full business mode, and she said, "Hey, important question. If you wanted to get the whole town together, fast, how would you do it?"

Gavin considered the question and said, "They have a town council meeting the second Tuesday of every month, but we missed December's already. I suppose you could put notices up everywhere and tell people you were calling a meeting."

Chase responded sharply, "Like we did for the lost dog? No, too slow. I mean a fast meeting, like tomorrow. How would you tell everyone to be someplace fast if you needed to?"

Gavin thought a second and said, "Honestly, there's no way to do that, Chase. Why? What's wrong?"

Chase came right back at him, "So you're telling me if there was an emergency you couldn't notify people? I know we're in the country, but this isn't 1850."

Gavin smiled at her salty tone and said, "Well, if it were an emergency you could have the sheriff send out a text, I suppose."

Chase asked, "Explain what you mean."

Gavin said, "Back when Hurricane Irene came up the coast it caused massive flooding in Vermont, washing out bridges and taking down homes along the river."

Chase was getting impatient. "Okay, okay, but get to the text part."

Gavin said, "Easy, pal, I'm getting there. After Irene we set up a system where people gave the sheriff their cell numbers, so in the case of an emergency or a tornado warning or something like that, he can blast out a text to everyone."

Chase smiled now. "And that worked?"

Gavin said, "Yep, far as I know everyone got it."

Chase then asked, "Do you trust me, Gavin?"

He didn't hesitate, saying, "Of course."

Chase continued, "I need you to call the sheriff and tell him to put out a text telling everyone there is a mandatory meeting in the town tomorrow night at six p.m. at the town square park."

Gavin was concerned now. "Chase, what's going on? You're scaring me."

His girlfriend then softened her voice, responding, "Listen to me. There's nothing to be scared about. I just need you to do this for me. It's important."

Gavin said, "More important than a tornado? 'Cause I have to tell you without more information there's no way Sheriff Harlan is going to send out a text like that."

Chase's voice got deadly serious now. "Yes, he will. Tell him it's for me. Then tell him three more words."

Gavin paused in silence, finally asking, "What three words?"

Chase said, "The third window."

Gavin's stomach turned instantly, sick with worry, as he asked, "So it happened again?"

"Yes," Chase said.

"And it is something bad?"

"No, not at all," Chase responded. "In fact, I think we've been looking at these windows the wrong way. Someone or something is trying to help us, not hurt us."

There was silence on the phone now as Gavin considered what to do.

"I need this, Gavin. We all do," Chase added.

Gavin, trying to hide his frustration, responded, "Okay, but can you just tell me what you saw?"

"Tomorrow, sweetheart. Tomorrow at six."

The two of them hung up and Chase waited. Three minutes later her cell phone buzzed, revealing a text message from an unknown number. The message said in bold type: MANDATORY TOWN MEETING MONDAY AT SIX. MONUMENT SQUARE. ALL REQUIRED TO ATTEND. IMPORTANT.

It was signed, Sheriff Erastus Harlan.

32
town gathers

Chase stood a good ten minutes, staring at the clothes that hung in her closet, wondering how to play this. Should she be herself and go with the designer jeans and Gucci belt and jacket? Or should she tone it down and make herself blend in better, be more approachable? She decided on a green barn jacket she once ordered from the L.L. Bean catalog, Lucky Jeans she got half off at Marshalls, and a pair of white leather sneaks she'd owned for a decade. Her words would be jarring enough to the people she'd be addressing in a few minutes; she didn't need her outfit to distract from the issue at hand as well.

Chase snapped Scooter's leash on his collar, and together they made the ten-minute walk to Monument Square at the center of town. She made certain to get there right at 6:00 p.m. so she could avoid too many questions if she arrived earlier. A rumble of voices greeted her as people were catching up with each other and of course asking if anyone knew what this mandatory meeting was about. Sheriff Harlan took a page out of Chase's book, being certain to arrive just as the nearby clock tower over city hall started to chime six bells.

Chase stood next to the sheriff, her eyes scanning the crowd and taking in, what were now, many familiar faces. Roddie from the funeral home was here, along with Shayla and Colgan from the diner. To her right she saw the Fosters, owners of the dairy farm where they rescued the puppy, and to their immediate left she saw Mrs. Witkowski, the blind woman who had showed her the neat trick about changing light bulbs. There was a burly man with a beard by her side holding her hand, her husband the invisible trucker, no doubt. Owen was there with Tommy, and she was happy to see Brenda, the very sweet waitress, standing next to them as well. Aunt Nolly was also there with Earl, both of them giving Chase a smile and a wave, which she quickly returned. There were also a lot of faces she didn't know, certainly not by name. They were people she'd likely seen in passing but hadn't had the chance to meet yet. Her eyes scanned the crowd further when she finally said, "There they are. I was afraid they hadn't come." She was looking at Ned and Abigail Farnsworth standing mostly out of sight behind a large maple tree.

The sheriff spoke first, thanking everyone for coming, then added, "With that said, I'm turning this meeting over to a special guest, Chase. And before she speaks, I ask only one thing from you; keep an open mind." With that the floor, or in this case the town square, was hers. Harlan had brought an empty apple crate, which was flipped over so the bottom faced the sky. It made the perfect step stool for Chase to climb up on so everyone could see her.

"Hi, everyone. First up I want to thank you for coming here on such short notice. My name is Chase Harrington. I'm a writer from Seattle who moved here about a month ago. How many of you have seen me or heard of me?" With that almost every hand went up in the air. Manchester was indeed a small town, and you couldn't so much as order an ice cream cone without half the town knowing what flavor you got.

With all eyes on her, Chase decided there was no point beating around the bush, so she jumped right into it. "By a show of hands, how many of you heard about the lost dog being found in the well and my part in it?" Most of the hands shot up in the air. Chase continued, "Okay, how many of you heard I knew the dog might be there because I saw it in a dream?" Again, almost every hand was reaching high in the sky. It made sense, really; the whole dream weaver nonsense was a pretty juicy morsel to leave out of the story as it spread around town. Chase then asked, "Not worrying about hurting my feelings even a little bit, how many of you thought the whole dream thing was complete BS?"

There was a momentary pause where no hands went up, and then one, two, five; soon more than half the hands that were up before were raised again.

Chase smiled. "It's okay, you didn't hurt my feelings. It was BS. There was no dream." Everyone started chatting amongst themselves, now asking what that meant or how she knew the dog was there, then. Chase didn't let them linger long with their doubts. "The truth is it wasn't a dream. It was a window. Back at the old church I'm renting and living in, one of the Tiffany windows showed me an image of a well with a dog collar sitting on top. I asked Owen, the Realtor, which property had one of those old wells where people used to drop the bucket down to get water, and he told me the Foster's place." Everyone turned to look at the Fosters, now not sure what to think.

Chase continued. "We went out on a whim, and sure enough Ruby was there, stuck in the well."

Maria Milington was there holding her dog in her arms and said loud enough for all to hear, "RUDY. His name is actually Rudy. And thank you, Chase."

A man Chase didn't know, who was dressed like an accountant, a suit with a vest underneath, asked, "Do you have proof of this? Did you take a photo of the window?"

Chase shook her head side to side. "Nope. I didn't get a picture. And I didn't get a picture when the second church window showed me something weird."

Everyone was riveted now when Earl, her bakery delivery partner, shouted out what everyone in town wanted to ask, "Assuming you didn't fall down the well and bang your head yourself and you're not talking gibberish, what did the second window show you?"

Gavin spoke up now. "It showed her a snowmobile that looked exactly like Nikki's sinking through the ice on the lake during the winter carnival." There was an audible gasp now, because everyone was there that day and saw Nikki Cheshire nearly drown.

Roddie Valenti spoke up. "You saw this window, Gavin? You saw it change like she said?"

Gavin looked away, not meeting his eyes, when he said, "No I did not, it had changed back before we got there."

Colgan Murphy from the diner asked, "We? Who's we?"

Sheriff Harlan stepped into this now, saying, "Me. When Chase saw the snowmobile sinking in the ice she called me, Gavin, and Owen."

Colgan came back with, "Owen? How does he figure into this?"

Owen stepped forward holding his son's hand and said, "Listen, my son, Tommy, rides on Nikki's snowmobile every year at the carnival. When Chase saw it sinking, she told me, and I made sure to keep him off the sled."

Gavin spoke again. "Good thing too after what happened."

Brenda was listening patiently to all of this, and suddenly a bell went off in her head as she said, "Wait a second. Is that why you tackled Tommy off the back of the snowmobile? I wondered why you'd do something so reckless."

Gavin turned to her and said, "Yes. That's why."

Owen added, "Good thing he did, too. I felt bad for Tommy toward the end of the day and told him he could have one ride, but Gavin didn't know that and yanked Tommy off the back. Thank God he did."

Sheriff Harlan said, "Listen everyone, I know how this sounds, and I was as skeptical as all of you are right now. But if you recall, I tied a rope to my sled the day of the carnival just in case Miss Harrington wasn't crazy, and when Nikki hit that hole in the ice it was a good thing I did."

Everyone started talking to their neighbors to the left and right again, to the point where no one could hear Mrs. Witkowski ask the million-dollar question. Harlan put two fingers in his mouth and made a loud whistle sound to get everyone's attention, then said, "I'm sorry we couldn't make out your question, Mrs. Witowski."

The blind old woman stepped forward while holding her husband's hand for support, and said, "Then I'll ask it again. Why are we here? Did something happen with the other windows in that church?"

Chase smiled and said, "You really are a wise woman. And the answer to your question is, yes, I did see something in the third window in the church, but it's nothing bad. Nobody falling into a well or going through the ice."

Mrs. Millington, still holding her small dog, asked gently, "Tell us what you saw, child." She gently gave a kiss to her dog on top of his head adding, "I'll believe you."

Chase had finally arrived at the point of this meeting and now, whatever she said, she needed to be convincing. One deep breath later she started. "The third window in the church is the one where the people are going to stone a woman and Jesus tells them not to. You guys know the window I'm talking about, I assume?"

Everyone nodded with an expression that said, okay, now get to the good part. Chase did. "Instead of holding rocks in the window, they were holding Christmas ornaments. There was a boy there who looked a lot like our friend Tommy here, and he was holding a star to place on a tree. And the woman they were judging had her face obscured, but you could see she had long red hair. She also had a T-shirt on exactly like one that used to be worn by Taylor Farnsworth." There was an audible gasp from the crowd when she said that last part.

Ned and Abigail looked at each other in astonishment, and Ned asked, "So that's why you called us last night. You saw our Taylor in one of the church windows?"

Chase looked at the innkeepers with kindness in her eyes and said, "Yes, I'm pretty sure it was Taylor."

Abigail spoke then, asking, "How is that possible, Chase?"

Chase shook her head slowly and said, "I don't know, Abigail."

Another woman she didn't know shouted from the back of the crowd, "And did you get a picture of this image, or are we supposed to just believe you again?"

Chase stepped down off the apple crate and started wading through the crowd, making her appeal more personal and genuine. "Listen, I get it. I wouldn't believe this either. And to answer your question, you in the back, no I didn't get a picture. I tried to but the camera wouldn't record what I could see."

The rumbling of the crowd started up again as people discussed the possibility that Chase was telling the truth or was just plain mad. Chase continued, "Here's the thing, though. This is happening. I didn't ask for it. I don't want it. Frankly, I have no idea why it's happening to me. I'm not the church-going type at all. But it's happening. And I'm not so sure that's a bad thing."

Aunt Nolly spoke for the first time. "What do you mean, Chase?"

She looked around at all their faces and said, "The first window helped get a lost dog home. The second window kept a child from falling into the ice and a woman from drowning. This third window, I think, is trying to heal this town."

Shayla from the diner asked, "Heal us how?"

Chase had rehearsed in her head how to say what needing saying next, but she wanted to be delicate or she'd risk offending the wonderful people of Manchester. "I don't know you. I'm a stranger to you," Chase began. "But when I got here I could see this town was hurting. As wonderful and joyful as you all are, and trust me, you are a joyful bunch, it's obvious you have been crippled by a terrible event that happened six years ago."

Brenda asked, "Taylor?"

Chase looked toward the Farnsworths and then back at Brenda and said, "Yes, Taylor. As horrible as her accident was, it was just that, an accident. But you all stopped celebrating Christmas, at least the way you used to. I think this window I saw, showing all of you holding ornaments instead of rocks, is a message. I think you are supposed to stop mourning what you all lost and start celebrating what you have."

No one said anything now; the crowd grew hushed as they thought about what she was saying, and they wondered secretly if this beautiful stranger to their town might not be right.

Chase then gave a final push to her argument, adding, "And I swear to God I think it's what Taylor wants. I don't think I saw her image in that window by accident. She wants this. She wants you to stop using her accident as an excuse to stop living."

Everyone in the crowd looked around waiting for someone to say something, and finally someone did. "I think you're right. I think it's time." It was Ned Farnsworth, squeezing his wife's hand with tears visible in his eyes. He then turned to his neighbors, many of whom he'd known all their lives, and said, "I decorated the house the other day. First time I've done that since we lost Taylor. It felt good to see the inn all lit up again. I also had friends over for pizza. Sorry I couldn't invite all of you, but that also felt good."

Ned then walked over to Chase and took her small hands in his. "I can vouch for this young lady. She's a good person, and I don't think she'd ever hurt or lie to us. I don't know why you were chosen to see these things, but you were, and we'd be foolish to ignore them."

The townsfolk in the park started talking louder to each other now, all agreeing that it did feel like it was time for Manchester to put away the sadness and celebrate Christmas the way they used to. Many of them had felt that way for some time but didn't dare say a word out of respect for the elderly couple who owned the inn and the loss they had suffered.

Gavin then said to Harlan, "So what do you say, Sheriff? Should we plan a bonfire and tree lighting for the Saturday before Christmas?"

Harlan rubbed his belly and said, "Well I don't know, that only gives us six days. Are you sure we can pull it off?" Harlan shouted to the crowd, "What do you say, folks? You want to have a proper tree lighting up on Mount Equinox?"

Without hesitation people started shouting "YES."

Chase was moved to emotion now. She looked away from the crowd so they wouldn't see the tears in her eyes, but Gavin saw them and moved closer, lifting up her chin in his firm, strong hands. He gave her a soft kiss on the lips, looked deep in her eyes, and said, "Thank you."

As every eye in town was on the lovebirds, the moment was broken when a child's voice asked, "Does that mean I finally get to put the star on the tree?" It was Tommy.

His father, Owen, picked him up with both arms, raising him as high in the air as he could and shouted, "You bet you do, sport. A deal's a deal."

He put Tommy down, and the boy ran over to Chase and gave her a big hug. He then turned to his father and said, "I wish Mommy could be there to see me light the tree."

Owen took Brenda's hand in his and said, "Something tells me she'll know."

The meeting broke up and Gavin walked Chase home, their faces glowing in the light of the lampposts that lined Main Street. As the old stone church came into view she said to Gavin, "Thank you for believing me and more important, believing *in* me."

Gavin drew her close and rested his head down on her shoulder, close enough to whisper in her ear, "I kind of love you." Chase's stomach twirled at the touch of his warm breath and the sound and meaning of his words, but she couldn't resist breaking his embrace, meeting his eyes and asking, "Just kind of?" Gavin pulled her tight and kissed her.

When Chase drove the three thousand miles to Vermont, she wasn't certain if she'd stay a day, a week, or a month. In that moment, safe in Gavin's strong arms, she felt like a woman who had surrendered her heart and just might stay a lifetime.

33

candle in the wind

The Saturday before Christmas came quickly in Manchester this year; after all, there was so much to pull together in just a few days. Gavin insisted he pick Chase up and drive her to the tree lighting, and when they reached the base of Mount Equinox she quickly saw why. It was a massive mountain, one of the highest in North America, stretching more than 10,000 feet or two miles into the clouds. There was only a single two-lane road that took you up and down, and it wound itself around the hillside like a large snake, bringing cars perilously close to the wooden guard rail that protected you from an unforgiving drop.

Gavin wanted to drive because he had a truck with a V-8 engine that could handle the incline and new enough brakes to negotiate the steep trip back down. Driving down Equinox was especially tricky because you were practically standing on your brake pedal the whole time. At the halfway point of the mountain there was a pull-off on the right-hand side, allowing drivers to rest their brakes, which often got so overheated you could smell the brake pads burning.

As Gavin and Chase slowly made their way up the hill, she could see the townspeople had been busy. Every eighth of a mile, there on the side of the road, someone had placed a torch that lit the way both up and down. She thought there was something both old-fashioned and charming about it.

When they were about three-quarters of the way up the mountain Gavin pulled his truck to the side of the road, put it in park, and pointed to a section of the guardrail just ahead of them, saying, "Do you see that?" Most of the railing that lined the mountain road was old and weathered, but Gavin was pointing to a small section where the wood looked newer, as if it had been rebuilt.

Chase knew instantly what that meant, and asked, "Is that where Taylor went over?" Gavin didn't say a word; he didn't need to. The sad look on his face gave Chase her answer. He then reached behind them onto the floor of the truck's back seat and grabbed a small brown bag. Inside was a tall red candle, the kind you'd see people lighting at church when they wanted to say a prayer for someone who was gone.

Gavin got out and carefully placed the candle on top of the guard rail in the exact spot she had crashed; then he struck a match. By the time he returned to the truck's front seat you could see the light from the candle flickering in the cold evening wind, bouncing off the thin branches that reached down from a nearby tree. "When her parents drive up here, I want them to see that and know someone remembered her, especially tonight," Gavin said in voice so soft it was almost a whisper.

As he put his hand on the shift lever to put the truck back into drive, Chase put hers over the top of his and said, "Wait, please. I should have said this before, but I'm sorry about you losing your friend. I'm so sorry."

Gavin gave her a hug and said, "Thank you, Chase."

The fastest a person could drive up Mount Equinox was about ten miles per hour, so it took a solid twelve minutes to make it all the way to the top. When Gavin and Chase arrived, they were greeted by a large crowd, tables filled with food and drinks and the sound of music. Just beyond all of this was a clearing and a beautiful pine tree about two-stories high which, up until eight hours prior, had been growing not far away in the forest. Some men had cut it down and spent the day securing it with ropes and stakes. "What a beautiful tree," Chase said to Gavin. Adding, "It's kind of like Rockefeller Center in New York City, without the traffic." The two of them looked around, taking in the beautiful view, and then looked up at the stars. They were so high up on the mountain it felt as if they could reach up and steal a star if they wanted.

Gavin responded, "Yeah, I'll take this over the big city any day."

As they made their way through the crowd, saying their hellos, Chase realized that the music she'd heard being played wasn't coming from a machine but a real live band off to her left. They were singing "Frosty the Snowman," so Chase only gave them a casual glance, but then she stopped and looked back again. Gavin knew what she was about to say. "Wait. What? Is that the country band Whiskey Highway?"

Gavin said, "It is, but no country tonight, just holiday music."

Chase listened to them all the time on Pandora so she could only stare in wonderment at their faces, finally asking, "But how?"

Gavin smiled and said, "Well, the lead guitarist is Steve Francis, and he grew up in Manchester. In fact, half the touchdowns I threw in high school went directly into his arms in the end zone. E.J., the lead singer, is from Poultney, Vermont—that's not even an hour north, and the guy on keyboards and drums, Jeb, is from Oswego, New York, a few hours away."

Chase responded, "So you just asked them and they agreed to play. I'm assuming for free?"

Gavin shot back, "Oh heck, yes, for free. You think I'm paying my old friends to sing 'Frosty'?" With that he laughed, then added in a more somber tone, "Look, they're my friends and when we decided on Monday night to have this tree lighting again I picked up the phone, told Steve what was going on and how important tonight is, so . . . here they are."

Chase nodded, understanding now, and said, "It's nice to have friends."

Gavin took her hand in his again and said, "Yes, it is."

For the next half hour there was more singing and potato salad and conversations among the townspeople, who rarely saw each other, with everyone being so busy in their lives trying to make a living. Finally, the guests of honor arrived: a large red Dodge truck with an extended cab came rumbling around the final turn before reaching the top. Owen was driving, Brenda and Tommy were sharing the front seat with him, and Ned and Abigail Farnsworth were sitting comfortably right behind them.

They all stepped out and took in the celebration, the older couple's eyes glistening with tears of joy. Owen approached Gavin and gave him a firm handshake, the kind shared by old pals, and said, "Sorry we're late. Someone put a candle on the side of the road where Taylor . . . well, you know. Anyway, they asked me to stop so they could say a prayer. I'll have to find out who did that and thank them."

Chase was listening to Owen and looked lovingly at Gavin; it was enough to give him away. "It was you, wasn't it?" Owen asked with admiration.

Gavin ignored the question and said, "Let's get you two some eggnog. We have regular, spiked, and then there's the batch Shayla from the diner made."

Owen laughed and said, "Let me guess, two cups of that one and you'll need to call an Uber?"

Gavin pointed at him and said, "Bingo." All four agreed to stick with the regular eggnog and let the enchantment of the evening be intoxicating enough.

Steve from the band then tapped twice on the microphone and said, "If I could have everyone's attention. It's time to do the ornaments." Then, without hesitation, one by one people in town reached into their pockets, each producing a single Christmas ornament. They were all different, each one carrying a meaning that was special to the person holding it in their hands. In no particular order they began walking over to the tree and placing them on the fresh branches.

The moment almost took Chase's breath away because it was exactly what she had seen in the third window at the church. Brenda saw her stunned expression and said, "Are you okay, sweetheart?"

Chase smiled and said, "Yes, I'm fine. It's just . . ."

Owen finished her thought: "Beautiful."

Chase nodded without saying it, wiping a tear from her eye. Gavin got closer so only she could hear him and asked, "This is what you saw, isn't it?"

Chase looked up into those deep blue eyes and said, "Exactly like this, except where is Tommy?"

As if on cue Tommy Johnson was led by his father over to the tree, and the mayor opened a small box and took out a beautiful silver star. It was the same one they used to put on the tree every year. Tommy took it carefully in his hands and put his foot on the first rung of the ladder. His father was hovering, causing Tommy to turn and say, "I'm okay, Dad. I can do this." Slowly he took one step after the other until he reached the top. An older man who Chase didn't know was already at the top and held tight to Tommy's waist as he learned over and attached the star to the top of the tree.

"How does it look?" Tommy yelled down to the crowd that had gathered in a half circle to watch this moment. Someone in the crowd whistled loudly with approval, and the rest of Tommy's friends and neighbors broke into spontaneous applause.

Chase was so taken with watching the joy on Tommy's face she didn't realize Gavin had taken out a small ring box he had hidden in his right jacket pocket. "Hey, gorgeous," he said to get her attention. Chase turned, looked down at the box and swallowed hard. This was not happening, she thought in that instant. Gavin saw a look of concern on her face and said, "OH NO NO, it's not that. Jeez, do you think I'm crazy? We've known each other six weeks." Chase finally started breathing again, but a small part of her was disappointed at the thought of what wasn't about to happen. So, if it wasn't that, what was it?

Gavin opened the box, revealing a small ring with a pretty green stone. "It's peridot, the birthstone for August, your birthday month."

Chase stared at the ring, wondering about its meaning, when she looked up and said, "I don't think I ever told you when my birthday was."

Gavin smiled like a small boy who had just been caught telling a fib and responded, "You didn't. Don't get mad, but I had Sheriff Harlan run your license plate so I could at least get the month right."

He took the ring out and slipped it on her left ring finger, saying, "When my dad fell for my mom he didn't have two bucks to his name, so buying her anything fancy was out of the question back then. But he saved up enough to buy what he called a 'promise ring,' which was his way of saying, hey, you're my girl and this is real. This is something that's gonna stick."

Chase looked down at her pretty new ring and said, "And you're telling me this is going to stick?"

Gavin smiled and said, "Well, I did put Krazy Glue on the inside of the ring, so yeah, I think you're stuck with it." Chase giggled, assuming he was kidding, but she started giving the ring a wiggle anyway. "I'm teasing," he said. "Listen, I don't know where all this is going but I do love you and you say you love me so I thought this might be a nice first step."

Chase considered for a moment, then gave Gavin a passionate kiss that seemed to last an eternity. She pulled back from his handsome face so she could look into his eyes and said, "Then a promise ring it is. And I promise to never take it off."

Just then the band started playing music again and singing a song that sounded strangely familiar—a tale of snow falling and children gathering for Christmas. Chase looked to the others nearby and said, "Wait, I know this song—how do I know this song?"

It was then she saw Tommy running toward the band, singing along, and Brenda said, "From the diner. You know it from the diner." Chase's face lit up with astonishment because she knew Brenda was right.

Owen added, "It's called 'The Gift.' He played it on the little jukebox the night you came to Manchester. Do you remember Tommy singing it in the diner?"

Chase smiled and said, "Yes, what a sweet moment. I remember it like it was yesterday."

Gavin pushed up against her shoulder and said, "That's when I came in and the real excitement began."

Owen and Brenda both took the napkins they were holding and threw them at him and said, "Oh, please." The four of them let out a hearty laugh that rose above the music drifting off into the clear night sky.

Suddenly there was a whoosh sound and a feeling of warmth on their faces, as someone threw a match onto the bonfire. The fire was so large it cast a red glow on all of their faces. Chase looked down at her promise ring and saw the reflection of the fire dancing in the stone. She looked up at the others and they back at her, and said, "This is the best night of my life."

34
christmas eve

When Chase was growing up, her family were Christmas Eve kind of people, meaning that's when everyone would go to church, get together to exchange gifts, and raise a glass to peace on earth. Christmas morning was reserved for sleeping in and staying in your new pajamas and fuzzy slippers until noon. She and Gavin were planning a quiet Christmas celebration out at his farm with dinner by candlelight in the loft above the barn. Normally the Bennetts would store hay up there for the winter, but they only had one horse left on the property, an old pony named Lulu, and she preferred dried oats and carrots to hay.

The loft was now used to store old tools, but Gavin cleared them out and set up a table with a white linen cloth and two antique black wooden chairs. He borrowed his parents' set of silver candlesticks and placed a vase with yellow roses and sage at the center.

The best part of the loft, and the reason he selected it, was the view. Two large doors slid back to reveal something so pretty it belonged in a painting. From their chairs in the loft they could look out at a pond with a weeping willow tree and a wooden swing held in place by some frayed brown rope. Beyond that sat a meadow with all manner of wildlife and a dirt road that led due west toward the Green Mountains. Chase stood in the loft, her hands on the hips of the pretty white dress she was wearing, taking it all in and thinking there must be mischief and romance afoot in those hills for the adventurous soul.

Gavin spent the afternoon working on the only dish he was qualified to make, chicken parm with angel hair pasta on the side. He surprised Chase when he arrived for their Christmas celebration in a three-piece suit. It was a gray Armani he had purchased for his best friend's wedding two summers ago. "WOW," Chase said, as she took a bite from a celery stick Gavin had placed out earlier with cheese and crackers.

"Oh, we approve?" Gavin said, his perfect face and tangled dirty blond hair serving as an always present and welcome distraction. Chase ran to him and did a very unsophisticated thing, jumping up into his strong arms and wrapping her legs around his waist. After a kiss hello she said, "Don't get me wrong. I love the suit, but aren't you hot?"

Gavin let out a sigh of relief and said, "Thank you, YES." He removed the jacket, rolled up the sleeves on his crisp white dress shirt and kept on the vest. He was still drop-dead gorgeous but more comfortable now.

They opened a bottle of Merlot and were about to raise a glass when footsteps came up the loft stairs. "I'm so sorry guys, I really am." It was Gavin's father. He had a concerned look on his face. "Abigail Farnsworth just called me and asked if we could pop over for a quick dinner." Gavin looked down at the table already set and his father said, "I know, I know. You have plans. But something is up. Something in her voice made it feel urgent."

Gavin looked away disappointed and didn't speak. He hated going against his father, but they were just there at Ned's place the week before. He shot his father a look and said, "I'm sorry, but I think we're going to pass."

His dad knew his son well, so he said, "How about this. The three of us all drive over and you stay for just a half hour and then you two lovebirds drive back and have your supper then. It will be more romantic with the sun setting and you'll have me out of the way too."

Gavin looked at Chase, then back to his dad, saying, "Oh, you're laying it on thick, old man."

Chase took his hand and said, "Ned and Abigail have been so sweet. It's just a half hour."

Gavin relented and said okay. As they made their way to the truck Chase said, "Besides, we can give him the gift."

Gavin's father turned to both of them and said, "You two should be so proud about that."

Chase smiled and said, "The whole town should be proud."

It was a short drive over to the Sleepy Panther Inn, and the three of them were surprised when they pulled up and saw a dozen other vehicles already parked outside. Christmas music was playing softly as they climbed the porch and let themselves in. Abigail greeted them warmly saying, "I know it's short notice and you must have already had plans, so thank you so much for coming."

Gavin and Chase joined the others in the parlor and noticed the guests all seemed older. Some Chase knew—the Fosters, Mrs. Millington, Harlan, Roddie from the funeral home—but others were strangers. Ned sat center court, sharing old stories and spending time talking to each guest. They listened and laughed, and the half hour flew by fast. Gavin looked twice at his watch and gave Chase a look that said, "We should get a move on, dear." When the conversation lagged, Chase interrupted and said, "Excuse me Mr. Farnsworth, I mean Ned. Gavin and I can't stay, but we have a Christmas gift for you."

She handed Ned a plain white business envelope and said, "Abigail, this is for you too." Abigail joined her husband, taking a seat next to his, with everyone in the room now hushed and watching for their reaction to what they knew was coming.

"We're sorry we didn't have time to get a card," Gavin said respectfully, adding, "This isn't from just us, it's from the whole town."

Ned struggled with the sealed envelope, so Abigail took it from his tired and shaky hands and slowly peeled it open. She then took out a long piece of paper with the words *Bank of Bennington* printed in bold ink across the top. It was a check.

Ned and Abigail read the check, and it said: To the Taylor Farnsworth Scholarship Fund. It was then that Abigail said, "Oh sweet Jesus, Ned, look at the amount!"

Ned took the check in his hands, drawing it closer to his eyes, and said loudly, "TEN THOUSAND DOLLARS!"

The elderly couple looked up at Chase and Gavin, confused, so Chase asked, "Do you know what a *Go Fund Me* page is?" Both the Farnsworths shook their heads.

Gavin interrupted, "We should tell them the other part first."

Chase agreed, responding, "Right, right."

Roddie from the funeral home spoke now. "When you two lost Taylor this whole town lost something. These two thought . . ." he said, looking at Gavin and Chase. "Well, we all thought it would be nice to bring some part of Taylor back."

Maria Millington added, "She was a wonderful artist. That was her gift."

Chase finished that thought. "And you told me, Ned, that you could only imagine what she might have done or created had she gone to art school."

Ned kept staring at the check as if it wasn't real, then said, "She was special."

Chase continued, "As a way of honoring Taylor we set up a fund-raising page where people could donate whatever they liked to a scholarship fund."

Abigail asked, "But when did you do this?"

Roddie replied, "The day after the tree lighting, so about seventy-two hours ago."

Ned was astonished. "How could you get so much money in three days?"

Gavin responded, "Because people care about you and they cared about Taylor."

Sheriff Harlan had been quiet all this time but finally joined in, explaining, "What we plan to do is tell the high school that if they have a child graduating who wants to be an artist, like Taylor, and if they get accepted to a college for that, they can use this money like a scholarship. If one student does that, they'll get the whole ten thousand. If we have a couple kids who qualify, then we'll split it."

Ned's eyes were filled with tears because he knew how much his Taylor would have loved this.

Chase said to him, "And don't worry, this isn't a one-year thing."

Gavin helped her saying, "No, we figure we'll make this a Manchester tradition. Right after the tree lighting each year we activate the fund-raising page and see how much we can get those few days before Christmas."

Abigail seemed confused, asking, "But so much money, how many people gave?"

Maria Millington said, "Everyone or near about. Some gave large amounts, like Nolly and Earl at the bakery, Roddie over there from the funeral home, Shayla and Colgan at the diner; they all donated a thousand bucks each. But most contributions were smaller—ten, twenty bucks. With so many people giving it added up fast."

Ned stood and put his arm around his wife and said, "You have no idea what this means to us."

Abigail added, "Especially this year." She looked at Ned, and there was a mixture of love and sadness in her eyes when she said that last part.

Chase said, "It was our honor to do it."

Abigail looked down at her left ring finger and saw the promise ring Gavin had given her at the bonfire. "Is someone getting serious?" she asked with a devilish smile.

Chase looked up at her handsome boyfriend and said, "Getting there for sure, I'd say."

With that Chase and Gavin said their goodbyes, but not before Ned pulled Chase close for a big hug, whispering in her ear, "I want you to know something. You coming to Manchester, you being here, changed everything. Somehow she knew."

When they broke their embrace, Chase looked Ned in the eyes, wondering who he was talking about. He just gave her a wink and said, "Merry Christmas to you both."

As they went back down the front porch, the holiday lights she'd hung with Ned only days earlier twinkling in the night, Gavin looked at Chase and said, "You okay?"

Chase took his hand in hers and said, "Yeah, I'm great. Just something Ned said. It's nothing."

As they made their way to the truck a light snowfall started floating down around them, making this Christmas Eve all the more perfect.

35

the last window

The night was still young when Gavin and Chase got into his truck to head back to the farm and have their Christmas Eve feast. Instead of starting the engine Gavin just stared out the front window like his mind was someplace else. "You okay, sweetie?" Chase asked.

Gavin turned to her and said, "Yeah, yeah, definitely. I was just thinking, do you really feel like driving all the way back to the farm to eat?"

Chase was surprised by the question and her tummy was rumbling, but she responded, "We don't have to. What do you have in mind?"

Gavin said, "Your place is only a few blocks away. If you have any wine and something to eat we could keep it simple tonight and have a cozy little dinner in front of your fireplace."

Chase thought about that image for a moment, then responded, "Wine, I always have in my house no matter where I live. As for food, I have one of those Stouffer's frozen lasagnas in my freezer; we can zap it in the microwave and be eating inside of ten minutes."

Gavin immediately started the truck and put it in drive, heading in the direction of the old church where Chase was staying.

Chase was happy to hear no barking sounds coming from inside her home once she and Gavin got out of the truck and were walking toward the side kitchen door. As she walked the twenty feet from the truck to the entrance her mind instantly went to the four windows inside and the realization that three of them had showed her something that was happening in town. Even though all of the visions she saw in the stained glass led to her helping someone, a big part of her hoped the fourth window would stay exactly as it was, quiet, and that this was the end of things in the empty old church.

Once in the house, the two of them decided to divide and conquer, so Chase heated up the lasagna while Gavin made a fire and opened a bottle of Yellow Tail Shiraz. As the food cooled down Chase raised a glass and said, "What should we toast to?"

Gavin didn't hesitate when he said, "To the beautiful young lady who got lost in the country and found her way onto my farm and into my heart."

Chase was so taken with his words she blushed. After taking a healthy sip she composed herself and said, "Darn, you're good, boy."

Gavin gave her a sly look and said, "You have no idea." They both laughed and held each other's gaze for so long, food seemed unimportant now.

"Hey, before we eat, do you mind if I grab something out of my truck? I got you a little something for Christmas," Gavin said.

Chase giggled and said, "That's funny. 'Cause I got you something too. Tell ya what, go grab your gift, I'll get mine, and we'll meet back here in sixty seconds."

Gavin rolled back the cover that kept his truck bed dry and pulled out a wide, flat package that was already wrapped. When he returned to the house Chase was waiting in front of the fire holding a large, clunky box wrapped in pretty white paper with a big bow.

"Merry Christmas," Chase said, as the two exchanged gifts, adding, "You go first."

Gavin slowly tore apart the pretty paper covering a large brown box. When he opened it up he said, "Oh wow. These are gorgeous. Wait, are these?"

Chase nodded, saying, "Tony Lama cowboy boots, yes they are. I asked your dad what size you wear."

Gavin was astonished, saying, "Do you know how much these things cost? Of course you do, you bought them. This is way too much, Chase."

Chase looked back with loving eyes and said, "No it's not. The day I met you I saw you had on that tan cowboy hat, but you were wearing work boots. And I've seen you in those same boots a half dozen times. If you're going to play the role of the handsome cowboy slash farmer, you need the right footwear."

Gavin smiled and pulled Chase in for a hug saying, "Thank you so much."

It was Chase's turn to open a gift, and she held the large, flat object in her hands, unable to imagine what it might be. "I have to warn you, it's not as nice as what you got me, but I think you'll like it," Gavin said hopefully.

Chase carefully peeled back the blue wrapping paper and realized it was some kind of framed picture. She was looking at the back and saw the Oropallo Frame Shop logo stamped on the back in black ink. She turned the frame over, and what she saw snatched the breath right out of her lungs. Gavin watched her as she looked carefully at the photo and then saw a single tear fall to the glass. Chase looked up, meeting his eyes, and said, "It's my calendar page. How did you do this?"

Gavin smiled, because he knew instantly that all the work he had done to make this moment happen paid off. Chase looked back down at the perfectly framed memory resting in her hands. It was Manchester at Christmastime, and it looked almost exactly like the page she had torn off a calendar back in Seattle twenty years earlier when she was a little girl, the page that was tacked up on her bedroom wall through most of her childhood.

It showed a wide view of the main street in Manchester, complete with lampposts wrapped in green garland, benches adorned with red bows, white lights in the trees, and beautiful wreaths on every door. All of it was covered in a dusting of snow that looked like freshly sprinkled powdered sugar. It was nearly identical to the one she had as she was growing up, but it looked more like Manchester as it was now.

Suddenly Chase was confused, asking, "I know I told you about the calendar page, but this photo, the way it was taken, the angle, it looks identical to the one I had. How is that possible? How could you know that?"

Gavin put his hands in the air as if surrendering to police and said, "Promise me you won't get mad, but I tracked down your mom back in Seattle and asked her if she had any photographs of the calendar page you loved of Manchester. At first she said no, but then she looked through photos in some old shoe boxes and she found one taken when you were about fifteen years old. In the photo you were holding up your report card, all A's, by the way, and over your right shoulder behind you on the bedroom wall you could see the calendar page you had tacked up there.

"She snapped a photo and sent it to me. I zoomed in on it, and that's how I knew what kind of picture to take."

Chase showed how astonished she was at the effort that went into the gift, and then asked, "So you took the photo? It's gorgeous!"

Gavin laughed. "God no. The only camera I have is the one on my phone. A buddy of mine, Jimmy Carras, is the photographer for the *Bennington Banner* newspaper. Once I had the photo of your calendar page I showed it to him, and he shot this picture in exactly the same way. I think he got really close."

"More like spot-on," Chase said, still wiping the tears from her eyes. She gave Gavin a hug and a kiss and said, "It's the nicest Christmas gift I've ever received. Thank you, love."

Gavin smiled proudly and said, "You're welcome. And I can't wait to wear my new boots."

The gift giving done, the two of them ate the lasagna, finished the bottle of wine, and retired to an old leather couch that sat directly across from the fireplace. Gavin turned all the lights off so the glow of the burning logs gave everything in the room a warm, magical look. Scooter assumed his usual place curled up in a tiny ball right in front of the fire, and Gavin leaned back with his arm around Chase as she rested her head on his firm chest. With every breath his chest rose and fell, giving Chase the sensation that she was on a ship at sea, rolling with the waves. It wasn't long before sleep took them both and arm in arm they drifted off.

The two of them would have likely slept until the sun came up if not for the antique clock announcing it was five a.m. and what happened next. The clock's chimes didn't wake Gavin; it was a sensation of being scratched on his knee. He opened his tired eyes, Chase still lost in dreams on his chest, and saw a paw reaching up again and again to gently claw and wake him. It was Scooter, sitting tall and scratching at Gavin's leg to get his attention.

"What's the matter, boy, you have to go to the bathroom?" he asked. Gavin got up, slowly easing Chase's head carefully down on a pillow in the corner of the couch. She never flinched as he lifted her legs up onto the cushions so she was lying comfortably now. Gavin walked toward the door to let the dog outside but realized as he rubbed his tired eyes and opened the door that Scooter was not with him. He turned around, wondering where the dog had gone, and saw the pup was at the other door that led into the empty church.

On previous occasions when something was happening with the windows in the church, Scooter was loud and aggressive, eager to get in there. This was different. He seemed almost melancholy as he brought his paw up to scratch the door, looking back at Gavin with sad eyes that said, "We have to go in here."

Gavin thought about waking Chase but decided to wait, thinking the dog might just be hot and wanting to continue sleeping on the cool floor of the empty space. He opened the door to let Scooter in and the dog walked slowly into the dark and vanished from sight. Gavin was about to return to Chase and see if she wanted to finish sleeping in her bed when he heard whining.

Gavin stepped into the dark, quiet church and searched for the light switch on the wall. After flipping it on he scanned the room and found Scooter lying flat on the floor, his sad eyes looking up at one of the church windows. Gavin approached and realized this was not one of the windows where Chase said she saw things appear before. He looked at the dog, then up at the Tiffany glass and said, "The last window."

It was the one depicting the Resurrection, with the image of Jesus in a beautiful robe, his hands raised in the air as if he was blessing the people looking up at him, and he seemed to be rising into the bright golden sky behind him. It really was pretty, Gavin thought.

Gavin had been in this church many times and remembered looking at this window more than once. As he searched every inch of it now, it looked exactly as it always had; there was no difference. He kept staring, trying to find a clue or something that would explain why the dog had woken him from a sound sleep to lead him here. His focus was so intense he didn't realize Scooter had gotten up and gone to get Chase.

"What's going on?" a groggy female voice said, echoing in the empty church. It was Chase being led into the room by her faithful furry friend.

Gavin whispered, "Nothing. Scooter woke me up and wanted to come in here. He lay in front of this window and cried a bit, but I'm looking at it and nothing is changed."

Chase slowly crossed the wooden floor in her gray wool socks, joining Gavin in front of the last window. She opened her eyes wide and blinked twice, trying to get the sleep out, and then focused her vision on the window above. Gavin looked at Chase's face as she examined the glass and watched her expression change to one of crushing sadness.

Chase reached behind her, grabbing the wall for support, and lowered her small frame down to the floor. She pulled her knees up to her chest, squeezing them, and started rocking back and forth for a moment like a child who was hurt. She didn't look up at the window or at Gavin; she just started to quietly cry. Scooter saw her tears and immediately walked over and started licking the salty water off her face. "Thanks, buddy, Mommy needed that," she said to her dog.

She then took in a deep breath and let it out, releasing the heavy emotions that literally forced her to the floor. "What's the matter?" Gavin asked. "What did you see?"

Chase patted the floor next to her and said, "Sit with me a minute."

Gavin did, taking the spot directly next to her on the dusty church floor, never breaking eye contact with her face. After a moment of silence, he said, "Chase, please. Tell me."

Chase looked up again and said, "You don't see it, do you?"

Gavin looked up again, and the window was exactly as it always was. He could only say, "I'm sorry, I don't. What do you see? Why are you so upset? What's happened?"

Chase took his hand in hers and said, "Ned Farnsworth died."

Gavin looked back at the window and then to Chase, asking, "How do you know?"

Chase stood up now, pointing up at the last window, and said, "Beyond Jesus in the golden sky above him, I see the image of an older man who is going to heaven."

Gavin considered her words for a moment, then asked, "But how do you know it's Ned? Maybe it's somebody else. Chase, we just saw him a few hours ago."

Chase wiped her last tear and turned to Gavin with a look that told him she was certain about what came next. "I know it's Ned because he's not alone. There's a beautiful woman with long red hair reaching out to take his hand."

Gavin felt his own eyes welling up now, and finally he said, "Taylor?" Chase nodded and said, "Yes, it's Taylor."

Gavin considered for a moment and asked, "Is there anything else?"

Chase looked up closely, examining every inch of the window, and noticed up in the clouds there was a small gray stone structure. It was too small to make out, so she said to Gavin, "No, that's it."

Without saying another word Chase started walking back to the kitchen and, without being called, Scooter instinctively followed after her. Gavin gave one last look to the window, which still looked the same to him, then went after Chase. "Where are you going?"

Chase turned and gave him a kind smile and said, "To make coffee. I can't sleep now. When the sun is up I want to call Abigail Farnsworth. We should probably call Harlan too, just so he knows what happened here."

Gavin put his arm around Chase, not certain what to say to make this better. He was still hopeful the window was wrong and that this one time what Chase said she saw wasn't true. As they sipped coffee and watched the Christmas morning sun rise over the snowcapped mountains to the east, Gavin knew in his heart Ned was already gone.

36
the final sketch

Chase and Gavin agreed it wouldn't be prudent to call over to the Sleepy Panther Inn at seven a.m. on Christmas morning without knowing for certain if something had even happened. What if the window was wrong or it was showing Chase something that might happen years from now? Waking up Ned and Abigail wouldn't be very nice, and what are you supposed to say? "Oh, sorry, we thought someone died."

Instead of calling, they grabbed Scooter's leash, bundled up for the frigid morning air, which was hovering around twenty degrees, and decided to walk over to the inn. If everything looked quiet they could let out a sigh of relief, loop back around, and have breakfast together in Chase's kitchen. Or better yet, hop in the truck and head out to the farm and have bacon and eggs with Gavin's dad, who must have been wondering where the heck they were.

There was no one on the cobblestone sidewalks that lined Main Street, being Christmas morning, so the brisk walk only took them a few minutes. As the inn came into sight both of their hearts sank, and Chase immediately felt her eyes fill with tears. There was a long black hearse in the driveway parked on the side of the inn. Sheriff Harlan's car was situated out front, and there were at least two other pickup trucks on the street that normally weren't there.

As Gavin and Chase got closer they heard voices and realized there were several people talking on the front porch of the inn. Harlan wasn't expecting any visitors at this early hour, so he was surprised to see the young couple walking up with the puppy in tow. "Good morning," the sheriff said, stepping down from the porch to greet them.

Without hesitation, Gavin asked, "Is it Ned?" His eyes tracked from the hearse up to the windows of the old house with the curtains drawn closed.

Harlan's face took on a surprised expression and said, "Yes. But how did you . . ." He stopped that sentence short and then glanced over to Chase, who looked like a four-year-old child who had just lost her best friend. "I see," Harlan said in a somber tone, deciding at that moment to drop any further inquiry.

Roddie Valenti came down the stairs rubbing his hands together, trying to get them warm, and Nolly and Earl from the bakery joined him on the sidewalk out front. Before any of them could speak, the rumble of a truck engine approached, and they all turned to see Gavin's father pulling up in front of the inn.

"Dad, what are you doing here?" Gavin asked.

"Ned and Abigail are old friends, Son," he responded.

As Gavin's father looked toward the others, Nolly said, "I was hoping he'd have more time."

Chase asked, "How did he die?"

To which Earl said, "Cancer, hon. Started in his liver and went everywhere it could find."

Nolly added, "Like water on a cracked sidewalk, that's how he described it. It found every place to seep into. He never had a chance."

Gavin put his arm around Chase and looked to the others asking, "You all knew?"

His father spoke for all of them, saying, "Son, Ned was a very private man. When he was diagnosed late spring he knew he had less than a year to live but he didn't want people treating him any different."

Nolly said, "We knew because we're old friends and he wanted to make sure a few people were aware so they could look out for Abigail."

Chase nodded with a mixture of pride and understanding, saying, "And people in Manchester look out for each other."

Earl smiled and said, "That we do, child, that we do."

Roddie then said, "I hate to interrupt, but I wanted to give you a game plan here." All of them turned their attention to the undertaker. "She wants to see the four of you." He was pointing toward Nolly, Earl, Harlan, and Gavin's father. "But she hasn't slept, so why don't you go in, but only stay a few minutes. Once you leave, I'll bring Ned out. She doesn't want an audience for that part. You understand."

All of them did, nodding in agreement, and slowly they started walking up the wide porch steps toward the front door. "Will there be a funeral service, Mr. Valenti?" Chase inquired.

Roddie responded, "No. Ned and Abigail decided what he wanted was to be cremated and his ashes spread in a special place."

Chase then asked, "Do you know where?"

Roddie was about to tell Chase that he had no clue when a voice in the distance said, "The ashes will be spread in a special field a couple of towns over." It was the priest, Father James O'Brien, the one Chase had met at the pizza party. He'd been in the house spending time with Abigail, consoling her. "Abigail says there is a field that is filled with bright yellow sunflowers every summer. Ned wants his ashes to be placed there so he will forever be part of something beautiful. He also mentioned Taylor liking that spot."

Chase looked at Gavin, knowing he carried a photo of Taylor basking in those sunflowers, carefully preserved in his wallet. She said, "Yes, that was a special place for them. Ned told me the story, and just recently he had a picture framed of Taylor in that field."

Roddie interrupted again. "Well, if you guys wanna say hi, you should do it now."

The four of them started into the home and Father O'Brien said, "I'm glad I saw you here, Chase. You saved me a trip."

Chase said, "I'm sorry, what trip?"

The priest fumbled with his hat and explained, "Abigail asked me to find you today and deliver a message. She'd like you and just you to come back to the inn later tonight at seven p.m."

Chase asked, "Me? Do you know why?"

The priest put his hat on his head to stave off the cold and said, "She didn't say. Just to tell you to please be here alone at seven. Oh, and to tell you it's important."

With that the others went in to see Abigail, Roddie Valenti lingered by his hearse waiting to perform his sad task, and Gavin and Chase made their way back to the old church to collect Gavin's truck and head out to the farm. "We can shower and change there and then have some breakfast. If you want, maybe we can all take a nap up in that hay loft. I think we're all going to be exhausted later, and it sounds like you have an important meeting."

Chase agreed, and they did as Gavin suggested. Even though it was Christmas day it didn't feel like it, and whatever they tried to do to take their minds off of Ned's passing it didn't work. Ralphie and *A Christmas Story* were on the television, but this year it didn't make them laugh. They tried playing a board game, but neither Chase nor Gavin could concentrate for very long. Chase kept looking at her cell phone and responding to the holiday greetings and text messages from family and friends as they trickled in, always keeping a keen eye on the time. Seven o'clock couldn't get there fast enough.

When the appointed hour arrived, Gavin drove Chase back to the Sleepy Panther and told her he'd take Scooter home and wait in the old church for her safe return. Chase hugged him firmly, uncertain what was about to happen, but feeling in her bones that life was about to change.

She knocked twice on the large wooden door and Abigail greeted her with a warm smile. "Thank you so much for coming, dear. Wine?" The older woman was wearing a pretty red sweater that one of her kids had given her some previous Christmas, had already opened a bottle, and had just poured her second glass. *If ever there was a day to have a drink, this is it*, she thought.

"Sit, sit," she said, handing Chase a glass of Merlot. "It's Bogle, a favorite of Ned's," she added. "We found it by accident one day when we took a long drive up to Bangor, Maine. Have you ever been there?" Chase shook her head. "Beautiful country, but my gosh, what a hike getting up there. 'Bogle in Bangor.' We used to laugh about that. We laughed about a lot of things. What a wonderful man. What a wonderful life."

Chase was quiet, taking it all in, but finally said, "I'm so sorry you lost him, Abigail. I had no idea he was sick."

Abigail took a healthy sip of her wine and said, "Not just you. Nobody knew except for a few people—you saw them here this morning." Abigail then walked over to the wall and looked at an old photo hanging there, of her and Ned together, taken at a wedding decades ago. She pressed her fingertips against the glass as if trying to touch him one more time. "He didn't want the pity. Didn't have time for it, he'd say to me. That was Ned. At least now the pain is gone. No more pills. No more pain."

She turned around, pointing at Chase now, and said, "And he liked you, Chase. Boy, did he like you."

Chase smiled. Just hearing that eased the heartache a bit. "He said, that girl . . ." Abigail stopped talking a moment, looking away as her voice started to crack, trying hard not to cry.

Chase wanted to hug her, to pull her close and tell it was all going to be okay. Instead she asked with a loving smile, "What did he say about me?"

Abigail composed herself and said, "Ned said to me, right after the big Christmas tree lighting, that this town is like one big beating heart. All of us connected. And after Taylor died the heart stopped beating. No more big celebration, no more lights for our home. People kept living, life went on here in Manchester, but it wasn't the same. The heart of it all just kind of stopped."

Chase listened quietly as Abigail turned, looking directly into her eyes now. "Then you came. This beautiful stranger, all five foot whatever, 130 pounds of you, and it's like you put those tiny hands of yours around the heart of this town and started to squeeze. And squeeze and squeeze. Ned said you squeezed so hard the heart started beating again."

She continued, "Then you found your way to us and our home. Did you know that since the accident we never rented out Taylor's room? Not once."

Chase was astonished at learning this. "No, I didn't know that," she said.

Abigail explained, "That's why it still had all her things in there, exactly as she left them that terrible winter night we lost her. And her paintings, we didn't have the heart to remove them, so there they sat on the closet floor."

Chase said, "They're beautiful. She was so talented."

Abigail seemed lost in a memory at that moment, then finally said, "Oh, thank you. Yes, she had a gift. Anyway, when you called a couple months ago from Seattle, looking for a place to stay for a few days, I was shocked when Ned said he was putting you in Taylor's room, but he looked at me and said it just felt right."

Chase responded, "I'm glad he did. It's a wonderful room. You can tell it was filled with love. I mean this whole house is filled with love that way."

Abigail crossed the room and was looking up the empty staircase now, when she said, "I remember the first night you were here. Just hearing a young woman's footsteps coming from that bedroom, it was nice."

Abigail then surprised Chase, adding, "I'll tell you something else too. I don't know if Ned would have made it to Christmas without you. I think meeting you gave him something to live for. You're important to Manchester. I knew it, Ned knew it. He once said even Taylor knew it."

As Abigail finished her wine a memory stirred in Chase from the night before, the impromptu Christmas Eve get-together. She remembered the way Ned said goodbye, pulling her in close for a hug, and then whispering something strange to her. Chase broke her train of thought and asked, "What did you just say about Taylor? She knew something about me?"

Abigail caught herself talking silly and said, "Oh, don't mind me. Ned said all sorts of strange things these last few weeks. He was on six kinds of pain killers and other medicine."

Chase said, "Abigail, I'm asking because when he hugged me goodbye last night, he whispered in my ear, 'She knew,' and I had no clue what he meant."

Abigail shook her head and said, "Who knows, Chase. Like I said, he was on a lot of medication and not above saying the odd thing now and again."

Chase paused a moment and said, "Well, please know I appreciate the wine and the talk. It is Christmas night and I should probably get back to Gavin."

Abigail said, "Oh, no, no, not yet. I didn't just have you by to chat with me, Chase. Ned left something for you upstairs. Well, actually two things. You'll find them both up on Taylor's bed in her room."

"For me?" Chase asked.

"Yes," Abigail replied, adding, "and he was very clear that whenever he passed I was to make sure you have them."

As Chase started walking up the stairs to make her way to the bedroom, her eyes were naturally drawn to all the pretty paintings of Taylor's adorning the walls. Before she reached the top she heard Abigail say to herself, "God bless him. I can only hope he's in a better place and Taylor was there to greet him."

With that Chase's stomach twirled as she stopped, turned, and said loudly, "OH MY GOD, I can't believe I forgot to tell you. Abigail, they are. Together. Ned and Taylor."

Abigail put her glass down carefully and walked toward the bottom of the stairs with a hopeful look, asking, "How would you know that?"

Chase didn't speak. For some reason the words were stuck in her throat. She just stared down at Abigail with eyes that said, *Trust me, I know.*

Then, Abigail's mind sorted through all the recent events, the lost dog, the trouble on the ice, the tree lighting; and suddenly what Chase just said raised an obvious question. "Did you see something in the church windows, like the other times? Did it happen again?" Abigail asked hopefully.

Chase smiled and said, "Yes. Yes, it did, in the last window."

Chase didn't bother coming down to Abigail. She simply collapsed her weight on the top step of the staircase. The hard oak with knots in the wood was not comfortable, but Chase needed to sit for what she told the old woman next.

"You know about the first three windows? Me seeing things and then those things coming true." Chase began.

Abigail nodded in the affirmative and said, "I'll be honest, Chase. I wasn't sure what to believe, but I knew what was happening couldn't be explained."

Chase agreed, saying, "Even I'm not sure what happened with those windows, but I know what I saw, and in all three cases, for those first three windows, what I saw came to pass, and in all three cases the information allowed me to help people in Manchester."

Abigail felt her emotions welling up again, and with a tired, thin voice asked, "And what did you see in the fourth window, child? Please tell me."

Chase stayed seated but extended her hands forward, urging Abigail to join her on the top step. She obliged, walking up the dozen or so steps until she could reach Chase and take her hands. She sat down directly next to her, both of them with tears in their eyes now.

Chase continued, "Oh, Abigail, I saw your Ned going to heaven and waiting for him, taking his hand, was Taylor."

Abigail let out a gasp that was a combination of crying and happiness at the same time. "You did. They're together?" she said, barely getting the words out.

"Yes, they are together in heaven. I'm certain of it," Chase said, squeezing Abigail's hands.

Abigail pondered the wonderful image in her mind, then asked, "Was there anything else you can tell me? Anything else you saw?"

Chase shook her head and then remembered the image she couldn't make out in the clouds. It was the same image from both the third and fourth windows in the church. "There was one thing, Abigail," she began. "Up behind them in the puffy white clouds was a small gray structure, a building of some sort, but it was too small to tell what it was or what it meant. I'm sorry I don't have more for you."

Abigail smiled at Chase and said, "But you do know what it is. Do you remember the night you called us when you saw an image of Taylor wearing the T-shirt with the girl on the front?"

Chase thought back and said, "Of course."

Abigail stood up on the top step now, pulling Chase up with her and said, "What was the name of the song from the Broadway show she loved? You played it over the phone for us."

Chase thought back and smiled now, saying, "'Castle in a cloud.' Taylor found her castle."

Abigail gave Chase a hug saying, "Yes, she did. Listen, dear; you just gave me the greatest Christmas gift anyone has ever received. Now I have something for you. Go into Taylor's room and see what Ned left you. I'll be here to talk after."

Chase wiped her eyes and went into the bedroom, closing the door behind her as if she was about to have a private conversation. In some respects, she was. There on Taylor's large fluffy bed, on top of a pink down comforter, rested some kind of notepad and a white envelope.

She sat on the bed and put the envelope to the side, taking up the good-size pad in her hands first. She opened it and instantly knew what it was; Taylor's sketch pad. She slowly thumbed through a few of the pages and saw drawings of beautiful things Taylor had either painted or planned to paint in and around Manchester. There was a picture of Main Street, one of the front of the Empty Plate Diner. There was even one of the old St. Pius church that Chase was renting. There were also many sketches that captured nature's beauty: mountains, streams, and meadows. She didn't look at them all. Instead, she placed it down next to her on the bed, wanting to see what was in the envelope.

It was sealed, but after two good tugs Chase managed to get it open without destroying the contents inside. Her fingers reached in and retrieved a single piece of white paper, folded in three, concealing a handwritten note. She opened it slowly; careful not to rip it, and saw it was a short letter from Ned Farnsworth.

✳ ✳ ✳

Dear Chase,

If you are reading this it means I am no longer here and that's a good thing. Cancer stinks and it hurts and I'm glad my suffering is over. This letter, if I've written it correctly, will serve two purposes. The first is to thank you. After Taylor died, I shut down as a person, I drowned in my grief and unfortunately like a lot of drowning men, I took others down with me who were only trying to help. Abigail, Nolly, Harlan, all my old friends tried very hard to shake me out of my grief but they couldn't do it. Then you came to town.

Do you know those doctor shows on TV where a patient dies and they use those electric paddles to shock them back alive? That was you. Helping me decorate the house was a big step for me. Then telling the town we needed to have the tree lighting again, that was long overdue and very much needed. The scholarship for Taylor you helped set up; all wonderful. Even now, just standing in her room you bring a life to this place that has been missing. Thank you for doing that Chase.

The second thing is going to shock you so you should probably sit down. Are you sitting? Okay, here goes. About a dozen years ago Abigail and I took a drive over to Saratoga Springs, New York. We were looking for something interesting to do and discovered a place called Yaddo. We had heard they had beautiful gardens in this private estate. What we didn't realize, until that day, is that Yaddo is an artist's retreat. That means artists of all kinds: painters, musicians, sculptors, writers; they go there and get to stay for free and work on their art. How great is that?

Anyway, we never really spoke about your writing, but after you left our inn and went to live in that old church, I Googled your name and found a bunch of your articles in some pretty impressive magazines. You are a fabulous writer, Chase! I mean that.

So, here's the part you need to be sitting for. Abigail and I don't exactly have a 'Yaddo' set up here, but we do have a room that once was the home to a brilliant artist. We lost her before she could achieve greatness. My biggest disappointment was that she didn't pursue art in school or at least have the time to work on her gift. I don't know what your plans are but if you are thinking of staying in Manchester, we would like you to pack up your stuff and move out of that dusty, empty church and come here to live in Taylor's old room. You can stay as long as you like, rent free, and write. Write poems, write more articles, write a book if you have that in you. We just want you to have the chance Taylor did not.

One last thing. I know a part of you is going to want to say no. You'll think what we are offering is too much, especially since we only met you recently. You may even think that your visit to Manchester should be over now or perhaps it was all just one big cosmic accident that you ended up here in our quaint little town.

Forgive me for saying it this way Chase, but you'd be wrong to think that. You do belong here and I have proof. Christmas Eve night when I hugged you goodbye, I whispered in your ear that 'she knew.' You asked me what I meant. And I winked at you, not wanting to spoil the surprise.

Well, now that I'm gone, I think it's time you knew I was talking about Taylor. Don't ask me how or why but there is an undeniable connection between you and my daughter. You told Gavin you came to Manchester as an adult because of a photograph you taped to your wall as a child. I'm telling you, you came here because this town was broken by a tragic death and you were the only one who could piece it back together. Taylor knew this. Don't ask me how but she knew.

Along with this letter, Abigail has given you Taylor's most prized possession, her sketch pad. On her last day alive, before the bonfire and tree lighting, Taylor sat in this room, on the very bed you're sitting on now, and did one last sketch. I didn't see it until the other night after the tree lighting, when I returned home and started looking through her things. I guess I wanted to feel connected with her again by looking at her artwork. That's when I saw it.

Chase, look at the last sketch in the pad. She knew.

With a kind and grateful heart, your friend forever,
Ned

✳ ✳ ✳

Chase put the letter down on the bed and picked up the sketch pad again, slowly thumbing her way through the pages filled with beauty and light. She then reached the last page and opened the pad up to see it full. If a person's heart could stop and start again in an instant, Chase's did.

The sketch was of a quiet country road with a big barn in the background. To the right of the barn was a field with an old man riding a tractor. He was stopped and had his hand up to his ear as if he was straining to hear something being shouted to him.

On the road, parked near the tractor was a vintage convertible Mustang with an attractive young woman standing on top of the front seat. She was trying to get the old man's attention. Sitting on the passenger seat next to her was a dog. At the bottom of the sketch was the date it was drawn, the day of Taylor's death. Next to the date was the title Taylor gave to her drawing "Lost and Found." Taylor drew this sketch a full six years before Chase ever made the drive from Seattle to Vermont.

Chase had to remind herself to breathe. She just sat frozen, her mind spinning with questions that she knew she could never answer. All Chase could do was run her soft fingers along the pencil drawing, touching the barn and field and car. She looked back toward Ned's letter still sitting to the side and said, "She knew."

Chase came down the stairs with Ned's letter in one hand, the sketch pad tucked under the opposite arm. Abigail was waiting with a hopeful look, and without prompting Chase said, "Yes, I will come live here and write."

Abigail gave her a hug, and without saying another word Chase slowly walked out of the inn and stood on the top steps of the porch looking up at the gentle snow drifting down past the glowing lampposts.

Her cell phone buzzed, and she assumed it would be Gavin wondering where she was all this time, but instead she saw her agent's name, DUKE, flash across the screen. Chase answered it, but before she could even speak, a hearty, "MERRY CHRISTMAS" boomed from the phone's speaker. "I'm not calling to pressure you; I just wanted to wish you a good holiday."

Chase drew the phone close to her ear, so he'd hear her words clearly and said, "No bother at all. It's good you called, because I have some news for you."

In a very happy voice her agent said, "Don't tell me you've written something? Is it another article for *Vanity Fair* or *Cosmo*?"

"No, I haven't written a single word but I'm about to and this time . . ." She paused a moment wanting to be certain of what she said next. "This time it's going to be a book—a novel."

Duke was overjoyed, asking anxiously, "Tell me, is it a romance? A mystery? Does our hero find true love at the end?"

As Chase strolled down the cobblestone sidewalk toward the old church to gather her things and kiss her boyfriend like she'd never kissed him before, she smiled and said, "YES, she does. Our hero does all those things and more."

Duke then asked, "And do we have any thoughts on a title?"

Chase considered his question carefully as she took in the perfect view of this town she'd come to love so much, all lit up like a Christmas village a child might place under the tree. "I do," she said with a hint of mischief in her voice. "It's called *Manchester Christmas*."

acknowledgments

I want to start by thanking my wife, Courtney. For years she has been encouraging me to write a book, and whenever I told her "someday," she'd look at me with loving eyes that said, "John Joseph, you can do this."

On January 6, 2019, when I sat down to start writing this story, I had no clue if I could actually do it or would even finish it. Every few days Courtney would ask me how the book was going, and that kept me focused and writing.

After it was finished and my agent started sending it out and we heard nothing, those were the tough months, because I wondered if all that work was for nothing. Again, Courtney told me not to worry, the right publisher would come along and love it, and all would be well. She was right all along.

I want to thank two editors. The first is Marlene Roberts, who took on the first draft of the book and polished up the roughest of corners. The second is Robert Edmonson from Paraclete Press, for taking my words and helping carry them the rest of the way home, without compromising my voice in the story.

Speaking of my publisher, Paraclete, there are too many on the fine team there to mention and thank, all having a hand in this book's success, but special thanks go to editor Jon Sweeney for taking the time to read it and believe in it, Michelle Rich, Sister Estelle Cole, Jennifer Lynch, Rachel McKendree, Charity Olsen, Lillian Miao, and Dan Pfeiffer. Paraclete is a family with a strong moral center, and an author or artist could not have a safer environment in which to share their work.

I want to thank Louise Underwood DeSare, a friend on Facebook, who saw me struggling to find a home for my words and put me in touch with a real-life Hollywood director.

That man is Brian Herzlinger, who also deserves my utmost thanks for taking the time from his busy schedule (and friendship with Drew Barrymore) to read my novel and tell me right out of the gate that he wanted to purchase the rights to turn it into a movie someday. Having someone of Brian's caliber validate my work, well, it means the world to me.

I want to thank my agent, Jim Hart from the Hartline Literary Agency, for reading my very first children's book and taking me on as a client. Jim and Joyce Hart both led me to Paraclete, and everything good happened after that.

I want to thank my high school English teacher and friend, David Kissick, for encouraging my writing at such a young age and making a 13-year-old believe that a moment like this could someday be possible.

I want to thank my parents for giving up so much so I could have a quality education, and for teaching me it is family and kindness that matter most in this world. I know they are in heaven looking down on this moment and smiling. And special thanks to my family and friends for encouraging me to chase my dreams.

I want to thank the lovely people of Manchester, Vermont, for always making Courtney and me feel so welcome. This story is fiction, but so much of what I've experienced in Bennington, Shaftsbury, Arlington, Dorset, and Manchester is alive in these pages. If you know Vermont you'll see things in this story, and you'll smile and say, "I know exactly what he's talking about."

I also want to thank Richard Paul Evans, the author of one of my favorite books, *The Christmas Box*, for reading my story and honoring me with such kind words of praise.

I want to thank my blind and deaf puppy, Keller. I have five dogs, but it is Keller who always lies by my feet whenever I write, and he was there for every single word of this novel. Whenever I got stuck, I need only reach down and touch his soft white fur to know I was on the right path and all would be well.

Last but certainly not least, I want to thank God. All of the blessings of my life come from above and I know much of the kindness and love in this story flows from the love of Jesus. Look inside this story and you'll see him everywhere.

God bless you all,
John

about paraclete press

Who We Are

As the publishing arm of the Community of Jesus, Paraclete Press presents a full expression of Christian belief and practice—from Catholic to Evangelical, from Protestant to Orthodox, reflecting the ecumenical charism of the Community and its dedication to sacred music, the fine arts, and the written word. We publish books, recordings, sheet music, and video/DVDs that nourish the vibrant life of the church and its people.

What We Are Doing

BOOKS | PARACLETE PRESS BOOKS show the richness and depth of what it means to be Christian. While Benedictine spirituality is at the heart of who we are and all that we do, our books reflect the Christian experience across many cultures, time periods, and houses of worship.

We have many series, including *Paraclete Essentials*; *Paraclete Fiction*; *Paraclete Poetry*; *Paraclete Giants*; and for children and adults, *All God's Creatures*, books about animals and faith; and *San Damiano Books*, focusing on Franciscan spirituality. Others include *Voices from the Monastery* (men and women monastics writing about living a spiritual life today), *Active Prayer*, and new for young readers: *The Pope's Cat*. We also specialize in gift books for children on the occasions of Baptism and First Communion, as well as other important times in a child's life, and books that bring creativity and liveliness to any adult spiritual life.

The MOUNT TABOR BOOKS series focuses on the arts and literature as well as liturgical worship and spirituality; it was created in conjunction with the Mount Tabor Ecumenical Centre for Art and Spirituality in Barga, Italy.

MUSIC | PARACLETE PRESS DISTRIBUTES RECORDINGS of the internationally acclaimed choir *Gloriæ Dei Cantores*, the *Gloriæ Dei Cantores Schola*, and the other instrumental artists of the *Arts Empowering Life Foundation*.

PARACLETE PRESS IS THE EXCLUSIVE NORTH AMERICAN DISTRIBUTOR for the Gregorian chant recordings from St. Peter's Abbey in Solesmes, France. Paraclete also carries all of the Solesmes chant publications for Mass and the Divine Office, as well as their academic research publications.

In addition, PARACLETE PRESS SHEET MUSIC publishes the work of today's finest composers of sacred choral music, annually reviewing over 1,000 works and releasing between 40 and 60 works for both choir and organ.

VIDEO | Our video/DVDs offer spiritual help, healing, and biblical guidance for a broad range of life issues including grief and loss, marriage, forgiveness, facing death, understanding suicide, bullying, addictions, Alzheimer's, and Christian formation.

Learn more about us at our website:
www.paracletepress.com
or phone us toll-free at 1.800.451.5006

SCAN
TO
READ
MORE

From the hills of Manchester to the streets of Manhattan—
wherever Chase Harrington goes, kindness, romance,
and mystery seem to follow.

ISBN 978-1-64060-671-5 | Hardcover | $24

"Chasing Manhattan is like a visit from a friend.
Filled with love and mystery, it is a sequel with
all the charm of the original."

—**Richard Paul Evans,** #1 *New York Times* best-selling author of *The Walk*

With her handsome boyfriend Gavin and her faithful dog Scooter at her side, Chase follows her heart on a new adventure, and finds love and healing amongst the most unlikely people and places.

Chasing Manhattan will make you want to grab a flashlight and a best friend and go searching for clues in the dark.

Available from your favorite bookseller
Paraclete Press | 1-800-451-5006 | www.paracletepress.com